Fatal Stand

by

Michelle Godard-Richer

The Fatal Series, Book Three

Fatal Stand

COPYRIGHT © 2024 by Michelle Godard-Richer

Cover Art by *Diana Carlile*

The Wild Rose Press, Inc.
PO Box 708
Adams Basin, NY 14410-0708
Visit us at www.thewildrosepress.com

Publishing History
First Edition, 2025
Trade Paperback ISBN 978-1-5092-5921-2
Digital ISBN 978-1-5092-5922-9

The Fatal Series, Book Three
Published in the United States of America

Dedication

To my family, both here and in Heaven.

Prologue

Four months earlier

Chris White, formerly known as David Hayes, and many other aliases along the way, put mango and rum in the blender with ice. He didn't stop there. To make his wife Emily's Friday night cocktail extra special, he added another ingredient—the tiny balls from inside the capsules of her prescribed sleep medication. The whirring of the blades smashing the ice camouflaged his guffaws.

Emily was a southern belle who exuded charm. But beneath the courtesy dictated by her upbringing hid an unscrupulous gossip who thrived on drama. If any of the women living in their neighborhood offended her in any way, she'd make sure the rest of her posse treated them as an outcast. She'd even driven her first husband so crazy; he'd hung himself to get away from her.

Her need to be in control and boss everyone around made her an exceptionally easy target. All women deserved to die for soiling and manipulating the superior male race, but bitches like Emily were even more worthy of punishment.

To lure her into his web, Chris had assumed the role of the meek, subservient man. The type of man the police would deem too weak to have the stomach for murder. Being the lonely widow, she'd bought his act. He let Emily make every decision from what they ate to what they watched on television all the while pretending to enjoy it.

But no more. Tonight, she would die.

Killing nasty women like Emily was doing all of mankind a service. No one would truly mourn her. Well, except maybe the single dad she'd been having an affair with down the street. Chris didn't mind in the slightest. It saved him from having to do the dirty deed.

He poured her drink into a martini glass and decorated it with a sprig of mint. He whistled as he carried her drink and a whiskey for himself up the stairs to their bedroom.

Emily leaned forward to take her drink, her breasts almost popping out of the tiny silk negligee she wore, and cooed. "It's about time you brought me my drink."

"I made your favorite, a Mojito with mango. Drink up."

"Thank you." She took a sip and smiled. "Delicious. You make the best cocktails." She treated him the same way she did the dog—demanding something and then giving praise as a reward. Her usual modus operandi.

He climbed into bed beside her and gazed into her brown eyes. "It's the secret ingredient."

"What ingredient would that be?"

"My love for you." The lie flowing so freely off his tongue turned his stomach with its sweetness.

"Oh, aren't you precious."

Chris cringed inside. He despised it when she talked to him the same way she did to Parker, her Bichon Frise. *Fake bitch.* He tipped his glass and the warm, burn of liquor slipped down his throat.

He smiled as she guzzled her drink.

She set her empty glass on her nightstand. "I feel

funny."

"Oh, poor thing. It's probably all that sun we caught at the beach earlier. Why don't you sleep? You'll feel better in the morning."

She lay down on her side and tugged the comforter to her chin. "Hold me."

"Of course." Chris snuggled up to her and wrapped his arm around her stomach, smiling triumphantly as he waited for her life to end.

Within minutes, her breathing deepened. Gradually, the rhythm of her breathing slowed, and her skin lost its warmth. He placed his fingers on her neck, and she didn't stir. Her pulse had dropped. *Not much longer.*

Parker's growls interrupted the silence of their bedroom as he dreamed on his dog bed in the corner with his paws moving. Did the dog sense his mistress's upcoming demise?

Emily's chest lifted as her breathing deepened and she inhaled three shaky breaths, then each breath grew fainter and fainter until her chest stopped rising and falling.

Chris didn't need to take her pulse to know she was gone.

****

In the wee hours of the morning, Chris wiped his prints off the bottle of Emily's sleeping pills, pressed it against her stiffening fingers, and sat them on the nightstand. He swapped her Mojito glass out for a half-full glass of water, then soaked the mojito glass and the blender in a sink full of dish soap and vinegar. His fingers turned red as he scrubbed and rinsed them repeatedly, then he dried the glass and put it away in the cabinet and returned the blender to its base.

Satisfied he'd left no traces of his crime, he phoned emergency services with the appropriate amount of sorrow in his voice to convey the appearance of the grief-stricken husband. He kept his story simple. He'd awoken to find his wife dead beside him in bed.

The doorbell rang.

Chris put his eye to the peephole. Two uniformed police officers, one male and one female, and a man in khakis and a dress shirt stood on his porch. He kept his face grim and opened the door.

The male officer asked, "Mr. White, I presume?"

Chris nodded.

"I'm Sheriff Jenkins." The male officer gestured to his colleagues. "This is Deputy Mischke, and the medical examiner, Dr. Hardaway."

Chris stood back. "Please come in."

Mr. Hardaway asked, "Where's the deceased?"

"My wife…" Chris paused for dramatic effect. "Is in our bed."

"Thank you. Sorry for your loss." Dr. Hardaway ascended the stairs.

Chris pointed down the hall towards the kitchen. "Would you like to sit? I think I made coffee. I'm not sure." He paused and swallowed. "This whole thing is such a shock. Emily was fine when we went to bed."

The sheriff patted him on the shoulder. "Lead the way."

Chris hunched his shoulders and pushed up his fake eyeglasses as he walked ahead of the two officers down the hall. "I didn't make coffee. I'm sorry I'll do that now."

Mischke said, "Don't worry about it, Mr. White. Have a seat with Sheriff Jenkins and I'll do it."

Chris took a chair at the table in the nook of his kitchen. "Thank you. The coffee is in the small canister on the counter."

Sheriff Jenkins sat across from him and pulled a small notebook out of his shirt pocket. "Can you tell me what happened starting with last night and moving forward to this morning?"

"Emily was fine at bedtime. She's had issues sleeping as long as I've known her, so she takes pills. I watched her take her medication last night, and then we both went to sleep." He hitched his voice. "When I woke up and called her name, she didn't answer. I touched her shoulder and that's when I noticed she was ice cold."

"Did she have any medical conditions?"

Chris shook his head. "Not that I'm aware of."

Mischke set three cups in front of them with the sugar bowl and spoons, then fetched cream from the refrigerator.

Chris sipped his coffee black while the officers fixed theirs. "So, what happens now?" He knew already that under the circumstances the medical examiner would do an autopsy. Thirty-year-old women didn't usually die in their sleep.

"Protocol dictates we need to collect evidence. Then we'll see what Dr. Hardaway says. Most likely he'll want to perform an autopsy to determine an official cause of death. Then Emily will be released to you, and you can make funeral arrangements."

Chris said, "Okay."

Mischke asked, "Is there anyone we can call? Family?"

"I don't have any family, but Emily's parents will need to be informed." Chris sniffled. "It's going to crush them. She's the youngest of three children and the only girl."

Sheriff Jenkins asked, "Would you like us to do the notification?"

"Maybe that would be best. I don't know if I'm in any state to drive and they live on the opposite end of town."

It wasn't long before the medical examiner had Emily's body removed from the house and sent to the morgue for an autopsy. The sheriff and his deputy collected the bottle of sleeping pills, and the rest of the pill bottles from the medicine cabinet, then left to visit Chris's in-laws who were as snooty as Emily.

****

Within a month, Chris had Emily's death certificate in his hand. The coroner had ruled her death an accidental overdose, and the police had seemed happy with that explanation. Having filed numerous insurance claims over the years, filling out the paperwork and submitting all the required documents had been a breeze.

Chris went through the motions of the funeral, wearing black, and crying when appropriate. He sure didn't pity Emily's snooty in-laws, or the group of her friends who thrived on the drama and cried crocodile tears.

In appropriate and courteous fashion, he put up with the constant visitors dropping off food and telling him how sorry they were for his loss. Before Emily's death, they'd hardly noticed he existed. Mostly, they did it for the sake of appearances because it was the right thing to do when someone died.

After the two-million-dollar insurance cheque came in the mail, he cleaned the house thoroughly from top to bottom, erasing any trace of his existence. He packed his stuff in the back of his black six-year-old Dodge Ram, then put Parker in the passenger seat. A sweet little dog would be the perfect gift for his next target, Amy Hunt.

Amy lived in Idaho, only one state away from his ultimate targets. The first target was Jessica Kent— the bitch who'd cost him a million-dollar insurance payout after sticking her nose where it didn't belong. She'd spied on him out her window and called the cops before he could dump Sarah's body on the side of the highway. And the second target was Jon Kent, who'd almost killed him and stopped him from killing Jessica.

Chapter One

Present Day
Jessica Kent sat in the middle row of the van next to her three-day-old daughter, Cassandra, as her husband, Jon, drove them home to their ranch in Lewistown, Montana. Jessica studied Cassie's sweet, sleeping face and kissed the tiny hand wrapped around her pinky finger.

I love you so much little one.

Her heart's capacity to expand and love another, so much, she'd kill or die to protect them, never failed to astonish her.

Jessica straightened as they approached their ranch. She struggled to keep her tone to a raised whisper. "Oh my—when did this happen? We've only been gone three days. How did you manage all this?"

The black iron horse perched on the top of the archway marked the entrance to the Kent Family Ranch. But beneath the horse where there used to be open access to the property, stood a tall, black, metal gate with cameras. The wire they used to keep the cows inside their property had been replaced with the same tall metal fencing, an empty guard booth, and cameras.

Jon met her eyes in the rear-view mirror. "FBI Assistant Director Georgia Pruitt footed the bill and coordinated all this while we were at the hospital."

"That was nice of her. We'll be safer. But home feels

more like a fortress now than a retreat."

Jon sighed. "I know. We'll get used to it."

"What do we tell Bryce when Aunt Debbie brings him home at dinner time?" Jessica's stomach twisted in a knot. Her nine-year-old son, Bryce, had been through too much for a child his age.

After his kidnapping they'd told him he was safe, and that David would never be able to hurt any of them again, because they'd believed him dead. But three days ago, the FBI had informed them David had somehow survived his tumble off the cliff. To make matters worse, David intended to come after them again.

How could they tell Bryce, after he'd worked past the trauma and the nightmares, that the same monster was loose and out to get them?

"We can keep Bryce safe without telling him, but..." Jon frowned, "he's smart. He'll know something is up."

"Maybe, but I don't think we should tell him anything other than we upgraded security."

He lowered the driver's window and pressed his thumb to a sensor. "Okay. But if we get a whiff of David being anywhere near us, then we won't have a choice but to tell him."

"Agreed." The sensor flashed green, then the gate creaked open. "Wow. That's some upgrade."

"It is. We'll have to program your thumb print into the system later. When a guest presses the big button below the sensor, it'll set off a chime on a panel in the kitchen and on our phones. The cameras will allow us to see who's calling before we let them in. The booth is there for emergencies if things heat up and we need an additional layer of security." Jon drove through the gate, and it closed automatically behind them. He followed the winding dirt road and parked in front of the house. "I'll get Cassie and the bags."

Jessica slid the door open, wincing as she shifted her tender body off the seat and out of the van. She stretched her arms over her head to get her blood circulating, then strolled up the porch steps and leaned on the railing to wait for Jon.

The mountains on the horizon and the welcome warmth of the midday sun kissing her skin melted away the tension of the past few days. The calendar would turn to September in another week, and the warmth would gradually dissipate, replaced with the chill of fall. She inhaled a deep breath of the clean air. "It's so good to be home."

Jon came up the steps with her hospital bag over his shoulder and Cassie in her car seat. "Since she's still sleeping, would you like to lie down?"

Jessica covered her mouth to stifle a yawn. "That would be amazing. Thanks." She reached for the knob, but then the door swung open. *So much for my nap.*

Cynthia, Jon's sort of ex-wife, as in she'd been declared legally dead while in hiding, held the door open looking gorgeous in a tank and cut-off jean shorts. "Surprise. I made you sandwiches and salads. There's a chicken casserole in the fridge for your dinner later."

Jessica's cheeks heated as she stepped through the door. She glanced down at her baggy tee and sweats and forced a smile. "Thanks. That was so kind of you."

Jessica liked Cynthia, despite the awkward nature of their relationship with Cynthia living in their guest house on their property with Agent Trent Cooper. But coming home from the hospital and finding Cynthia in her home, fresh as a bakery loaf of bread, without an invitation—it made Jessica want to turn around and hide in the barn until she left.

Jon came in behind Jessica with Cassie. "Jess, go on ahead to bed. I'll bring you lunch."

"I'm exhausted. I'll see you later, Cynthia. Thanks again." Jessica trudged along the carpeted hallway, dragging her heavy, exhausted feet. She sprawled in bed, leaving the door open in case Cassie woke needing to nurse.

"Thanks for all this." Jon's voice carried down the hallway. "Jessica hasn't been sleeping. She just didn't have it in her to sit and have lunch."

"Ah, poor Jess. I understand. If she needs any help with Cassie and Bryce, let me know. You go on and have your lunch. I'll see myself out."

"Text Trent and get him to walk you home. It isn't safe."

Jessica rolled on her side and clutched her pillow. Jon was just being a gentleman. His concerns had nothing to do with Cynthia being his ex. Or did they?

Cynthia said, "I'm a big girl. I even have my own gun."

"No one should be going anywhere alone. David is one of the sickest bastards I've come across."

Jessica couldn't agree more. She shivered and tugged her comforter to her chin.

Chapter Two

Jon sat at the kitchen table with his laptop open and the baby monitor nearby while Jessica tried to catch a nap. They'd gotten five measly months of peace after Hugh Jones came after them, seeking revenge for the losses Jon caused him while working undercover for the FBI.

And surprise, surprise, David Hayes, alive and well, had led Hugh Jones to their doorstep. To make matters worse, after Hugh Jones' assassin failed to kill Jon, David had promised to murder Jon and Jessica himself.

Would the waking nightmares never end? And why would David come after them again?

The last time a witness got in his way the same way Jessica had, he'd fled, had plastic surgery, then moved on. He never went after that witness. Did he have another motive that they were unaware of? Or were Jon and Jessica cursed?

Jon had retired from the FBI and moved back to his ranch in the middle of nowhere to escape evil, yet it followed him as if he was a lit beacon drawing darkness in. Destiny kept pointing a finger at him and his family, seemingly desperate to thwart their happiness. But Jon wouldn't let that happen. The love he shared with his wife and their children was worth fighting for.

The FBI had reopened the investigation into David Hayes, but he'd evaded them for so many years. And after the FBI had failed to protect Jon's identity, then failed to protect his family from Hugh Jones, he couldn't trust them to apprehend David in time.

His phone vibrated across the table with a call from an unknown number. With a new baby in the house, he'd silenced the ringtone. He caught it an inch away from the edge of the table, then put the phone to his ear. "Hello."

"Jon Kent?"

"Yes."

"It's Agent Kato Chen. Remember me?"

Jon sat up straighter in his chair. "Yes, we crossed paths on a case years ago." Chen was one of the good ones.

"I just finished interviewing a bunch of inmates at Leavenworth. Hugh Jones' former crew. I'd like to fly to Montana to compare notes. I think we have a better chance of tracking down David Hayes as a team."

"That would be amazing. Do you have any leads?"

"Yes, actually. Hugh Jones sent a crew to evacuate David from a cave in the mountain and flew him to a clinic in Colombia called Belleza de Sol."

"That's something to go on." Jon jotted down the name of the clinic. "I'll pick you up when you land in Great Falls. There's plenty of room for you at the guest house with Agent Cooper and Cynthia. I'd offer up my guest room, but we have a newborn crying at all hours."

"I heard. Congratulations. I'll text you my flight info."

Jon ended the call, then typed the name of the clinic into a search browser. He hung his head and sighed.

Dammit. Not again.

It wasn't a run of the mill medical clinic, but rather a fancy, secretive resort for the rich and famous. David had plastic surgery to alter his face in the past to evade the FBI, and Jon wagered he'd be coming for them with a different face. They had no idea what he looked like anymore, and that needed to be rectified as soon as possible.

Worse, he'd have to tell Jessica about it.

Cassie's cries came through the speaker of the baby monitor. He ran to her hoping Jessica was getting some sleep. She'd need every minute of rest she could get to cope with this latest update.

****

Jessica stood in the shower and sighed as the hot spray warmed her sore muscles. During the newborn phase, survival was the main goal. While Cassie slept and her hands were free, she needed to shower and eat while the going was good.

The fog in her brain had lessened after a decent nap, but after foregoing caffeine during her pregnancy, she craved a cup of coffee like nobody's business. One cup every few days wouldn't affect Cassie's milk too much. She wrapped her long, blond hair in a towel, pulled on her dark blue, chenille bath robe and tiptoed past Cassie's room to the kitchen.

Jon sat at the kitchen table with furrowed brows and his gaze focused on his laptop screen. She stuck a coffee pod in the machine and pushed the brew button. "Did Cassie stir?"

He lifted his gaze to meet her eyes. "I changed her and fed her the bottle of milk you pumped at the hospital last night maybe half an hour ago. She went right back to sleep."

"That's great. She seems to be an easy baby so far." Jessica savored a sip of her vanilla-flavored coffee as it warmed her throat on the way down. "What are you working on?"

"I'm sure you can guess, sweetheart."

She sighed and sat in the chair next to him. "David."

"I have some news on that front."

"Oh."

Jon frowned and ran his hands through his hair. A tell-tale nervous habit of his. Whatever he had to say wasn't good news. "While you were sleeping, I got a call from Agent Kato Chen. He's flying here tonight from Kansas City. He found out Hugh Jones transported David to a clinic in Colombia." Jon opened a new browser window and typed in Belleza del Sol. "This is it."

Jessica read the description of the clinic and cringed. This had to be the worst-case scenario. "A plastic surgery resort? Now we don't know what he looks like. He could walk right up to us, and we wouldn't know the difference."

"If ever a strange man does cross the path of our cameras, we can use facial recognition software. David can't alter his retina no matter what." Jon rubbed her knee. "I'm sure Kato will be getting in touch with the authorities in Colombia to try to get David's medical records and hopefully, that will lead to his current alias."

Tears prickled Jessica's eyes, and she forced them away. "That might not be possible. Celebrities sneak off to these resort clinics, so people won't know they had work done. These places are extremely protective of their patients' privacy."

Jon ran his hands through his hair again. "Not only that. Law enforcement agencies here don't have the strongest relationship with the Colombian authorities.

Drugs make up a huge part of their economy, so we don't exactly see eye to eye."

"How do we get David's records? We need to find out what he looks like."

"I could fly to Colombia, case out the clinic, and try to track down the surgeon that operated on him. Persuade them to talk. But I think there's an easier way. A hacker. Maybe we'll get lucky, and photos of the patients will be uploaded electronically. If not, we'd at least get our hands on his records."

"Doesn't Cynthia have some experience?"

"Getting into a phone is one thing but hacking into a secure server at a clinic is another. We could've really used Thomas' expertise right now. I still miss him. I have a list of his online friends from the memorial. Maybe one of them could help us."

"I miss him too." Jessica swallowed around a lump in her throat, flooded with the memory of Thomas laying on the basement floor in Oahu missing half of his head. Dead because he'd helped them. "Okay. We find a hacker on the list. And if that doesn't work. Then we'll go from there."

"I'll need to pick up Kato in Great Falls tonight around midnight. Will you be okay on your own for five or six hours? I can ask Trent and Cynthia to come over."

Jessica stomach churned at the thought of Jon leaving. Having his ex-wife and Trent stay in the house, instead of the rental on the same property, may seem extreme to some. But with what David was capable of, it made perfect sense. "Sure. Cynthia and Trent can stay in the guest room. She did volunteer to babysit."

As overwhelming as the situation with David was, in combination with giving birth, she needed to face it.

Part of protecting her family involved letting Jon do what he needed to do. If she'd listened to him and let him go after Hugh Jones in the first place, it might have prevented her kidnapping. Aunt Debbie wouldn't have gotten shot in the liver, and Thomas might still be alive.

Jon took her hand. "Having Kato here and us working together is a good thing. In my opinion, he's one of the best agents the FBI has."

"I'm glad. We need all the help we can get." A few hours, she could handle. Bryce would be coming home for dinner, so she'd have the two kids to keep her busy. Time would fly by, right?

Chapter Three

In anticipation of Aunt Debbie's arrival with Bryce, Jessica turned on the oven to heat the chicken casserole Cynthia had made. She still wasn't sure whether to be grateful or annoyed that Cynthia had let herself in and cooked without asking.

Maybe a combination of both since Cynthia's heart was always in the right place, but her presence within their home was innerving, at least from Jessica's perspective. Without asking Jon, she couldn't be sure how he felt about the situation, and she hadn't yet mustered the courage to ask.

Jessica glanced down at her cozy bathrobe and sighed. Finding clothes to fit would be a challenge. She padded down the hallway to the walk-in closet in her bedroom and flipped through hangers. Besides cotton leggings, which would highlight the extra weight she was carrying, none of her pants would fit. She grabbed a summer dress with an empire waistline that would camouflage her midsection then tied her still damp hair into a ponytail.

Back in the kitchen, she sliced a loaf of bread and set it on the table with butter. Then she filled the kettle with water and rested it on the stove for tea, Aunt Debbie's favorite beverage. Jon hadn't even left, and she already needed to keep busy to cope.

The new panel for the security gate buzzed on the

kitchen wall. On the camera feed, she recognized the old, red Ford pickup truck, and Aunt Debbie behind the wheel with Bryce in the passenger seat. Jessica pressed the button to open the gate, then turned the gas burner on beneath the kettle.

Cassie's cries carried from down the hall. "Coming, baby girl."

As Jessica strode down the hallway, the crying stopped.

Jon's baritone voice reached her ears. "It's okay, Cassie. Let's get you a clean diaper, then find your mommy. Oh, boy what a mess."

Jessica chuckled and her heart warmed. She loved the sight of Jon and Cassie together. "That's babies. Adorable but smelly."

Jon scrunched his nose as he stepped on the pedal of the garbage can and dropped the dirty diaper inside. "You're telling me. This is why I didn't babysit my nephews until they were potty trained." He snapped Cassie's onesie shut.

Jessica picked Cassie up from the changing table and sat in the rocking chair in the corner of the nursery. "Oh, crap. The kettle is boiling in the kitchen for Debbie. She buzzed just as Cassie started crying."

"No worries. I'll get them settled and make tea."

Jessica locked eyes with Cassie. "How are we going to manage without Daddy around for six hours? I guess we don't have a choice. Do we, little one?"

Cassie's eyes fluttered once she had her fill of milk. Jessica shifted her onto her shoulder with a burping cloth and patted her back as she wandered down the hall to the kitchen.

Aunt Debbie, Bryce, and Jon sat at the kitchen table

together with mugs. The scent of chicken and vegetables from the casserole steaming on top of the stove made Jessica's stomach rumble.

Bryce turned his head and smiled. "Can I hold, Cassie?"

Jessica said, "Sure. But you have to give me a hug first. I missed you."

Bryce ran over and wrapped his arms around Jessica's waist. "I missed you, too."

"Okay, buddy. Sit in your chair and crook your arm, then I'll hand you your baby sister."

Bryce sat, eyes shining with excitement.

Jessica placed Cassie in his lap. "That's right. Keep her head cradled by your elbow. If she gets too heavy let me know." Tears prickled her eyes as Bryce looked down at his baby sister with love in his gaze.

Aunt Debbie rolled the sleeves of her denim blouse up to her elbows. "After Bryce, it's my turn to hold her. Jess, why don't you go ahead and eat while we have her?"

Jon stood. "Good idea. You sit, and I'll dish out dinner."

The love and warmth of her family surrounding her served as a reminder of how hard she'd fight for these precious moments. Nothing and no one, serial killer or otherwise, could be allowed to stand in the way.

****

Later that night, after Debbie had gone home, Jessica tucked Bryce into bed and kissed his forehead. "Sweet dreams."

She wanted to make sure he still got special moments of her time where her attention was on him and only him. That way he'd enjoy having his sister around, rather than resenting Cassie for needing so much care. Jessica still remembered feeling like an outcast when her parents brought her sister home from the hospital.

"Good night, Mom." He rolled over and faced the wall.

As always, within minutes his breathing deepened. Bryce had always been a heavy sleeper. It was good in one sense because he'd sleep through Cassie's cries in the night, but bad in the sense that fire alarms and gunfire didn't wake him either.

Jon came out of their bedroom further down the hallway. "I should head out. Don't want to keep Kato waiting." He brushed a quick kiss against her lips. "Trent and Cynthia are on their way over. You and the kids will be fine."

"Of course we will. Don't worry about us. You focus on what you need to do." Their kisses in passing were sweet and well-intentioned, but the fire behind them had dwindled in recent months as her pregnancy progressed. They'd have to remedy that before long. She couldn't let her closeness with Jon slip away.

A soft knock sounded on the front door. "That would be Cynthia and Trent. Bye, sweetheart." Jon walked through the kitchen and out the back door.

Jessica stared at the closed door, missing Jon already. She sighed, then scurried through the main living area to the front door. "Hey, Cynthia. Come in. I just put the kettle on. Where's Trent?"

"He wanted to do a perimeter check before coming inside."

Jessica ignored the distinctive tingle of fear crawling up her neck. "Makes sense." She set mugs and tea bags on the table while the water heated.

"How are you? Recovering?"

"I'm getting there." Jessica took the steaming kettle off the burner.

Cynthia flipped her hair behind her shoulders as Jessica poured water into their mugs. "I'd like to help you get back into shape and teach you how to fight."

Jessica placed the kettle on the stove and sat across from Cynthia with the baby monitor. "That's kind of you. I know my basic self-defense and Jon taught me to shoot."

"Did he teach you hand-to-hand combat?"

"No."

"Me neither. Because Jon can't bear the thought of you in that situation, and he wants to carry the role of protector alone."

Jessica sipped her tea. "Well, he's good at it."

"He is. But do you feel like you can protect yourself and the kids on your own?"

"Not entirely."

"See, I get that. That's how I felt after Henson kidnapped me and sent me into hiding." Cynthia pressed down on her tea bag with a spoon. "When Trent taught me how to fight, I felt safe and in control again. I want to share that with you."

Jessica envisioned the effort and pain required to achieve that goal, but the idea of feeling in control was too irresistible to pass up. "I want that feeling. Let's do it. We'll start tomorrow."

Cynthia beamed. "Great."

"Thank you for doing this. I knew I needed to get back into shape fast. I just didn't know where to start." Jessica sipped her tea. It scalded her tongue on the way down, but it warmed her insides.

"What about Bryce?"

"We put him in Taekwondo lessons after David kidnapped him. It helped with the nightmares."

"Smart. Martial arts are the best self-defense for kids. What did you tell him about all this?"

"Bryce asked about the security gate at dinner. We decided to tell him we upgraded security and nothing else." Jessica frowned. "He had nightmares after David kidnapped him, so it seemed like the best course of action. I'm concerned about school."

"Oh, yeah. I meant to tell you. There's an opening at the school for a learning support teacher and I applied."

"Really? That would be perfect. I thought you were done with teaching."

Cynthia shrugged. "I'm still undecided. I loved working with special needs kids before Jones uprooted my life. I figured with him dead, I'd give it a shot and see how things go."

Trent came in the kitchen door, kicked off his cowboy boots, then sat beside Cynthia. "The ranch is secure." He took off his cowboy hat and set it on the table.

"Good," Jessica said. "Can I get either one of you anything before I go to bed?"

Cynthia shook her head. "You go on to bed. Trent and I can take care of ourselves."

"Thanks again, guys. I really appreciate this." She took the rest of her tea and her phone to the master bedroom, then checked on Cassie in her nursery. She'd kicked her blanket off at some point, so Jessica covered her again, then went back to her own room and climbed into bed.

Staring at the empty spot in the bed beside her stirred up a sense of unease. All the more reason to embrace Cynthia's offer. She scrolled through active wear on her phone and added some compression leggings and baggy, breathable tees to the cart in a few sizes. That way she'd always have something that fit. Once she accomplished her goal of returning to her pre-pregnancy size, she'd reward herself with some fitted shirts and zip-up jackets.

Next time you come after us, David. I'll be a force to be reckoned with.

Chapter Four

Jessica slept for a few hours before Cassie woke for her midnight feed. Cassie went straight to sleep after being changed and fed. Jessica placed her in the crib, then tiptoed into the hallway, and eased the door shut.

She yawned and glanced at Bryce's door. He always slept through Cassie's cries, but she had the urge to look in on him. She opened his door, wincing as the hinges creaked, but Bryce didn't stir. He slept facing the wall the way he always did, his chest rising and falling in a steady rhythm.

Out of the corner of her eye, something moved outside, past Bryce's window.

With the house being a single-story, the windows were too accessible. Her heart thudded against her rib cage. With the alarm system, motion sensors, and the security gate, her reaction seemed unfounded, but nonetheless, the hair on her arm stood on end.

She forced herself to cross the room and peer out the window. The clear night sky, unobscured by clouds, illuminated the hayfield outside. In the center of the field, stood a tall man with dark hair. The hay stalks concealed him from the waist down. She covered her mouth to smother a scream.

Oh no! Not David. Please, it can't be.

He turned around and faced the house.

Unable to believe her eyes, she pressed her face to

the glass and strained her gaze for a better view.

Adam?

In the dark, at such a distance, she couldn't be sure, but he closely resembled her first husband who'd passed away nine years ago. On occasion, Adam appeared to her, but usually in the same room, and never at a distance.

He turned his back to her and walked away, seeming more solid than ghost.

What if the man outside was someone else?

She sprinted through the kitchen and past the dining room to the guest room at the opposite end of the house. She made a fist and knocked on the door.

"Coming." Trent swung the door open dressed in a white tee and shorts. "Is everything okay?"

She swallowed back the instinct to tell him she thought her husband's ghost wandered the field. He'd take her more seriously if she kept that part to herself for now. "I'm not sure. I just saw a man in the hayfield outside Bryce's window. He was heading south away from the house."

He came out of the room and shut the door. "I'll go check it out." He stepped into his cowboy boots, grabbed the rifle off the top shelf of the closet by the entrance, and slung it over his shoulder as he headed out the front door.

Jessica locked the door behind him, then sprinted to the window in the eating nook tucked into an alcove near the kitchen. That window faced the same direction as the one in Bryce's room.

The beam of Trent's flashlight illuminated the golden hay stalks as he wandered through the rows. The man she'd spotted was nowhere to be seen. Once Trent crested the hill in the distance, only his flashlight beam was visible over the hay stalks.

Assuming he'd be a while, Jessica filled the kettle and set it on the stove to boil. Once the water heated, she poured it into a mug over an herbal tea bag. She cradled her tea in her hands and returned to the window to wait for Trent.

The panel for the security gate chimed. On the camera feed, Jon drove his black Dodge Ram through the gate. *Thank God!* He had a passenger she couldn't make out on the feed. It had to be Kato. She set her tea on the kitchen counter and dashed out the front door to wait for Jon on the porch.

Gravel kicked up as he rounded the bend in the road and parked in front of the house. Jon and Kato climbed out of the truck. The newcomer was a head shorter than Jon and trim, but his biceps strained against the sleeves of his tee. He carried the confident air of law enforcement in his movements.

Jon bounded up the steps smiling, wrapped his arms around her waist, and kissed her. His lips lingered for a change, long enough for her to taste a hint of coffee. "Hey, sweetheart. I missed you. I was hoping you'd be sleeping." He gestured to the other man. "This is Agent Kato Chen."

Kato held out a hand and smiled warmly. "It's nice to meet you, Mrs. Kent." He had a slight accent, pleasing to the ear.

She shook his hand. "It's nice to meet you, too. Call me Jess."

Jon asked, "Where's Trent and Cynthia?"

"Cynthia is in bed. I woke Trent about ten minutes ago after I spotted a man in the hayfield."

Kato asked, "Which way?"

Jon pointed in the direction of the field. "South of the house."

"I'll go help Trent." Kato jogged down the porch steps.

Jon's brows furrowed. "Did you recognize this man?"

"It's hard to be certain at a distance, but I think it was Adam. I sent Trent out as a precaution."

"Are you sure you weren't dreaming or imagining things?"

Jessica tensed and took a step away from Jon. "No. And I can't believe you're questioning what I saw when you've seen Adam's ghost before."

"I'm sorry. Don't take it the wrong way. But you're exhausted. A tired mind can play tricks on anyone."

"I suppose it's a possibility. I've never been so tired."

"None of the motion detectors were tripped, and I'm assuming the alarm on the new gate didn't go off?"

"No."

"At least Kato is here now. We'll figure it out." Jon wrapped an arm around her shoulders. "Let's go inside and check out the cameras. You're shivering."

"Sure." She hadn't noticed the chill in the night air until Jon mentioned it. Maybe this whole episode was the product of exhaustion.

They went into the house and sat beside each other at the round table in the kitchen nook. Jon pulled up live camera feeds on his laptop. Only four different camera angles displayed at a time out of the forty cameras around the property. Jon clicked through the ten sets of feeds one at a time.

Her gut churned. "What's the purpose of all these cameras when we can't watch all the feeds simultaneously?"

"That's where the motion sensors and the alarm on the gate come in. If someone trips a sensor, then the security program will zero in on the relevant camera feed." Jon clicked on a button and the feeds alternated to different cameras. "No one so far."

A light knock sounded on the back door in the kitchen.

Jon stood, glanced out the peephole, then opened the door. "Did you guys find anything?"

Trent frowned at Jessica and shook his head. "Nothing."

"Footprints?"

"Some, between the rows. But between the staff, Kato, and me running out there more worried about an intruder, I don't know how reliable that would be."

"Makes sense. I'd be more in a panic to cover the area as well. Hopefully, there won't be a next time, but if there is we need to be more diligent about the evidence trail."

"I don't see how anyone could bypass that security." Trent rubbed his eyes. "I'll get Kato settled at the rental."

Jessica crossed her arms, barely refraining from huffing. *Neither one of them believes I saw that man.*

The men left and Jon locked the door behind them. "Want to search through camera feeds or call it a night?"

"We can watch the footage in the morning. If there was a man on the property, he's gone now anyhow." Jessica glanced out the window at the empty hayfield one last time.

No. That man wasn't a figment of her imagination. The camera footage would prove it.

Chapter Five

At six the next morning, after putting Cassie down, Jessica pulled on sweatpants and an old baggy tee. She covered her mouth to smother a yawn and stared at her comfortable bed. Sleep appealed to her much more than the workout she'd planned with Cynthia, but she needed to face the reality of her situation. Being postpartum and out of shape made her far too vulnerable.

At least the men were out working on the ranch, so she'd have some privacy for her first workout in a long time. Too long. Not to mention, she still resented Jon's implication that she'd hallucinated the man in the hayfield. With any luck, Cynthia wouldn't bring it up.

She jogged in place. Her tired muscles warmed and some of the fog cleared from her brain. As she wandered into the main living area to find Cynthia, she seesawed her head to loosen her neck muscles.

Cynthia had placed two chairs facing each other in the middle of the floor between the living and dining rooms. She wore fitted black leggings and a matching cropped tank showing off her perfect physique. "Oh, hey. Come sit. You're still recovering, so today we'll start with a chair workout and ease you into low-impact cardio after you've had a few more days to heal."

Jessica did her best not to think about her frumpy sweats and her soft, flabby stomach as she sat. Cynthia, the picture of fitness and David the maniacal serial killer combined were the perfect motivation to work out as much as possible. "A chair workout sounds interesting. But how much can you get done sitting?"

"You'd be surprised. We'll start with arms then move to leg exercises with weights." Cynthia handed her a small set of two-pound dumbbells then picked up a five-pound set. "Carrying Cassie around as she gets bigger will strengthen your arms and core muscles naturally, but we want to speed that process along in case you need to defend yourself."

"Makes sense."

"Okay then. I know you're exhausted, so I'll go slow. Just copy what I'm doing." Cynthia curled her arms and lifted the weights until they touched her shoulders, revealing sculpted muscles.

Jessica copied her movements through a series of different positions with the weights. Sweat dripped from her neck down the center of her spine, and her arms and shoulders ached and trembled, but she pushed through the pain, mild in comparison to the marathon of labor. She wanted a body like Cynthia's, strong and dependable, with the ability to subdue a man double her size the way Cynthia had in the airport washroom the first time they met.

Cynthia set her weights on the floor. "Great job, Jess. Feeling the burn?"

"Oh, yes. My arms are like spaghetti."

"Shoot. I overdid it. I'm sorry. If it's too much tell me next time."

Jessica shook her head. "No. I want to push myself. Time isn't on our side. It's already been almost six months since David said he'd come for us. I need to be ready for him. He outsmarted us last time. I need to be prepared for that to happen again when I least expect it."

Cynthia frowned. "I understand. Are you up for moving onto legs?"

"Yes. Let's do it." It might only be the first workout of the many she needed to get into shape, but it was a solid step on the right path. The path that would lead her to never being anyone's victim ever again.

****

Later that afternoon, once work around the ranch had wrapped up, Jessica sat in the chair next to Jon at the kitchen table. Kato had been in Jon's office on the phone all morning trying to make headway with the Colombians. So far, he'd struck out.

Cassie, a sweet and welcome distraction from Jessica's sighting the previous night, slept, cradled in her arms as the camera footage played on the laptop from the night before.

It would be difficult to pinpoint when the man entered the property, as he could have done so at any point in the day. To shorten the timeframe, they played footage beginning at the time Jessica had spotted him and went forwards thirty minutes to when Trent and Kato were positive no one was on the property.

Throughout the past four hours, they'd watched thirty-six of the forty camera feeds and so far, nothing. Each time Jon clicked on his mouse and started new feeds, Jessica doubted her sanity a little bit more. They were down to the final four.

"Would it be possible for someone to manipulate the feeds and the motion sensors to avoid being caught on camera?"

"With a system this sophisticated, it would be extremely difficult. But nothing is impossible. Anything relying on a computer and internet is hackable."

The last few minutes of the footage wrapped up, revealing nothing.

Am I losing my mind? No.

She wouldn't allow her thoughts to travel down that rabbit hole. She didn't conjure up the sighting out of her imagination.

Jon minimized the security program. "I don't know what you saw, sweetheart. But there was no one on our property."

"It had to be Adam, then. There is no other explanation. What if he was trying to warn us that David is nearby? Remember how he told me he'd lose his connection with me if he said too much? Maybe that's the problem. Maybe he's desperate to tell us something but can't speak."

"I'm not discounting that possibility. Adam saved our lives with his warnings in the past. Our guards have been up since we found out David was alive, and they'll stay there."

Why couldn't he just say he believed her? She shoved aside her frustration and moved on. What else could she do? Hopefully, if it was Adam, he'd figure out a way to get his message across.

Chapter Six

Over the past three months, Chris White, now Nathan Kirk, had settled into daily life in Ketchum, Idaho. He climbed the five concrete steps to the entrance at The Community Library, where Amy worked, and went inside.

The wood-burning fireplace in the center of the room always stopped him in his tracks. It wasn't because of the eye-catching, grey, stone façade that comprised the hearth and chimney all the way up to the vaulted ceiling with dark wooden beams, but rather that on chilly days the firebox held fire.

Shutting his eyes, he pictured the flames and the sweet aroma of burning logs. What would happen if the screen was left open? And there happened to be a stack of books resting on the wooden mantle?

Sparks might fly from the fire, fed by the extra oxygen, and land on the books. Their pages would flame, creating more sparks. If the ventilation kicked in, it would blow more sparks around the room. The books on all the bookshelves surrounding the fireplace would flame, hopefully in unison. What a magnificent sight that would be.

Nathan sighed. As much as he wanted to make his dream a reality, he couldn't take the risk and draw attention to himself. Instead, he'd have to be content with trapping Amy in his web on the path to revenge. She was proving to be more difficult to woe than he anticipated. If it wasn't for her location being convenient to Montana, he'd move on to a new target.

One more big insurance payout. That's all he needed.

He wandered over to the true crime section and ran his hand along the spines while browsing the titles. He wasn't an avid reader as he'd led Amy to believe during their online chats. But he didn't mind reading about other killers and their crimes. They provided him with a source of inspiration and creativity.

A small hand touched his forearm. "Hi, Nathan."

He turned to face Amy and forced a smile. "Hi, darling. Just stopped by to see you and grab some books." Her small frame hid beneath a dark, frumpy dress, and her long, dark curls covered most of her face from the almost permanent slouch in her shoulders from hanging her head and avoiding people.

She clasped her hands together. "Need help finding anything?"

"Got any new books in this week?"

She adjusted her glasses, then pulled a book from the shelf. "This one just came in. It's about a serial killer who embalmed his victims before leaving them to be found."

He took the book and wrinkled his nose. *Gross.* He'd learned to take pleasure in the smell of burnt flesh over the years, but formaldehyde? No thank you. "You have to wonder what goes on in the mind of someone that warped."

"Is that why you read these books? To try to figure it out?"

"Yes. I like to understand humanity in all forms.

Both good and bad." He took her hand. "Would you like to have dinner after you're done work? Afterwards, maybe we could go for a walk and stop for hot chocolate at that bakery you like so much for dessert."

She smiled and her cheeks reddened as she glanced down at her sensible loafers. "Uh-huh."

After six months of chatting online and three months of dating in person, Amy still got flustered in his presence. Her lack of self-esteem proved to be the biggest roadblock for him to overcome. He'd need to use a different tactic to shift their relationship into something less casual and more serious—lie through his teeth to boost her self-esteem.

He placed a finger under her chin and raised her head to face him. "Chin up, love. You're beautiful." The green eyes behind the thick lenses of her glasses gave her face some charm. With her looking down all the time, he hadn't noticed them before. Maybe she possessed some redeeming qualities after all.

****

Nathan pulled his truck to the curb at the library to pick up Amy. She bounded out the front doors before he came to a complete stop. Her enthusiasm was a positive sign, but he sensed she didn't fully trust him yet.

Why, he couldn't be certain. Some people possessed keener instincts than others. Although she didn't rebuke him, perhaps on some level she sensed the danger hidden behind his smile. Or maybe, like many lacking confidence, she feared getting too close to him, believing he'd reject her.

Either way, he needed to work past whatever was holding her back. He needed to test her to decipher the root cause of her hesitation.

She climbed into the passenger seat. "Hi, Nathan."

He reached into the backseat for the bouquet of roses he'd picked up on the way there. He kissed her cheek. "These are for you."

"Oh, thank you. They're beautiful."

Time to attempt his first test. "You're welcome. Did you want to stop at your place to feed Parker?"

She fingered the petal of the one rose that had already opened. "Yes, then I won't feel bad about making him wait for his dinner."

He drove the few blocks to the small apartment building where she lived and pulled into the visitor's parking space. "Here we are."

She placed her hand on the door handle. "Did you want to come with me and say hello?"

"Sure."

So, she trusted him enough to invite him into her space. Maybe trust wasn't the issue. This was a step in the right direction for their budding relationship.

They took the elevator up to the third floor.

She unlocked the door to her apartment and Parker's little wagging tail greeted her. She rubbed the fluff on the top of his head. "Hi, baby. Mommy missed you."

Nathan stepped inside the apartment behind her, and Parker stared at him, bared his teeth, and growled. "He probably doesn't like me because I took him away from his first owner."

Amy cradled Parker in her arms and kissed his head as she took him into the kitchen. "Poor boy. Let's get your dinner. I bet your first Mommy misses you. But she couldn't take you to the old age home, pup."

For a descendant of Eve who showed weakness in the Garden of Eden, Amy wasn't as evil as most women.

She paid a lot more attention to the dog than Emily ever did. But given time and experience, she'd use her wiles to manipulate men. All women poisoned the male race and made them weak, some worse than others.

Amy dished fancy wet dog food into a bowl and filled Parker's water dish. "Here you go. Mommy will be back later." She smiled at Nathan. "Ready?"

Nathan drove them to the best Italian restaurant in town close to North Main Street. They had the most tender and mouth-watering filet mignon around. Having had a crappy start in life, and no one to teach him to cook, he'd never learned beyond boiling water or turning on the oven for frozen, pre-made food. Emily, may she not rest in peace, with her southern upbringing, had cooked tasty dishes. Her peach pies were to die for.

He chuckled. *Haha. To die for.*

Amy glanced at him. "Thinking of something funny."

"Yes." He lied. "I watched a funny comedy this afternoon. Enjoying my days off."

"That sounds fun."

"We should watch a movie together sometime at my place."

A flush spread across Amy's cheeks and her gaze travelled to her loafers.

"What's the matter? Why do you always get bashful around me?"

She picked at the hem of her long cardigan. "Well, I don't exactly have much experience with physical relationships. Zero experience, actually. And you're well—you're so handsome, so I'm sure you have expectations."

"I figured that out already. Don't worry. I can wait

until you're ready."

"Why would you want to wait for me?"

"Why not? You're smart, sweet, and beautiful underneath all the layers you hide behind. But you don't need to hide from me, darling."

Tears welled in her eyes as she smiled. "I like how you see the real me."

He clasped her hand. "I do. And I'm lucky you're mine." And just like that, her walls had started to crumble. *Got you, Amy.*

Chapter Seven

Jon rode his favorite horse, Daisy, at a jog around the cattle fields. He needed to see with his own eyes that all his animals were healthy heading into the colder seasons, although the weather belied their approach.

The sun shone in a vast, cloudless sky on a warmer than normal day for late summer. His sweat-soaked hair stuck to his head inside his dark brown cowboy hat, but he didn't mind. Summer tended to let go in Montana without any warning.

His phone came to life with an incoming call. He shifted the reins to his left hand and hit the accept button. "Kato. Any progress?"

"No. The Colombians are being assholes. We might be on our own unless you want to wait months for the information."

Jon ran a hand through his hair and tugged on the ends. "We were expecting this, but it still sucks. I put out feelers amongst our old pal, Thomas' friends to see if any of them can help us hack into the server at that clinic."

"I need to pretend I didn't hear that."

Jon chuckled. "Right. I never mentioned a hacker." Kato had never been one to let rules stand in the way of nabbing the bad guys. That's what made him one of the good agents. He cared more about saving lives than keeping his job.

"Oh, you know me, I'm okay with bending the rules

if it means getting a killer off the streets. If the hacker can't help, and you end up deciding to go to Colombia, I'll take a few days off and go with you unofficially. Don't go down there and sniff around by yourself, whatever you do."

"I'm hoping it won't come to that. But if it does, I'll let you know."

Jon hung up and gently squeezed Daisy's sides. "Let's head back to the stables, girl."

After removing Daisy's tack and giving her a quick grooming, water, and an apple, he went inside and booted his laptop on the kitchen table. He clicked on the mail icon and scrolled through his new emails.

One of Thomas' friends, Beachgirl71, had responded.

—Thomas would've wanted me to help you. You were one of his closest friends. Send me the details, and I'll see what I can do.—

Jon typed a response giving the name of the clinic and the parameters. David had switched identities in the past, so they needed to narrow down the search through the patient files. Fortunately, they knew exactly when he'd fallen off the side of the mountain, and thanks to Hugh Jones' minion, they also knew he'd suffered a severe leg break.

He hit send, then shut his laptop and went in search of his family. Bryce's laughter carried through the open windows in the sitting room from the porch that wrapped around the front of the house.

Jon shifted the curtains and smiled. Cynthia was facing Jessica and Bryce, leading them through a series of yoga poses while Cassie slept in her stroller. Never in his wildest dreams had he ever imagined his first wife, presumed dead, would be on the porch with his family. Although Cynthia was family, too.

Cynthia had gone back to her natural auburn hair, looking more like the version of herself from when they were married. The kind, sweet, woman she'd been back then was still in there, but with an edge she'd never had before because of him.

His chest tightened as guilt reared its ugly head. His career as an undercover FBI agent had bled into the lives of the people he loved. It caused Cynthia's abduction, then Jessica's kidnapping, and ultimately cost his friend Thomas his life. Reminders lingered in the faces of his loved ones, creeping up on him when he least expected them.

But he refused to let those negative emotions hold sway, preventing him from enjoying life and loving his family the way they deserved to be loved.

He stepped out onto the porch as Jessica and Cynthia rolled up their yoga mats. "Nice day for some outdoor exercise."

Cynthia tucked her yoga mat under her arm. "It is. This was fun. I'll see you guys, tomorrow. Same time, Jess?"

"Yes, please. Thanks so much, Cynthia."

Bryce asked, "Is it okay if I go visit Daisy?"

Jon ruffled his hair. With the fencing and cameras, they didn't have to worry about Bryce wandering the property. "Sure." He wrapped his arm around Jessica's shoulders. "How are you feeling today? Better?"

She leaned into him. "Yes. I'm getting my energy back. I think the daily workouts with Cynthia are helping. We'll have to move them to after school next week."

"Why?"

"She got a call from the principal this morning. They've officially hired her as the learning resource teacher for the year."

"I was hoping that would work out. It'll be good for her and for Bryce's protection."

"You seem awfully concerned about your ex-wife when she's perfectly capable of taking care of herself. First, she needed Trent to walk her home, and now this job is good for her."

"Of course. Why wouldn't I be? What are you trying to say?"

"It makes me uncomfortable that you care so much. She's living on our property looking amazing, and I just gave birth."

"Sweetheart, I'm only in love with you. And that's not going to change. We've talked about this before. Yes, I have feelings for her, but nothing like what I feel for you. What you're seeing is my guilt. I'm responsible for all the danger she's encountered and having her life ripped apart."

"I'm sorry, Jon." Tears filled Jessica's eyes. "I know how you feel. I inflicted David on everyone."

"Everything will be okay, sweetheart. We'll figure this out." He held her close and rested his head on hers, inhaling the strawberry scent of her shampoo. "One of Thomas' friends responded. Beachgirl71 is going to help us."

"Good. This has to end."

"Yes, it does." He needed to find David, and then David needed to die.

Chapter Eight

Jessica shut her eyes and leaned into the soft cotton of Jon's shirt, letting him reassure her as they stood together on the porch. He claimed he wasn't in love with his ex-wife, but she had a hard time believing him after the way he'd looked at Cynthia through the window before coming outside. He wouldn't intentionally deceive her, but he might be deceiving himself.

Cynthia hadn't been an issue living a state away in Colorado with Trent. Jessica assumed after they tracked down David, or he found them, everything would go back to normal when Cynthia and Trent returned home. But now that Cynthia had accepted a position for a full school year, who knew how long she'd stick around?

Regardless, Jessica could feel Jon's love for her in his warm embrace. And he'd made the conscious decision to be her husband and a father to their children. And Jon's best quality was his unwavering loyalty. He wouldn't stray, even if it got in the way of his own happiness. And that bothered her even more because she wanted Jon to be happy.

Cassie stirred in her stroller, scrunched up her face, and started to cry.

Jessica left the welcome comfort of Jon's arms. "She'll be interrupting us for the next eighteen years."

Jon chuckled. "Probably."

Jessica unclipped the straps holding Cassie into the

stroller and cradled her baby in her arms. "I'll take her to the nursery and feed her again."

"Okay. How about I fix us some lunch?"

"Sure." Jessica hummed a lullaby to Cassie as she carried her inside. "Almost there, baby. We'll get you fed." She settled into the glider inside the nursery and let the rhythm of Cassie feeding ease her worries.

With Jon home, a protective cocoon settled over the house and their family. She continued to let him take on the role of protector while she cared for everyone's basic needs because he had such specialized training and abilities. But last spring, Jessica had learned a valuable lesson about herself—in the face of a threat, she could step into that role. She'd shot a mobster to prevent him from shooting Jon. While his life hung in the balance, she hadn't hesitated to take a life, and she could do it again.

Cynthia's presence created an awkward atmosphere, but she was right about Jessica needing to be able to fill the role of protector on her own. She would be forever grateful to Cynthia for offering the gift of empowerment. Someday far into the future, after surviving the wrath of Hugh Jones and David Hayes, she'd pass on that gift to her own daughter. Cassie would never need to be dependent on anyone for her safety.

****

After putting the kids to bed later that night, Jessica sat up in bed trying to read a book but was unable to focus on the words to make sense of them. Beside her, Jon had his computer resting on his lap. He clicked on his email icon once again. He'd checked his inbox once an hour since lunch.

She asked, "Anything?"

"Actually, yes. I have a reply from Beachgirl71. She narrowed down the patient files to two sets, one belonging to Chris White and another to Frank Conklin. The bad news is neither one of them had images filed electronically. But maybe those names will lead us somewhere."

"Maybe. Why is nothing ever easy for us?" She set her book on the night table, switched off the bedside lamp, and lay on her side facing Jon.

He rubbed her shoulder. "Don't lose hope. He may not have switched identities when he left the clinic, having just switched on the way there."

Jessica shut her heavy eyes, serenaded by the methodical clicking pattern of Jon's fingers on his keyboard.

"Hot damn."

Jessica's eyes flew open. "What?"

Jon's lips shifted into the lop-sided grin that she'd always found hot.

"You found something." She scrambled into a sitting position beside Jon.

"Frank Conklin has social media accounts, and he's too short to be David. Which leaves Chris White. Chris White is a common name, and I would've been stuck searching through thousands upon thousands of records. So, I did a keyword search combining Chris White and death." He turned his laptop in her direction. "I found this."

His computer screen displayed an image of an attractive woman named Emily White accompanied by her obituary dated April 24th, 2023. A lump rose in Jessica's throat. Emily White was born on April 15th, 1993, to Heather and Matthew Evans. She had no children but was survived by her parents, a sister Nathalie Evans, and her husband Chris White.

"It doesn't say how she died. Just that it was unexpected. This doesn't prove anything." Jessica shivered violently. "But it feels like someone walked over my grave."

Jon set his computer aside and pulled her into his arms. "That's your instincts kicking in. It's him. I feel it too."

His warmth seeped into her bare skin, and the trembling slowed. "What's the next step?"

"The article came from a newspaper in Morgan County, Georgia. If you're okay with it, I'd like to fly there tomorrow with Kato and investigate. Kato could also go alone if you need me here."

She interrupted. "God, no. I don't trust anybody else with this. You need to do this yourself."

"Okay. You sleep. I doubt I'll find anything, but I'm going to search the DMV to see if I can find a driver's license for him, then I'll alert the FBI."

She nodded and shut her eyes.

Are you Chris White now, David?

Could they really have stumbled onto his trail? Hope bloomed. But the real possibility of disappointment existed. Emily had passed away four months ago. If David was responsible, he'd be long gone.

During his previous rampage, after he followed Jessica to Lewistown, Jon and Thomas had investigated him, unraveling a disturbing pattern. They'd never discovered David's real name, but they did identify a string of ten dead wives in his past who died under suspicious circumstances after he took out life insurance policies on them.

After each claim had been paid out, he'd moved locations and changed his identity, then he'd marry another woman. He shifted his money all over the place and in various accounts in the Cayman Islands, making it impossible for them to trace his location. And he knew to use cash wherever he went to avoid leaving a trail.

With a head start, they'd have to pray he'd left some evidence somewhere along the way. And if he had, Jessica trusted Jon to find it.

Chapter Nine

The following day in the middle of the afternoon, Jon and Kato deplaned at Hartsfield-Jackson Atlanta International Airport. Jon's search through the DMV records and the local newspapers in Madison, Georgia had turned up nothing. Without a face or a description of the vehicle Chris White was driving, he couldn't search for camera footage. His best bet would be old-fashioned police work.

Assistant Director Pruitt had notified the field office in Atlanta of the potential connection between David Hayes and Chris White. But with crime in Atlanta at an all-time high, it would take a few days for a local agent to be assigned to the case. Thank God, Kato was the lead agent on the investigation enabling him to step in.

Kato signed the paperwork for a rental car and accepted the key. "Where to? Do you want to go to the hotel or start canvassing?"

"I think we should canvass. I'd like us to interview witnesses ahead of the agents from the field office before they get annoyed with the questions and clam up."

"Agreed. This lead is too promising to allow someone else to mess it up on us."

Jon strode next to Kato as they made their way through the airport to find the exit closest to their rental car. "I'm so relieved Pruitt assigned you to this case. Thanks for letting me join in. It means a lot."

Jon used the maps app on his phone to navigate the sixty-five-mile route from the airport to the small city of Madison in Morgan County while Kato drove. Emily and Chris White had lived in a home owned by Emily's parents in Madison's Historical District.

Kato took his eyes off the road for an instant and glanced at Jon. "Did you get the file I sent you from the local police on Emily's death?"

"Yes, it did appear to be a classic accidental overdose. Emily had her own prescription and alcohol in her system, and only her prints were on the pill bottle. Them not fingerprinting Chris White was a major oversight. Disappointing to say the least."

"I agree. Protocol dictated they should have gotten Chris White's prints."

Jon rested his phone in the console. "Take the next right. Then we'll be on Emily's old street."

Kato signaled his turn. "Okay."

Interesting and distinctive bungalows lined both sides of the street. No one house resembled another. Most had two stories and columns with covered porches and lots of windows. Well-manicured lawns, gardens in full bloom, and old, tall trees gave the neighborhood an air of safety. A place where you didn't need to lock your doors or worry about letting your children play unsupervised.

But no place was ever safe. Monsters hid behind smiling faces all over America. A strong possibility existed that Chris White had hidden here unbeknownst to anyone.

Kato parked at a curb near the middle of the street and Jon climbed out.

The humid, muggy air in Georgia hung much

heavier than what he was used to in Montana. The calm winds offered no reprieve from the hot almost suffocating sun blanketing Jon in uncomfortable warmth.

Kato came to stand beside him on the sidewalk and pointed to a house across the street two houses down from where they stood. "Chris and Emily White lived in number sixteen."

Jon crossed the street, stopping in front of the house.

Wisteria wound itself up the brown brick covering the facade and the four columns holding up the entrance and the front porch, running all the way up to the chimney.

Jon climbed the stairs to the front door with Kato behind him. A layer of dust covered the matching, wooden rocking chairs on the porch, and the flowers in the black iron planters flagging the door were long dead.

Although he doubted anyone was living there, he knocked on the door anyway and waited.

A male voice with a pleasing southern drawl and long vowels said, "No one lives there anymore. Not since the husband packed up and left."

Jon turned. An elderly gentleman in a linen shirt and shorts with a straw hat on his head, stood on the sidewalk, shoulders hunched, leaning on his cane. If no one lived there, maybe they had a chance of finding some DNA or a fingerprint. The FBI had David's DNA for comparison on file, but not his prints which could lead to unraveling the mystery of his real identity.

Jon smiled and approached. "Hello, sir. I'm Agent Kent, FBI. And this is Agent Chen."

"It's a pleasure to meet you fine gentlemen. I'm Herbert. I live across the street with my wife Martha."

Jon asked, "Did you know the couple that used to live here?"

"Everyone knew Emily. She had to be in charge of everything and everybody." Herbert let out a small laugh. "Including her husband."

Jon pressed on. He needed more. So much more. They had so few pieces of the puzzle that made up David, and they needed more of them to put together a clearer picture of him. "She wore the pants. But what was Chris like?"

Herbert shrugged. "Barely noticed him. He kept to himself and walked with his head down everywhere he went. If you said good morning to him, he'd look at you out of the corner of his eye, say hello back, and then go about his business. He wasn't one for polite conversation."

Jon asked, "Did you ever get the impression that he was dangerous?"

"Dangerous? No. Not at all. More like terrified of his wife."

Jon nodded. "Would you happen to have any photos of him?"

"I don't think so. I'd have to check with Martha. She's the one that takes the pictures." Herbert turned and called over his shoulder. "Come along, y'all. I'll get Martha to make us some of her famous lemonade."

Kato walked alongside Herbert as he hobbled along with his cane. "That sounds nice, thank you."

Sweat drenched Jon's back and his tie felt like it was cutting off oxygen. He let Herbert and Kato walk ahead of him, then unknotted the tie and shoved it in his pocket. After opening the two top buttons of his shirt, he could breathe easier.

Herbert led them onto a covered porch spanning the width of the front of the house. "Have a seat, gentlemen. I'll fetch Martha."

Jon sat on the end of a wicker sectional couch. In the shade, away from the punishing afternoon sun, the warm air comforted rather than suffocated. "It's hot for late August."

Kato dabbed his forehead with a handkerchief. "You'll get used to it."

"I'm hoping not to be here long enough to adjust. I hate not being on the ranch protecting my family."

"So, what do you make of Herbert's description of Chris White?"

A bead of sweat ran down Jon's forehead. He wiped the salty moisture away before it landed in his eye. "During our interactions with David, I picked up on arrogance, egocentricity, and instability. He believes himself superior and smarter than everyone else around him which we used to trap him the last time."

"Well, he has avoided detection for over a decade."

"He made no effort to disguise his true nature when he came after Jess. But he must be an expert at masking himself or women wouldn't keep marrying him. That's why the questions about his personality are so important."

The door opened and Herbert hobbled out ahead of a woman with short silver hair and thick eyeglasses carrying a tray. "Gentlemen, this is Martha."

Martha smiled. "It's nice to meet you. Herbert says ya'll are law enforcement agents." The ice cubes clinked together inside the four glasses of lemonade as she set them down on the table. "Help yourself."

"Thank you, ma'am." Jon picked up a frosty glass

and sipped delicious lemonade. "Yes, we're with the FBI. We were discussing the Whites with Herbert."

Martha shook her head and frowned. "Such a shame what happened to Emily. A horrible accident, they say."

Jon asked, "Ma'am, do you think she was the type of person to do something careless enough to lead to her death?"

Herbert squinted at Jon behind his glasses. "Careless?"

Jon nodded. "Yes, sir. She allegedly took a prescribed sedative she'd been taking for over five years while drinking and the combination killed her. Seems to me she would have known better."

"You don't think she did it on purpose, do you?" Martha said. "She had her friends and Chris. There's no way she'd kill herself."

Herbert asked, "Why the questions about the husband?"

Jon glanced between them. "Because we think he's responsible for her death. We're searching for a serial killer who moves around marrying women, and then makes their deaths look like accidents to cash in insurance policies. We think Chris White may be him."

Herbert stared at him and went silent.

Martha gripped the arms of her chair. "Oh, my goodness. How awful."

Jon continued. "I'm sorry to have dropped that on you, but that's why I was asking Herbert if you had any pictures of Chris White. He disappeared off the radar when he left here three months ago."

Martha stood. "Wait here. I'll dig out the photo album."

Kato dug a notebook out of his pocket and a pencil.

"Sir, could you tell me what Chris White looked like? Was he tall?"

Herbert set his glass on the table and adjusted his position in the chair. "He always had his shoulders hunched, but yes, he would've been quite tall. Maybe six feet? And big. Not fat like a lineman. More like a sturdy linebacker."

Kato scribbled down notes. "You mean muscular but not fat?"

Herbert chuckled. "Yes, sir. You don't watch football, do you?"

"Unfortunately, no. I'm usually busy with work." Kato flipped a page in his notebook.

Martha came out the front door with a photo album in her arms. "I found it." She sat next to Herbert and opened the album.

Jon leaned forward in his chair and stayed silent, following Martha's finger as she carefully studied each photo before flipping to the next page. She made it through the whole album and Jon's hopes melted like the ice cubes in his almost empty glass of lemonade.

Martha flipped back a few pages, then handed the album to Jon and pointed to a photo. "I have this one of him from behind."

Chris White's head was turned away from the camera, blocking his whole face. But his height and build resembled David. Between the medical records and the photo, they were definitely on the right track. "Thank you, Ma'am. This looks like the man I'm looking for. The problem is he had plastic surgery on his nose and chin since I saw him last."

Martha said, "Maybe one of the other neighbors will have a better picture. We could introduce you to the couple a few doors down from us. They have a few young ones, so the wife, Shelley, is always taking pictures on that mobile phone of hers."

"That would be lovely. Thank you." Jon forced a smile. "There is another important question we're looking for an answer to. Do you know how Emily met Chris?"

Martha shook her head. "No. Did you ever hear about how they met Herb?"

"No."

Jon resisted the urge to groan. The chances of David, if indeed he was Chris White now, getting caught on camera were slim to none, but the man beneath the vile personality was human, and humans made mistakes. Besides, this was only the first interview of many.

Chapter Ten

After Trent and Cynthia had settled into the guest room for the night, Jessica put the kettle on to boil for chamomile tea. She wanted to turn in and get some sleep before Cassie woke again, but her unsated thirst from producing milk and her racing mind with Jon out of town wouldn't allow it.

She poured boiling water over her teabag, closed her eyes, and inhaled a deep breath of the lemony steam wafting from her mug. *I'm okay. The kids are okay.*

Jon had hired a private security guard to man the booth by the gate while he and Kato were out of town. And if somehow David made it past the gate, Trent and Cynthia were down the hall.

With her tea in hand, Jessica tiptoed past Bryce's door and Cassie's nursery to her room. She sipped her tea and opened her book. Her eyelids drooped and she abandoned her book and curled up under the covers.

Later that night, Jessica's eyes flew open, struggling to adjust to the dark as the hair prickled on the back of her neck. She scrambled out of bed and picked up her phone from the nightstand. Three in the morning, and Cassie wasn't making a peep.

What had woken her and set her on alert?

The kids.

She rushed into the hallway and pushed open Bryce's door. His chest rose and fell in sleep. Jessica stepped over the toy cars he'd left on his floor and peered out his window. Hay stalks swayed in the field that was otherwise empty. No creepy man. Maybe the memory of the last time Jon was away overnight had weighed on her subconscious mind.

Jessica left Bryce's room, shutting the door behind her, and stepped across the hall. The door stood open a crack from when Cassie had woken an hour earlier to feed. She peered inside and smiled at the calm expression on her baby's sleeping face.

Satisfied all was right with her world, Jessica went back to bed. With any luck, she'd catch another few hours of sleep before Cassie woke again. She curled her arm under her pillow and shut her eyes.

"Jessica," a male voice whispered.

She leaped out of the bed and searched the dark corners of her room. Nothing.

The same spine-chilling whisper came from the baby monitor. "I see you, Jessica."

Her ears rang and her pulse raced. *Cassie! Jesus!*

She yanked open the drawer of her bedside table. Her clammy hand slipped on the grip of her revolver. She wiped her hand on her pajama bottoms, picked up the gun, and ran into the hallway.

With her bare foot, she pushed open the nursery door, and with the gun poised to shoot in front of her, she dashed inside. She swept the room fast, the way Jon had taught her. No one. But she still needed to check the closet. Steeling herself, she crossed the room. The closet door creaked as she tugged it open. Nothing except Cassie's baby clothes.

Bryce!

She shut the door to the nursery, then swung open

Bryce's door, and charged inside, gun at the ready. No one except Bryce, still fast asleep. Her foot landed on one of his toy cars. The metal pressed into the sensitive skin covering the ball of her foot. Resisting the urge to cry out, she swung open the closet. She shifted his clothes around. Thankfully, no one hid behind them.

Jessica took a deep breath to slow the tremors in her hands. The kids were safe.

What next?

She stood in the hallway between the two rooms, heart in her throat, and forced her brain to work. Two receivers came with the baby monitor. One sat on her bedside table and the other was on the kitchen counter. That made sense for an intruder because the back door was in the kitchen.

She didn't want to leave her children. But with no one in her room or the kids' rooms, the intruder couldn't be behind them. The only room between her and the kitchen at the opposite end of the hallway was the main bathroom.

Jessica could scream for Trent and Cynthia, but they were in the spare room on the opposite side of the kitchen. Besides, if someone waited in the kitchen with Trent and Cynthia unaware, they could walk into a trap.

With the gun steady in her grip, Jessica hurried the few feet down the hallway to the door of the bathroom. The door stood ajar. From the hallway, she could see the shower stall and toilet reflecting in the mirror over the vanity. Again, no one.

Saliva pooled in her mouth, and she swallowed around a lump in her throat. *Oh, God. Now the kitchen.*

She plastered her back to the wall and sidestepped along the hallway toward the kitchen. Luckily, the carpet muted the sounds of her movement. Steeling her nerves for whatever was to come, she stepped around the corner with the revolver raised.

The kitchen was also unoccupied, and the baby monitor sat where she'd left it beside the coffee maker. With the open floor plan, she could see into the living and dining areas, and they were also clear. If the voice didn't come from either receiver or Cassie's nursery, then where the heck had it come from?

The basement needed to be searched and she couldn't move that far away from the kids. She sprinted to the guest room door. What if the intruder had killed Trent and Cynthia in their sleep? Jessica pressed her ear to the guest room. Trent's snores carried through the door. Jessica exhaled the breath she'd held and knocked on the door.

Cynthia cracked the door open and yawned as she leaned against the door frame in shorts and a tank top. "Hey, Jess. What's up?" Her eyes widened. "What's with the gun?"

"A creepy voice on the baby monitor whispered my name. He said, 'I see you, Jessica.' I already checked on the kids and the rest of the main floor. I found no one. But I need someone to clear the basement."

"Stay with the kids while I wake Trent. Okay?"

Jessica nodded and retraced her steps with the gun at the ready in case someone slipped behind her during her initial search. Her eyes roamed the dark corners of the living room and the kitchen as she passed. Along the hallway, she checked the main bathroom again. No one.

She moved onto Bryce's room. The door was shut as she'd left it. She opened the door and stormed in with the gun raised. Bryce was the only one in the room, still asleep in his favorite pose on his side facing the wall.

Leaving the door open, she crossed the hallway to Cassie's nursery. She opened the door. No intruder. But the curtains danced, and a breeze lifted her hair. Jessica's pulse raced as she shut the window and engaged the lock.

She was one hundred percent positive she hadn't opened the window. Maybe Jon had opened it the previous afternoon after changing Cassie to air out the room, and with the mild weather and calm winds, she hadn't noticed.

While she waited for Trent, she stood in the hallway between the two rooms with the doors open so both children were visible.

Cynthia approached with a gun in both hands trained at the ground. "Did you backtrack to your bedroom yet?"

"No." Jessica gulped. In her determination to protect the kids, it hadn't occurred to her that someone could be lurking in her own room.

"I'll check it out." Cynthia moved past Jessica and continued down the hallway.

Bryce's room. Jessica stepped over his toy cars to his window. Locked. Would Jon have lapsed in safety and left Cassie's window open? Not likely. Something was off. But if things panned out the way they did with the man in the hayfield the other night, no one would believe her.

Cynthia returned. "No one. I even checked your window. It's locked."

"It's interesting you mentioned the windows. Because just now, Cassie's window was wide open. I shut and locked it."

"Trent texted the security guard on gate duty before heading to the basement and asked him to check the outside of the house just in case. If someone went out that way, he should find them."

Jessica couldn't suppress the bitterness in her voice. "That's good. But he's not going to find anybody."

Cynthia's brow raised. "How can you be so sure?"

"The man I saw the other night in the hayfield. No one found him and none of the cameras picked him up. Why would tonight be any different? The same person would have to be responsible for both."

Cynthia shrugged. "Maybe."

"You don't believe me. You think I'm losing my mind."

"Jess, you aren't crazy. But you have endured a massive, ginormous, steaming pile of crap in the past year and a half. And you're exhausted. It's possible you're having waking dreams with all the stress you're under."

"Waking dreams?"

"Yeah. Where you think you're awake, and maybe you are half awake, but you're actually drifting off to sleep."

Jessica paused to consider Cynthia's words. "Maybe. But during both incidents, I felt on edge and sharp. No drowsiness involved."

"That wakeful state could be a part of your dream. It would explain all this."

Jessica had her doubts. "I don't know."

"It's a lot more believable than the idea of someone getting over that high fence without setting off the security system and roaming the property."

Jessica swallowed back the angry response on the tip of her tongue. Insomnia and lack of sleep were things she'd grappled with for years after Adam died. And she'd never departed from reality.

Trent approached them from the direction of the kitchen. "There's no one in the basement or on the grounds. We're safe. Let's hit the hay."

Jessica put the safety on the revolver and tucked it in the waistband of her snug pajama pants. "Thanks. Sorry to disturb you." She retreated down the hallway and shut the door to her bedroom.

She leaned against the door and clenched her fists until her nails pierced her skin to stop from screaming. *Waking dreams? Really? Am I losing my mind?*

Chapter Eleven

Jon woke early the next morning in the room at the inn Kato had booked, his tee and boxers were soaked and glued to his skin. The air conditioning unit in the window was making loud noise and producing a cool breeze, but not enough to make a dent in the oppressive southern heat.

He turned the shower to lukewarm and climbed in to wash away the layer of sweat that would no doubt return almost the minute he stepped outside. He couldn't wait to catch his flight that evening to return home to the more temperate climate in Montana. He'd take the cold and snow over the heat any day.

Hopefully, by the time he caught his flight, he'd have more to work with in the hunt for David. He'd spent the rest of the previous afternoon and evening interviewing more of the neighbors with Kato at his side before it got too late to continue.

So far, they hadn't come across any pictures of Chris White. Everyone they'd interviewed described the same passive man who acknowledged greetings but made no effort to befriend anyone. As a result, no one really knew him. And no one knew the answer to another important question—how Chris and Emily met. That could lead to answers on how he was finding victims.

A buffet breakfast was included with the room, so after putting on fresh clothes and running gel through his hair, Jon headed to the elevator with his packed bag in tow. Refreshing cold air greeted him as he stepped off the elevator in the main reception area.

He checked out at the concierge desk, then followed the signs and the alluring aroma of bacon to the dining room. A few other guests were scattered throughout the room at tables, but the atmosphere remained quiet and peaceful. A nice way to start the day.

Two staff members were in the process of putting out pans of steaming eggs, meats, and hashbrowns. His stomach rumbled. What a blessing not to have to forego his usual hearty breakfast. He filled his plate, poured himself a cup of black coffee, then sat with his bounty at a table in the corner.

With his fork hovering over his plate, it occurred to him that in his hurry to escape his hot room, he hadn't checked his phone. Given the time zone difference, it was only five in the morning in Montana. But maybe with Cassie up at all hours, Jessica had messaged him.

He abandoned the fork and pulled his phone out of his pocket. While inputting his passcode, he munched on a thick, salty, maple flavored piece of bacon.

He frowned at the text message he'd received from Trent in the middle of the night.

—*Jessica had another episode. Claims she heard a male voice talking to her on the baby monitor. There was no one.*—

Getting onto the same frequency as a baby monitor wasn't as far-fetched as breaching their security and roaming the hayfields. But still. David didn't seem the type to do something so trivial. He preferred to start fires or plant car bombs.

Jon didn't want to face the most logical conclusion,

but he didn't have a choice: his poor wife who he loved more than anything in the world was under so much stress, her mind was breaking, causing her to see things that weren't there. *Damn you, David.* If he could just get his hands on the bastard and kill him once and for all, most of Jessica's stress would be relieved.

In the meantime, the workouts with Cynthia would boost Jessica's serotonin levels, but maybe that wasn't enough. Jessica might need a therapist to help her work through her stress. One that specialized in these sorts of situations. Maybe Assistant Director Pruitt could set them up with one the FBI used to debrief agents.

A chair squeaked across the table and Jon flinched. He glanced up from his phone into Kato's smiling face. "Good morning."

"Morning. Everything okay? You look rattled."

"I'm fine. A hiccup on the home front, but nothing I can't handle."

Kato nodded. "Good. Because I heard back from Emily's parents, Heather and Matthew Evans. They're meeting us at Emily and Chris' house and allowing us to have a look around."

"Maybe they believe their daughter's death was fishy."

"That's the impression I got."

"They'll want to help us then." Jon's interest in his breakfast had waned since reading Trent's message, but he'd need the fuel, so he spooned a large mouthful of scrambled eggs into his mouth.

"We won't be able to put off talking to the local police afterwards. They'll be unimpressed about us investigating on their turf without talking to them."

"It all comes down to how you approach a situation

like this. Once we explain that David has foiled multiple law enforcement agencies, including the FBI, they won't have their hackles up. You'll see."

"I hope so."

After breakfast, they headed to the former White residence and parked along the curb to await the arrival of Emily's parents. Still headachy from roasting in bed the previous night, Jon stayed in the passenger seat with the air conditioning running while Kato waited outside on the porch steps.

Jon had the messaging app open on his phone. He'd started typing a message to Jessica asking how she was a few times before erasing it. The last thing he wanted to do was make her feel like he wasn't taking her seriously. She needed him more than ever. He typed a sweet message and hit send.

—Hi, sweetheart. Hope you have a good day. I'm about to meet Emily's parents. I'll let you know how it goes. Love you.—

Bubbles appeared on his screen as the rumble of an engine came from directly behind him. He glanced in the side mirror. A police cruiser. Jon stuffed his phone in his pocket. So much for nosing around the place in peace.

Oh, well. Guess I can milk two cows at the same time with Emily's parents and the local police. Saves a trip to the station.

Jon climbed out of the car and went to stand next to Kato.

An officer climbed out of the cruiser and ambled up to them with a neutral expression on his face. At least he wasn't scowling. A good sign. As he got closer, Jon noticed the sheriff's badge on his belt.

Jon held out his hand. "Good day, Sheriff. I'm

Retired Agent Kent, FBI. It's a pleasure to meet you."

The Sheriff had a strong grip as he shook. "Sheriff Jenkins, Madison P.D." He shifted his gaze to Kato. "And you are."

"I'm Agent Kato Chen, active."

Sheriff Jenkins said, "Okay, gentlemen. Let's get to the heart of the matter. We got a request for the file on Emily White without much of an explanation. And Emily's parents asked me to meet y'all here."

Kato said, "Yes, sir. Would it be okay if we explained when the Evans arrive? What was your take on Emily and Chris White?"

"Answers can wait for their arrival," Sheriff Jenkins said. "Emily was—well, the polite way to put it would be very spirited."

Kato grinned. "Yes, the neighbors said the same. And that Chris appeared shy and meek."

A new, red SUV pulled to the curb behind the squad car. A slim woman with shoulder-length dark hair and large, black sunglasses wearing a pink dress climbed out of the passenger side. And a man with silver hair and transition eyeglasses wearing khaki shorts and a light green linen golf shirt walked around from the driver's side to join her.

Sheriff Jenkins waved. "That would be the Evans's."

Emily's mother attempted to smile. Her lips raised for an instant before falling again as she held out her hand to Kato. "I'm Heather Evans, pleased to meet you."

Kato shook gently. "The pleasure is all mine. I'm Agent Chen, and this is my colleague, Agent Kent. We're both very sorry to hear about your daughter's passing."

Heather said, "Thank you."

Jon held out his hand. "Pleased to make your acquaintance."

Emily's father shook with Jon. "I'm Matthew Evans. So, what can we do for you today? You said on the phone you were investigating Chris White and looking into our daughter's death."

"Yes, sir and ma'am. That's what we've come to do," Jon said. "I apologize for the lack of information up until now, but we only happened upon a clue leading us here the day before yesterday. We're on the hunt for a dangerous serial killer. His last known alias was David Hayes, and we believe he changed his name to Chris White while undergoing facial reconstruction in Colombia before returning stateside."

Sheriff Jenkins blinked but otherwise didn't react. "Chris White is a common name. Why are you looking into this particular Chris White?"

Jon said, "Modus operandi. He targets lonely women. Convinces them to marry. And then takes out big life insurance policies on them. Afterwards, they have an unfortunate accident resulting in their death. He's gotten away with it in six different cities that we know of so far across Western Canada and the USA using a different alias in each one. Sound familiar?"

Heather covered her mouth with her hand. "I always thought something was off about him. He was polite but too quiet, and I always wondered what he was really thinking. And Emily met him on one of those dating sites and you can't trust those."

Matthew nodded. "I agree with my wife. I never approved of him for our Emily."

A dating site. That could yield some key

information. "Would you happen to know which dating site she met him on? That could lead us to his other potential victims and his location."

Heather said, "Sorry, no. He took her computer, and we never found her phone."

Jon held in a string of curses. "I don't suppose you know her username or password to any of her accounts."

Matthew said, "No. I wish we did. Maybe she wrote them down somewhere. We kept some of her stuff. I'll go through it when we get home and let you know if we find anything."

Jon prayed they'd find something. Without more to go on, that line of investigation was dead.

Sheriff Jenkins asked, "What are you hoping to accomplish here today, gentlemen?"

"Because of the plastic surgery, we don't have a face for him. We already checked the DMV. He never had a valid driver's license while he was here. We were hoping someone got a picture of him." Jon cleared his throat. "Also, since this house has been vacant, maybe we'll find DNA for comparison with the sample the FBI has on file to verify that Chris White is indeed David Hayes. We also haven't gotten his fingerprints, yet, which is standing in the way of figuring out his real identity."

Heather glanced at the dead flowers in the planter on the porch then faced Jon again. "I don't have any pictures of Chris. He didn't like having his picture taken. When they got married, Emily had photos taken of herself alone, without him."

Kato said, "Would you folks be willing to meet with a sketch artist?"

Heather said, "Of course. Anything you need."

Sheriff Jenkins pulled a handkerchief from his

pocket and mopped his forehead. "I apologize for not taking a closer look at Chris White when we responded to the initial call. He appeared genuinely distraught."

Jon said, "You did nothing wrong, Sheriff. The only reason we're on to him is because of a witness. We need to find him before he kills again."

Matthew handed Jon a key. "Go on ahead inside. Heather and I will leave, so you're not distracted. Anything you need. You let us know. If Chris is your man, and he killed my daughter, I want to see justice served. And like I said. If we find anything in her belongings that might help, we'll let you know."

Jon closed his hand around the key. "Don't worry, Mr. and Mrs. Evans. I'll make him pay for his crimes."

Chapter Twelve

Jon waved to the Evans's as they drove away. Sheriff Jenkins stared at the front door with his hands on his hips. Would he stay to keep an eye on them? Or would he let them search the house for evidence in peace?

Kato broke the awkward silence. "I'll get my gear from the trunk of the rental car."

Jon strategized as he stood on the porch waiting for Kato to return. David had successfully wiped his prints from the scenes of his crimes in the past, but this was the first time Jon had the opportunity to be present at a scene, albeit months after the fact. Maybe, just maybe, he'd find something others had missed.

Kato shut the trunk, then came up the walkway with a case in his hands. "I have flashlights, gloves, baggies, and my brush and powders for fingerprinting."

Jon stuck the key in the lock. "That should do it." He took a deep breath, then walked inside.

Refreshing cold air greeted him inside the house. A small miracle. In the sitting room to the left of the entrance, a couch with blue floral print rested against one wall across from a window seat with matching upholstery. Knickknacks and books were displayed on a white shelving unit, and a pair of reading glasses rested on a round glass table in the corner beside a coaster.

Jon almost expected someone to come home and

curl up on the window seat with a book.

Kato handed Jon and Sheriff Jenkins each a pair of gloves. "So, shall we divide and conquer?"

Jon nodded. "Our suspect has a history of meticulously cleaning up after himself, so we need to be thorough. I doubt we'll find anything in the usual spots. Look under furniture and the crevices of cabinets for something he may not have noticed."

The sheriff handed Kato back his gloves. "I don't have time for anything this extensive. Why don't you lock up behind you and drop off the key at the station?"

"Sure, Sheriff. We understand." Kato said, "Okay, I'll take the kitchen."

Jon put his foot on the first step at the bottom of the staircase. "I'll do the upstairs."

Kato nodded and they headed their separate ways.

Out of curiosity, in case Chris left in a hurry, Jon dipped the brush in black fingerprint powder and swept the bristles along the banister as he ascended the staircase. Nothing. Not a single print. It spoke of David and his usual meticulousness.

At the top of the stairs, the first open door he came across led into the master bedroom. He dipped the brush in black fingerprint powder and swept the doorknob on the inside of the door with the brush. Again, nothing.

The room gave off a distinctive feminine air with pink frilly bedding and white and grey furry cushions. Even the curtains were bright pink. The decor spoke of feminine dominance and told the same story about Emily White that the neighbors had described.

Jon dusted the light switch, the posts on the bedframe, the picture frames, the lamps on the side tables, and all the drawer pulls. He found no prints. Not even a partial. Every drawer had been emptied.

Jon moved onto the adjoining bathroom and checked all the usual surfaces. The toilet flusher, the mirror, the taps. Once again, he came up empty. He wandered back into the master bedroom and did another visual sweep.

I wonder.

He dropped to his knees beside the bed and lifted the comforter. The flashlight on his phone illuminated only the cream-colored carpet rather than the dropped or discarded item he sought. He crawled to the nearby side table and shone it into the small gap between the base of the table and the carpet.

A black, cylindrical item, most likely a pen, rested on the carpet. It had probably fallen and rolled beneath the table unnoticed. Jon placed the table lamp on the bed, then lifted the table and set it on the carpet further away.

He kneeled and picked the pen up by the ink tip with two fingers. His hand trembled slightly as he dipped his brush in the powder and dusted the pen. The dust adhered to the oil from a finger revealing a partial print.

Jon carried the pen down to the kitchen. "Kato. I found something."

Kato was only visible from the waist down. The rest of him was hidden inside the cabinet under the kitchen sink. "Give me a second. The cabinets were emptied. I'm checking the crevices." He backed out of the small space on his knees, then stood. "Nothing in this one."

"I found a partial on this pen. It rolled under the bedside table in the master bedroom. Want to lift it and compare it to Emily's from the autopsy file?"

"Sure."

While Jon held the pen steady, Kato used lifting tape

to collect the print, then stuck it to the glossy side of the lift card.

Kato took his gloves off and pulled a file folder out of his bag. "It's a decent partial, but not ideal." He flipped open the file and pulled out a sheet of paper with Emily's prints on it. He took a magnifying glass out of his bag and held it over Emily's prints, then the one they lifted from the pen. "Take a look."

Jon took the magnifying glass and studied the grooves of Emily's prints compared to the one they found. "These don't match at all. With any luck, it belongs to David and not someone else who happened to use this."

"I don't know that it'll be enough to go on. We better keep searching."

"For sure. I'll continue with the upstairs, then join you down here."

A few hours later, Jon took off his gloves and shoved them in his pants pocket. "Well, that's it."

"I agree. We didn't miss anything. There's nothing to find."

Between him and Kato, they'd checked every crevice and surface in the house. Besides the one partial, the whole house had been wiped clean. And they found no sign of any login credentials for either Chris or Emily White.

Kato gathered his equipment. "What's next? Do you want to stay in Georgia and interview more witnesses?"

Jon shook his head. "With Martha smoothing the way, we talked to every neighbor on the street. They all promised to double-check their photos. I think the Atlanta field office can take it from here. I need to get home to my family. I can't shake the feeling that David's closer to the ranch than we are."

Chapter Thirteen

Nathan browsed the selection of engagement rings at the local pawn shop. With how often he bought rings, and how little time his wives had left to live while wearing them, it made no sense to pay full price.

He drifted towards the shiniest and biggest diamond engagement band with a matching wedding band. They would do the trick. Flashy enough to impress Amy, yet they wouldn't break the bank.

He pointed to the rings and glanced at the clerk. "I'll take these and your finest ring box."

The clerk fumbled around inside a drawer for a box. "Right away, sir." He dropped the box. His hands trembled as he picked it up and placed the rings inside the notch in the satin display cushion.

The clerk's anxiety made no sense. He'd never met the man before or crossed paths with him. Perhaps the clerk sensed a killer nearby. Some people possessed much stronger instincts than others like Jessica's Aunt Debbie, the old bitch who shot him in the leg.

Nathan rolled his eyes and pulled a wad of cash out of his pocket. He paid for the rings, stuck the small square box in his pocket, then strode to his truck in the parking lot.

Overhead, more grey clouds had moved in since he'd first entered the shop. They sagged with the threat of rain, and the smell of moisture clung to the air.

Thankfully, he'd placed a takeout order for Chinese food from Amy's favorite spot for their dinner to bring to her apartment. An outdoor picnic would have been a bust.

He couldn't invite her back to his horrible basement apartment. It reeked of mold, and the forest green carpets were so thin they were bare in patches. Not to mention, he'd swear a mouse ran over his foot one day while he was watching his small television, sitting on his floral-printed grandma couch.

But with no references or credit history because of his fake identity, there were no other rental options in the current hot market besides seedy motels. Those types of places didn't scream romance either. Hopefully, Amy would invite him to move in with her soon.

He picked up the food and pulled into the visitor's parking beside Amy's building. As he stepped outside his truck, the patter of rain on the pavement sounded in the distance and a few drops of rain landed on his face. He sprinted across the lot and inside the building. As the main door shut behind him, sheets of rain angled into the glass.

Nathan had missed getting soaked by a few seconds. A good omen for the rest of his evening.

He rode the elevator to the third floor, then knocked on Amy's door.

She opened the door and looked into his eyes, smiling rather than avoiding his gaze. A sign of progress. "Hi, Nathan. Thanks for dinner." She still hid behind her clothes. Her blouse was a size too big and buttoned up to her neck, and it hung almost to her knees. Over the past while, she'd grown less timid.

"You're welcome, darling."

She kissed his cheek and took the brown paper bag

from his arms. "Yum. Chinese. I could smell the eggrolls and sweet and sour pork when you got off the elevator." She led him to the small, round table tucked in the corner of the main space that doubled as a living and dining room. "Beer?"

"Yes, please." He sat and unpacked the paper containers holding the fried rice, pork, eggrolls, and his favorite, chicken chow mein. He left the fortune cookies in the bag for later.

Amy brought plates and two bottles of light beer to the table, then sat. "Need anything else?"

"No, I'm good. Thank you." He handed her a set of chopsticks.

They ate in comfortable silence. Of all his past targets, Amy annoyed him the least. She didn't complain about calories or nag for details about his day, nor did she feel the need to fill the silence with meaningless, annoying chatter about the neighbors and the latest gossip.

Their knees brushed beneath the table. He met her gaze. Her cheeks flushed and she smiled. A twinge of guilt fluttered through his consciousness as he thought of her impending demise. She still hadn't shown any signs of the evil women possess. She'd never tried to use her feminine wiles to get anything from him. She'd never even killed a fly in his presence.

It could be she was one of the rare, innocent gems, like his childhood rescuer Mrs. DeGuire. But he couldn't deviate from his plan and let her live. Not when he was so close geographically to the Kents and they still believed him dead. The most he could do for Amy was ensure her death was quick and painless. He needed one more sizeable payout before killing them, then disappearing.

She set her chopsticks down on her plate. "I'm stuffed. Thanks again for dinner."

He pulled a fortune cookie out of the bag and handed it to her. "Here. Dessert."

"I don't know if I can squeeze it in right now."

"That's okay, darling. Just open it and read your fortune. I have a good feeling about these fortune cookies." He tore open the plastic on his cookie and snapped it open. Only her cookie had a predetermined message in it. His would be a surprise. The tiny slip of paper read: *Enjoy yourself while you can.*

Amy watched him read his fortune as she cracked open her cookie. "What does your say?"

"Pretty boring. Enjoy yourself while you can. What about yours?"

Amy pulled the tiny slip of paper out of her cookie and burst into laughter. "This is hilarious. It says someone is about to propose marriage to you."

Nathan pulled out the ring box, opened it, and held it out to her. He couldn't be bothered with getting down on one knee. It hurt too much to get back up since he'd broken his leg badly in his tumble down the mountain at Judith Peak. "So, what do you think? Will you make me the luckiest man in the world by agreeing to be my wife?"

Her eyes widened and her mouth formed an 'o' shape, but she didn't respond.

Had he misread the situation and popped the question too soon? He didn't have all year to sit around waiting, but maybe he should've given it a few more dates. "Are you okay? Is it too soon? Talk to me, darling."

Amy's blank expression gave nothing away. "I don't know what to say. This is a big surprise."

For the first time in all his years, after proposing to numerous women, he couldn't predict the outcome. He needed to put her at ease. "Take your time thinking about it. No pressure. There's no need to answer me right away."

She smiled and her green eyes lit up behind the frames of her glasses. "You're so sweet and kind, Nathan. And you see the real me. What more could I possibly want?"

"So…?"

"So, yes. I'll marry you." She took the engagement ring out of the box and placed it on her ring finger. "It's a perfect fit."

He reached across the table for her hand and ran his fingers along the edge of the diamond. "It is. See, it's meant to be." *What a relief!* His trap lay open, waiting to cage her inside.

"To celebrate, we'll have to visit my parents to introduce them to you and tell them the good news."

He resisted the urge to roll his eyes. "Of course, darling." *Parents. Great. More schmoozing.*

Chapter Fourteen

Jessica slapped ham on bread for Bryce's lunch while Cassie slept in a sling nestled against her chest. Bryce sat close by at the round kitchen table eating scrambled eggs and toast. But he wouldn't be close enough for her to shield for much longer.

The three weeks since Cassie's birth had flown by, and the day she'd been dreading most, the first day of school had arrived. At least Cynthia would be driving him, but during school, Cynthia couldn't watch him every minute of every day.

After the man in the hayfield, and the creepy voice on the baby monitor the night before last, Jessica wasn't convinced the ranch was any safer than a public school full of adults and children. Especially with Jon and Kato away from the property.

She couldn't help but consider Cynthia's improbable suggestion of waking dreams, because the idea of someone getting past the tall, metal fencing barricading them into the ranch seemed equally as impossible.

Cynthia came into the kitchen wearing a cardigan over a blouse and a pencil skirt. "Good morning. You almost ready to hit the road, Bryce?"

Bryce glanced up from his plate. "Uh-huh. I don't get why I can't take the bus like always."

Jessica didn't want to answer the question and give

her son nightmares. Instead, she handed Cynthia a to-go mug filled with coffee. "Here, I made this for you. Do you want breakfast?"

Cynthia sipped from her mug. "The coffee is good. Thanks, Jess. I'll grab a quick bowl of cereal before we go."

"Sure. Help yourself." Jessica zipped Bryce's lunch bag. "Can we work out later?"

"Of course. We'll start hand-to-hand fighting skills after school."

"I'll look forward to it." Jessica's muscles ached a bit, but not nearly as much as they had after the first few workouts. Once Cassie went down in her crib for her first nap, Jessica planned to attack the hand weights on her own. Maybe she'd even take some swings at Jon's punching bag in the basement.

Somewhere, hopefully far away from them, David was preparing to come after them. And Jessica needed to be ready to protect her family when he did. Her guard sat on high alert and would remain there until the nightmare ended.

Bryce placed his dishes in the dishwasher, then slipped into his shoes and grabbed his backpack. "See you later, Mom."

Jessica swallowed around a lump in her throat. "Come here. I need a hug before you go."

Bryce smiled and wrapped his arms around her waist and rested his cheek against his sister.

Jessica soaked in the comfort. "I love you. Have a good first day at school."

"I will."

Cynthia smiled. "Bye, Jess. I'll take care of him. I promise."

Jessica nodded. She stood by the kitchen window as they walked out the door and climbed into Trent's truck parked in the gravel beside the barn. Then they drove away, taking a piece of Jessica's heart with them. The anxiety she'd experienced since Bryce's kidnapping didn't cripple her in the same way it used to when separated from him, but it still wasn't easy to let him go anywhere without her.

****

After Jon and Kato landed in Great Falls, they hit a drive-thru for coffee and breakfast sandwiches. Jon couldn't bear the idea of stopping anywhere and delaying his return to the ranch. As it was, they wouldn't get back until lunchtime.

Jessica needed him home to chase away the scary thoughts causing the bizarre episodes she'd been experiencing whenever he left the ranch.

Once they merged onto the highway, Jon floored the accelerator of his truck.

Kato asked, "Are you okay?"

"I'm worried about Jessica is all. With everything we've been through, she's never seen or heard things that weren't there before."

"The man in the field I found hard to believe until you told me about her dead husband. Where I'm from in Japan, after the tsunami, ghosts are everywhere. My brother drives a taxi there, and he swears he's picked up passengers that have vanished out of the backseat a mile down the road."

"You don't think she's hallucinating?"

"No, I don't. Think about it. The baby monitor could have been an electronic voice phenomenon."

Jon switched lanes to pass a car. "I had a dream

encounter with Jessica's first husband. My mind is open to the paranormal, but after that night in Hawaii, his visits stopped. He's always used dreams, so why would he switch tactics now? Besides, wouldn't Jess recognize his voice?"

"No. Go on the internet and listen to some E.V.P.s. The voices all sound the same. Not human."

"It's a possibility. I'd rather believe that's what's happening, but it feels wrong. I'm also not convinced Jess is losing it either, but just in case it makes sense to maybe find someone for her to talk to."

Kato balled up the empty wrapper from his sandwich and shoved it in the empty food bag. "I'm sure the FBI would have someone on staff she could talk to. But may I give you some unsolicited advice?"

"Any time."

"Tell her you believe her. If you question her experiences, she'll feel isolated. With a madman on the loose and gunning for your family, the last thing you want is any division on the home front."

"True. We all need to stick together." The longer Jon spent with Kato, the more he liked him. It bolstered his confidence in their ability to catch David. "Any results from the partial print yet?"

"No matches. Once that sketch is done, it's going out to law enforcement everywhere."

"Damn. The print getting a hit was too much to hope for with how clean this bastard is. Just law enforcement with the sketch, right? If it's made public, he'll figure it out." A light bulb went on in Jon's brain. He glanced at Kato, then returned his eyes to the road. "Wait a second. You know there's one thing we haven't tried. I can't believe we didn't think of doing this during this rampage."

"What?"

"Genealogy sites. He doesn't strike me as the type to visit family, but maybe we could figure out his real identity from a relative's DNA profile and get a fuller picture of who he really is."

"Of course." Kato slapped his thigh. "We've blown up a ton of cases that way. I don't know why I didn't think of it either. When the case on David Hayes was closed after we presumed him dead, the evidence, including that DNA sample was filed away but preserved."

"I have the profile at home from when Thomas and I got a sample of David's blood after Debbie shot him."

Jon accelerated, easing the speedometer up another ten miles per hour.

****

In the schoolyard at recess time, the sun shone in a cloudless sky, and laughter carried on the breeze to Bryce's ears. As he ran past the playground structure to the field, the back of his long-sleeve tee stuck to his sweaty skin under the sun's rays. But that didn't dampen his mood. He hadn't seen some of his friends since school ended. He'd missed his best friend, Ty, the most.

Ty carried a soccer ball as he ran alongside Bryce and four of their other friends. He dropped the ball on the grass and sent a sideways pass to Bryce. "Bryce and Iain are on my team. Kasper, Nick, and Sam, you're on the other team." Since the ball belonged to Ty, the schoolyard rules dictated that he got to choose.

The boys split into their teams. Iain stood in a net on one side of the field while Bryce and Ty ran down the field towards the other net where Sam stood fidgeting with a string hanging from his tee.

Bryce pretended to kick the ball to right. After Nick moved in that direction, Bryce passed the ball to Ty. "Go for the goal."

Ty kicked the ball past Sam, who made no effort to stop the ball from sailing past him.

"He shoots he scores!" Ty held up his hand for a high five.

Nick groaned, "Sam, dude. What the hell? You didn't even try."

"I wouldn't have been able to get to the ball anyway. It was too far away." Sam jogged over to the ball, then shovel-passed it to Nick.

Bryce turned and ran back to his end of the field with Ty to wait for Nick and Kasper to come closer to attempt to intercept the ball. A prickle ran up Bryce's spine and he turned towards the fence alongside the soccer pitch.

Behind the fence in a small forest, a man stood beneath a tall ash tree staring straight at Bryce. The stranger was tall and muscular with dark hair and eyes. Something about the man triggered recognition in Bryce's memory, yet he felt certain he'd never seen him before.

Ty said, "Lookout, Bryce. Kasper's almost on top of you."

Bryce turned just in time to stick his foot out and sweep the ball away from Kasper. He ran ahead with the ball and passed it to Ty.

Ty kicked the ball in the net. "Yeah, goal."

Bryce glanced over his shoulder at the forest. The man was gone. He touched Ty's arm to get his attention. "Did you see a guy standing behind the fence watching us a minute ago?"

Ty turned, stared at the forest, then squinted. "No. I didn't see anyone."

"Psych. I was pulling your leg."

Ty narrowed his eyes at him, then smiled. "Weird joke, dude."

Bryce glanced back towards the forest. The man had disappeared, but the sensation of being watched persisted. Unbidden, the photo of his biological father, hanging in the hallway at home, flashed in his mind.

Dad. Was that you?

After recess, Bryce stopped at his locker to stow his hat. He hung it over his jacket on a hook. As he shut the door, a piece of paper on the bottom of his locker caught his eye. He picked it up.

I'm alive. It's a secret. You can't tell anyone, or they might get hurt. That's why I've stayed away. We can't talk in person now, but we can talk online. Type this website into the browser and it will take you to my chat room.

https://www.chatnow.com/adam523467

Love, Dad

Bryce folded the note and stuck it in the front pocket of his backpack. His mother wouldn't lie about his father being dead. Unless someone lied to her, and she didn't know any different. She hated lies more than anything else; nothing upset her more.

The man behind the fence looked so much like the one in the portrait of his father in his uniform, hanging on the wall at home. It had to be him.

Chapter Fifteen

Jon clenched the steering wheel as he and Kato came upon the ranch. The black metal gates defined his property, and he couldn't adjust to them. They destroyed the welcoming atmosphere and instead said, "Keep out."

He couldn't wait for David to be apprehended or, even better, killed. The minute the nightmare ended, the cage around his property would be yanked out of the ground, concrete footings and all. He may not be able to erase David from their minds, but he could erase the evidence.

His thumb on the sensor triggered the gate to open, and he drove up the gravel road and parked at the back of the house. "It's good to be home."

"I bet." Kato smiled. "I'll bring my bag to the guest house and unpack, then meet you back here."

"Great. Thank you."

Chip, his lead ranch hand, waved to him from across the field and approached.

Jon climbed out of the driver's seat and held his aching lower back. He strode towards Chip, to get the blood flowing in his aching legs. "Hey, Chip. How are things?"

"Good. I just wanted to let you know I have things under control here, boss. You can keep doing what you need to do."

"No signs of trespassers?"

"No. Not a one. Having Trent around again has been great. He's been helping out while you were gone."

"Where is he now?" Jon inhaled a deep, cleansing breath of cool, clean mountain air.

"In the barn mucking the horse stalls."

"Thanks, see you later." He lifted his hand to tip his hat to Chip like he usually did, then realized he wasn't wearing one. He needed to get out of the chinos and golf shirt and into his plaid and jeans.

In the barn, Trent whistled as he brushed Daisy, Jon's favorite horse. "Oh, hey, Jon. You're back. Find anything useful?"

The familiar, sweet smell of hay and leather greeted Jon as he rubbed Daisy's neck. "A partial print that returned no hits, but I'm convinced Chris White is David Hayes. One of the neighbors had a photo of him from behind. That combined with the modus operandi—it has to be him. The field office in Atlanta is getting a sketch artist out to the neighbors to circulate around the various law enforcement agencies."

"That's not much to go on."

"It's not. But I have another idea, and I need your help. Could you meet me in the kitchen with your laptop?"

"I'll be there in a jiff."

Jon left the barn and headed for the house. He shut the kitchen door behind him softly. Silence greeted him. He set his laptop case on the kitchen table. Then with his suitcase in hand, he slipped off his shoes and padded softly along the carpeted hallway to the nursery. The door stood open a crack. Inside, Cassie slept with her mouth open and her arms over her head.

As he neared the bedroom he shared with Jessica,

the sound of the shower running reached his ears. He dropped his suitcase in the closet and stood near the bathroom door. Some of Jessica's new workout clothes lay scattered on the bathroom vanity.

She'd started working out on her own. A good sign. They'd been through a few hellish years, and throughout that time she'd grown stronger, not weaker.

He stepped inside the bathroom. "Hi, sweetheart. I'm home."

She turned the water off, pulled the shower curtain, and wrapped herself in a towel. Her shoulders and arms looked more defined already. "Hey, we missed you. I'm glad you're home."

He took her in his arms and kissed the top of her head. "I missed you more."

She stepped back and laughed. "I'm getting your clothes wet."

He unbuttoned the cuffs of his dress shirt. "That's okay. I need to change anyway. Chinos aren't my thing." He tossed his shirt in the clothes hamper.

Jessica wandered into their closet. "How was Georgia? Find anything?"

"Georgia was gorgeous but stinking hot. We didn't find much, unfortunately. But we have a new plan." He told her about the genealogy sites.

"Oh my gosh! I should have thought of that. Adam was adopted. He sent his DNA to one of the more popular ones to try to find his birth parents."

Jon grabbed a plaid shirt off a hanger and slipped it on. "Really? Did he find any relatives?"

Jessica zipped up a hoody. "His birth father died of cancer a year before Adam started using the site. He found some distant relatives on his father's side and that was it. He never found his birth mother, or anyone connected to her."

"That's too bad." As she walked past him into the bedroom, Jon admired the way her athletic pants sculpted her bottom. He didn't object to the change in style at all with that view. Jessica always wore jeans and dresses sometimes in the summer, but never athletic wear.

"It is. But his adoptive parents are amazing people. Adam had a great relationship with them, and Bryce loves them."

"This is just a suggestion. Take it or leave it, sweetheart. It doesn't mean I don't believe you heard someone on the baby monitor. But with everything that we're going through, I could get you set up virtually with a PTSD therapist from the FBI. It might help to talk to someone that's removed from this crazy situation we're stuck in."

"I'll think about it. Working out is reducing my stress."

"That's great. You look amazing, too." Jon pulled on a pair of jeans. "I'm meeting Kato and Trent in the kitchen."

"Okay. Cassie fed maybe ten minutes before you got home. She should be good for a while. I'll dry my hair, then put on a pot of coffee."

He brushed a delicate kiss against her lips. "I'll see you out there then."

She smiled, then turned and headed back into the bathroom.

When Jon returned to the kitchen, he found Trent and Kato sitting at the round table chatting. Their computers sat in front of them ready to go.

Jon sat in the chair across from Trent, then zipped open his computer bag. "These sites usually work by sending out a kit to collect a sample."

Trent said, "I went this route on a case about a year ago. Before I was assigned to the Hugh Jones investigation. We'll have to submit special requests with David's DNA profile to each individual site."

Jon asked, "Did you run into any red tape?"

Trent shook his head. "None. Law enforcement requests are a common thing now."

Kato said, "Yes, the information on those sites is now considered public domain. We shouldn't have any problems."

Jon nodded. "Good. Let's divvy up these websites and get requests in."

****

Bryce leaned his head against the window of Cynthia's car on the way home. He didn't bother talking to her, and he'd given up on asking to take the bus. Something was wrong again, and his parents were keeping it from him. Whenever he entered a room, his parents, Cynthia, and Trent stopped talking or changed the subject. Not to mention the new fences around the ranch.

Whatever it was, he hoped no one would get hurt and they wouldn't drag him out of school and across the country again. Since finding the note in his locker, he wondered if it had something to do with whatever his father had warned him about in the letter.

Cynthia hummed along to a song on the radio. "You're really quiet. Are you tired."

"A little."

Cynthia pressed her thumb on the pad beside the big

metal gates and they swung open. She drove along the winding road leading to the house and parked. He climbed out of the car, ran to the kitchen door, and eased it open. Since Cassie was born, they all took care to make less noise. Occasionally, he caught the odd snippet of conversation, but he hadn't overheard anything useful yet.

His parents, Trent, and Kato were sitting around the table with their computers, not talking. So much for learning anything new.

Mom smiled. "Hey, buddy. How was your day?"

"Fine. I played soccer with Ty." Bryce had a hard time staying angry at her with the warmth in her eyes. She always took care of him, and she never lost her temper and yelled at him the way she did other people, including Dad.

The temptation to tell her about the note in his bag ate away at him. But the note said that if he told anyone, they could get hurt. It made sense. Adults made such a fuss about everything all the time. If he told his mother, she'd search for Adam no matter what the note said, like the time she'd gone after David with Sheriff Hank.

"There's a plate of cookies on the counter for you. A special first day of school treat," Mom said. "Why don't you take them to your room with some milk?"

"Thanks, Mom." Clearly, they wanted to get rid of him so they could do whatever it was they didn't want him knowing about. He poured himself a glass of milk, adjusted the strap of his backpack to keep it on his shoulder, then carried the plate and the glass to his room.

Bryce sat on his bed and stared at the piece of paper as he chewed a soft and warm chocolate chip cookie. Something about the idea of talking to his father made the cookie stick in his throat a little on the way down. It felt like a betrayal, but talking in a chat room wouldn't hurt anyone.

He picked up his tablet and typed the web address into the browser. The page loaded, and a message waited for him.

—Hi Bryce, I've missed you so much. You have no idea how hard it's been living away from you. You're so good at soccer just like your old man. Soon, once I make sure the bad people after me are taken care of, I'm coming to see you.—

Bryce chewed on his lip. He didn't know what to think of Adam coming to visit. What would Mom do? She was married to Jon, and they had his baby sister. Jon was his dad now, and Adam was a stranger.

Not sure of how to reply, he closed the browser window without typing a response. He didn't want to be in the middle between his parents, and his loyalty was to his current family. If Adam wanted to visit, then he'd have to talk to his mother and Jon about it himself.

Chapter Sixteen

A few weeks later, Nathan stood across from Amy at the town hall in Ketchum. She wore an old, lace wedding gown from a thrift store that hugged her curves in all the right places. He couldn't fathom why she hid her beauty behind the baggy clothes. It didn't make sense. Women who looked like Amy used their appearance to get what they wanted, corrupting the men around them.

An officiant stood in front of them with a book open, reciting standard wedding vows.

Amy repeated them. "I take you, Nathan Kirk, to be my husband, to have and to hold from this day forward, for better, for worse, for richer, for poorer, in sickness and in health, to love and to cherish, til death do us part."

Nathan held his breath and bit his tongue to contain his laughter. The part about death always cracked him up considering his wives never lasted long after reciting their wedding vows.

For the sake of expediency, he recited his vows without prompting from the officiant. His voice shook with laughter at the end. "...til death do us part."

Amy beamed at him, clearly misinterpreting the irony of the situation, and assuming his laughter originated from marital bliss.

The officiant also smiled. "I now pronounce you husband and wife. You may kiss the bride."

Nathan wrapped his arms around Amy's waist. Rather than giving her one of their routine chaste kisses, he pulled her close and pressed his tongue into her mouth. She yielded to him, and her knees buckled. He held her upright and tasted sweet hints of mint and chocolate on her breath.

He broke the kiss and held her hand. "Come on, Missus…" He meant to tag on his current fake last name, but it temporarily escaped him. "Time for our honeymoon."

Her cheeks flamed and she giggled, radiating innocence. "I'm looking forward to it."

After their wedding night, how much of that innocence would remain intact? Perhaps she'd learn about the power of feminine wiles and then reveal her true nature.

Nathan led her outside to his truck in the parking lot. He lifted the hem of her dress off the ground as she climbed into the passenger seat, so she wouldn't trip. He shut the door, and a smile spread across his face from ear to ear. After they went back to her place, now their place, to change, they were bound for Montana. He couldn't wait to get there.

****

Jessica wiped her forehead with a towel to keep sweat from dripping into her eyes. Since school had started, she'd gotten into a routine of running on Jon's old treadmill in the basement and beating his punching bag into submission. After school with Cynthia, she'd be continuing hand-to-hand combat lessons.

Jessica's muscles burned, but she craved the addictive exertion of the exercise and the sense of power as she grew stronger by the day. Despite the lack of sleep from feedings, her energy levels had improved drastically in the month since giving birth. The exercise did a lot more for her than talking to a psychologist could with the constant unsettled state she lived in with David on the loose and out to get them. No matter what anyone thought, she was completely sane and mentally stable.

She'd come a long way since the night in Cochrane when she'd witnessed David loading his wife's body on his truck and landed on his radar. If she ever had the misfortune of coming face-to-face with that animal again, he'd be seeing a whole new version of her.

She ran up the basement stairs to the kitchen and filled a glass with water from the dispenser in the door of the refrigerator. She chugged half of the cool liquid, then set the glass on the counter. As she was about to head to the shower, a knock sounded on the door a few feet away from her, and she jumped.

Jessica checked the peephole, then opened the door. "Hey, Trent. Come in. How's it going?"

Trent stepped inside and took off his cowboy boots. "Great. I have news. Where's Jon? I'd like to tell you both at the same time."

"He's out in the fields somewhere. Why don't you shoot him a text?" Jessica sat at the kitchen table and pointed to an empty chair. "Sit."

"Okay. Ah, heck. I'm too excited to wait. I'll just tell you." Trent sat. His fingers flew across the screen of his phone. "I got results back from one of the genealogy sites. David's maternal uncle, Marc Kingston, sent his DNA to the site and added a family tree. He only had one sibling—a sister. David's mother was Heather Kingston. I did a quick search of her name, and something crazy came up."

Jon barged through the kitchen door. "I got your text. What's this big news?" He hopped on one foot as he yanked off his cowboy boot, then ran to the table.

Trent said, "I think we're about to blow this case open, Jon. I got a hit on the Family Match website. As I was just telling Jess, David's mother's name was Heather Kingston. I say, was, because she's dead. We wouldn't have found her if her only sibling, a brother named Marc, hadn't used this site. Bradley has another match to a maternal half-sibling, but that person's identity is hidden. I don't see the point in trying to get through the red tape to find this person. Whoever he or she is may come up in an investigation of Heather Kingston anyhow."

Jon asked, "How did she die?"

"That's where it gets interesting. I typed her name into a browser window, and it brought up a newspaper article. She died in a house fire, ruled an accident in 1995. Her son, Bradley, was home at the time and ran to the neighbor's house for help."

Jessica's ears rang, and Trent's voice sounded as if it travelled through a tunnel before reaching her. An arm wrapped around her shoulders. Stars danced in front of her eyes as she faced Jon.

"Trent, grab that glass of water off the counter. I think she's in shock." Jon shook her and tapped her cheek. "Stay with me, sweetheart. Breathe."

She inhaled slow, deep breaths, then her head cleared. "I'm okay now. It's just…holy crap! We knew he was sick, and we know he likes fires after he torched Debbie's barn. But to murder his own mother?"

Trent nodded. "I know. There's a lot more research to be done on this before we can be sure about Bradley

Kingston's profile."

Jessica asked, "What more could you possibly need to know to draw a conclusion?"

Jon patted her shoulder. "A lot of killers have horrible childhoods. I'm not saying it's an excuse, or that all people with a bad childhood turn into criminals, but the stats prove it. Digging into his past and interviewing people who knew him will yield important information."

Jessica guzzled the last half of her glass of water. "What's next?"

Jon shifted his gaze to Trent. "Where is Bradley Kingston from?"

Trent said, "A town in Eastern Ontario, Canada called Vankleek Hill."

Jon faced Jessica.

The solemn expression on his face, given the huge break they'd gotten, could only mean one thing. She sighed. "You don't have to say it. I know you want to go there. Take Kato with you. I'll be fine with Trent and Cynthia."

Jon clasped her hand. "Are you sure? Kato could go."

"Yes." She squeezed his hand gently. "It'll drive you crazy staying behind. Besides, this genealogy thing was your idea."

"You know me so well." He smiled. "Without a Canadian law enforcement badge, it won't be as straightforward, but the FBI and the RCMP share information all the time. But now that we know we're looking for Bradley Kingston, we can dig into public records. And possibly track down people that knew him at different points in his life."

Jessica said, "In the article, did it mention any other

relatives? A father? Anything?"

Trent shook his head. "No. And if there was an obituary, I couldn't find it."

Jessica spun her wedding band around her finger. "I wonder where and who he ended up with after the fire. If he landed in the system with children's social services, there may be records."

Jon said, "That's a strong possibility. If we find out he did end up in government care, Kato or Trent could get his file through official channels."

Jessica smiled. They didn't have a way of tracking David, no Bradley, she needed to get used to calling him, Bradley. But his identity was no longer a mystery. Whatever dirty secrets lay hidden behind that name would be brought to light. She prayed that information would lead them to Bradley at long last.

Chapter Seventeen

Nathan's heart soared like a firework set free to burst in the sky as they crossed the state line into Montana. Another nine hours of driving lay ahead of them before they arrived at the hotel in Lewistown.

Amy smiled. "The mountains are beautiful. It's been a pretty drive, but I'm glad we're in Montana now. I can't wait to get to our destination."

"Lewistown is a special little town. You'll love the western feel. It'll be a wonderful honeymoon." The closer he got to the Kents, the more his adrenaline kicked into gear. With his new face, he could walk beside them on the street, and they wouldn't recognize him.

But having Amy in tow would complicate matters. He'd have to get creative to sneak away to accomplish his goals. He didn't yet feel ready to tackle the fortress that the Kent Ranch had become. They went overboard after their encounter with Hugh Jones.

Hugh's failure to kill them would complicate his efforts, but that didn't mean he'd give up. He couldn't bear to walk the earth knowing the Kents lived, raising Bryce to be kind and loving when the boy had the potential to do so much more good for the world by carrying on Nathan's work.

Until he had a life insurance policy out on Amy, and enough time passed to stage an accident, he couldn't cash in. That meant he couldn't kill the Kents on this trip. But doing some reconnaissance and getting revenge elsewhere could satisfy him for the time being.

He could hit Jon and Jessica where it hurt without having to go anywhere near them or their ranch. It would be the highlight of his trip.

Amy yawned. "I think I'll try to take a nap. If that's okay? I didn't sleep well last night with the excitement of the wedding."

"Of course, darling."

With what he had planned, Amy would be well-rested by the time they returned home from their honeymoon. If she were to bear witness to his plans unfolding, he'd have to kill her which would derail his timeline.

After they stopped at a diner for some dinner, then a drive thru for donuts and coffee, they arrived at the hotel in Lewistown in the wee hours of the morning.

Amy climbed out of the truck and stretched her arms. "This is a quaint little town. I love the brick buildings and the western charm."

He stepped out of the truck and a gust of wind slammed into him. He snatched his ballcap as it lifted off his head and threw it on the dash of the truck. "Are you still tired?"

"I am. But it's our wedding night. Well, technically our wedding morning now."

Nathan grabbed their luggage from the backseat. "Why don't we make tonight our special night? I wanted to set the scene for you with candles and flowers."

Amy blushed. "That sounds so romantic."

"Great. It's settled. We can catch up on sleep, then find a nice spot to eat."

After checking in, he lay next to Amy on a

comfortable pillowtop king-size bed. Before booking them a place to stay, he ensured the bed would be comfortable to entice his bride to sleep. To speed the process along, he'd dumped a capsule of Emily's sleeping medication into Amy's coffee at the last rest stop while she was in the bathroom.

Her chest rose and fell, and after ten minutes she appeared to be in a deep sleep.

He checked his watch. *Two in the morning. Perfect.*

Nathan eased himself out of the bed, taking care not to jostle Amy. He tugged on his pants then patted his pocket to ensure the room key was still there. He slipped into the hallway and out to the parking lot. In preparation for the trip, he'd done his research.

Oh, how he longed to pay Aunt Debbie a visit, but that would be too obvious, and she was too smart and perceptive. He would take care of her later. Instead, he drove to Sally Kent's house close to Main Street.

He parked a street away, tugged his hood over his ballcap to keep it in place, then set off on foot with his backpack of tools slung over his shoulder. Keeping his head low, he hunched his shoulders to avoid having his face appear on any doorbell cameras that may be in the area.

The street around Sally's house was deserted and the windows were dark. To be on the safe side, he slipped around the side of her house to the back door. He studied the simple deadbolt and selected a lock pick from his set. He slipped it in the keyhole and shifted it around until the lock disengaged.

Child's play.

He put the lock picks away in his bag, then turned on his signal jammer in case the alarm system was armed. Slowly, he turned the knob and opened the door. The weatherstripping made a whooshing sound, but the hinges didn't squeak. He slipped out of his shoes, padded across the kitchen floor to a hallway, then turned on his flashlight as he descended a staircase to the basement.

In his search for the utility room, he passed through a family room with worn carpeting and an old floor model tv from the eighties. He swept the beam of his flashlight around and discovered a door at the back of the room. On the other side of the door stood an old hot water tank and a new furnace.

He ran his beam along the connections of the hot water tank. One of the gas line connections was a bit corroded.

Yes! It'll appear accidental.

Nathan used a wrench and tugged on the connection slightly and a hiss of air escaped before the pipe became silent again and with any luck, deadly.

His steps made little noise as he crept up the stairs and out the back door. He locked it on his way out so nothing would appear amiss. No other vehicles passed him on his way back to the hotel. He slipped the key card in the lock and eased the door open.

Amy lay in bed on her side in the same position he'd left her in.

He climbed in beside her and fought to keep his laughter silent as he reveled in the sweet, uplifting feeling of revenge.

Chapter Eighteen

The next morning, after caring for her horse and cows, Debbie drove to Sally's house. They'd made plans to go shopping together for baby gifts for Cassie. She had plenty of stuff, but how could anyone resist those cute little outfits with how fast babies grew and the amount of clothing they soiled?

She parked behind Sally's blue Ford Focus, then knocked on the door. A few minutes passed, and Sally didn't answer.

Debbie pounded on the door. "Sally, are you there?"

Sally wouldn't forget they'd made plans with how much she loved to shop. What could be keeping her?

After another few minutes passed, Debbie stood on the edges of the flower bed, careful not to trample Sally's annuals which hadn't yet succumbed to frost and peered inside a window. There were no lights on, yet Sally's car was in the driveway.

Something isn't right.

Debbie's hands shook as she dug inside her purse for her key ring. She pulled it out and sorted through her keys for Sally's spare. She stuck it in the lock and opened the door. "Sally! It's me, Debbie."

The alarm system blared in response.

Darn.

Debbie didn't know the code, but that didn't matter. A foul odor of something rotting smacked her in the face, and she wrinkled her nose. Figuring out where the awful smell was coming from could wait. She needed to find Sally. The kitchen was empty, and her sense of unease grew. She ran to the hallway where the bedrooms were located.

The door to Sally's bedroom stood open, and Sally lay in bed, unmoving.

Debbie shook her shoulders. "Sally, wake up!"

Sally's eyes remained shut.

"Oh, God. Oh, no. What's wrong, Sally?" Debbie placed her hand on Sally's neck to check for a pulse. Nothing. She grabbed her phone from her pocket, dialed 911, and hit the speaker icon to free up her hands. "I need an ambulance at 10 Aspen. My friend Sally isn't breathing, and she doesn't have a pulse. I'm beginning CPR now."

****

Jon packed business casual for another trip he didn't want to take away from Jessica and the kids. His instincts screamed that this was a horrible idea. He chalked it up to the last few incidents with Jessica claiming to see and hear things no one else saw or heard.

But if anything did go wrong Trent and Cynthia would be there for her and the kids. He still cringed at the memory of Jessica and Cynthia hiding behind cars in the parking garage while engaged in a shootout with Hugh Jones' men. Thank heavens, he and Trent had been nearby to help. They'd all emerged unscathed except for poor Sam, his former FBI colleague, who hadn't stood a chance with where he stood when the bullets began to fly.

Jessica came into their bedroom with a steaming mug in her hand. "Bryce is off to school with Cynthia, and Cassie just went down again. Hopefully, she'll sleep for a while. Last night was brutal. Something I ate must have given her a gassy stomach, and she couldn't settle. When are you leaving?"

Jon glanced at the alarm clock. "In about an hour." His phone vibrated on the bedside table. "Hello?"

"Jon. It's Hank. I have some bad news." Sheriff Hank's voice quivered in an uncharacteristic way.

Jon's knees buckled and he sat on the bed. "What happened?"

Jessica set her mug down, sat on the bed beside him, and leaned in to listen.

"You need to come to the hospital. It's your mother." Hank sighed. "There's no easy way to say this. She's in a coma. If Debbie had found her even five minutes later—thank God for Debbie—Sally would be dead. Carbon monoxide poisoning from a corroded gas connector on her hot water tank. The doctors are running tests to assess her condition now."

Jessica's face blanched as she wrapped a comforting arm around his shoulders.

"I'm on my way, Hank." Jon resisted the urge to panic. A coma was better than dead.

Jessica asked, "Do you want me to get Cassie ready? We could go with you to the hospital."

"It's better if you stay here, sweetheart. It might be hours before they can tell us anything, and we don't want Cassie picking up germs. As soon as I hear anything at all, I'll call." He wrapped his arms around her and breathed in the natural smell of her skin combined with the faint whiff of breast milk. "I'll have to call Kato on the way. He'll need to fly to Ottawa without me. We can't put off the investigation, and I can't focus until I know what's happening with my mom."

"Of course. When Cynthia and Bryce get home, I'll come join you at the hospital. I love you, Jon. I'm so sorry about what happened to Sally. Give Aunt Debbie and Hank my love and tell them I'll be there later."

"I will."

Jon's stomach clenched as he climbed behind the wheel of his truck and used the Bluetooth to dial Kato. He felt torn in half. His mother needed him but the only way to keep everyone safe was to find Bradley Kingston.

What a nightmare.

Chapter Nineteen

That afternoon, Jessica rocked Cassie as she nursed her. The innocence in her daughter's sweet blue eyes, combined with the rhythmic creaking of the rocking chair, soothed the tension in her muscles in a way nothing else could.

Jon still hadn't received any updates on Sally's condition, but at least he wasn't alone. Aunt Debbie, Hank, and Jon's brother Jamie were with him at the hospital. Jamie's wife Patricia was on duty as an E.R. nurse as well, and she'd be paying special attention to Sally.

Please let Sally be okay.

Jessica had texted Cynthia earlier to let her know what happened, and Cynthia had agreed to stay with the kids. The thought of leaving them with someone else, even Cynthia and Trent who she trusted, chilled her to the bone. Under the circumstances, it couldn't be helped.

Cassie's eyes fluttered and she stopped suckling.

Jessica stood slowly and placed her in the crib. She ensured the window was locked, then stepped out into the hallway, closing the nursery door behind her. She took a deep, shaky breath and leaned her forehead on the door. As much as she dreaded leaving her, Cassie would be good for a few hours. There were two pouches of breast milk in the fridge to tide her over until bedtime.

Milk had leaked onto the front of her shirt. She

hustled to her closet, dumped the tee in the hamper, then pulled on a green knit sweater. Once the sun started to set, the temperature would drop fast.

Back in the kitchen, she reheated potato and leek soup and slathered butter on a stack of soda crackers. As she inhaled the last delicious spoonful of her favorite soup, the kitchen door opened, and Bryce came inside followed by Cynthia and Trent.

Jessica stood and brought her dishes to the sink. "Hi, Bryce. How was your day?"

Bryce dumped his backpack on the floor beside the kitchen table. "Good. Cynthia says you're going out."

Jessica rested her hand on his shoulder. "Yes, I'm meeting Dad at the hospital. Grandma Sally is sick."

Bryce frowned. "Is she going to be all right?"

"We don't know yet. But stay positive. She's in good shape, and she has a lot to live for. You know how much she loves us." Jessica shifted her gaze to Cynthia and Trent standing nearby. "I'll be home to put the kids to bed. Cassie has milk in the fridge."

The corners of Cynthia's mouth lifted in a half smile. "We'll be fine. If you learn anything about Sally's condition, let us know."

Jessica slipped her running shoes on. "Of course. Thank you. There's soup in the fridge or help yourself to whatever."

She stepped outside and shut the door behind her and hustled to her minivan. A hollowness carved out all other emotion as she glanced in the back at the empty car seat. She wasn't used to being alone anymore and she hated leaving her babies behind.

****

Jessica found Jon, Debbie, Jamie, and Hank in the

waiting room of the critical care unit.

As she approached, Jon turned his head and smiled. "Hi, Jess."

Aunt Debbie stood and hugged her. "Thank you for coming. It must've been hard to leave Cassie."

"It was. But Cynthia and Trent will take care of her." Jessica sat next to Jon. "Any news?"

Jon held her hand. "Her condition is unchanged. She's still in the coma, but she hasn't been having seizures so far which they think is a good sign. The neurosurgeon on her case is supposed to update us when he gets out of surgery."

Hank shook his head. "I'm replacing that hot water tank. I can't believe your mom didn't keep up on the maintenance. I blame myself for never taking a closer look at it when I was over there."

Jamie said, "Mom had it serviced every year. You'd think the technician would've told her to replace it if it was that corroded."

An unfamiliar female voice interrupted them. "Jon and Jamie Kent."

Jon turned. A doctor stood at the front of the waiting area. Jon approached her. "I'm Jon Kent."

Jessica followed and took Jon's hand, and the others gathered behind them.

The doctor said, "Your mother sustained some brain damage which resulted in her coma. But it isn't severe. I expect she'll wake and recover. The thing to keep in mind is that some patients with carbon monoxide poisoning experience continued neurological deterioration for up to six weeks. Until she wakes, we won't know the extent of the impact. She could be fine, or she may experience issues with memory, language, movement, cognition, and behavior."

Jessica inhaled a deep breath. At least Sally had survived. She couldn't imagine a life without Sally and her upbeat personality. The kids adored her.

Jon said, "Any idea how long until she'll wake?"

The doctor closed the file she carried. "It isn't an exact science. We can never be sure, but based on her condition, anywhere from a few days to a month."

A month. Jessica swallowed around a lump in her throat. Sally needed them close, and Jessica wanted Jon to be there for her, but they couldn't halt the search for Bradley that long. He would be coming for them, and they were sitting ducks.

"Thank you, doctor," Jamie said. "At least Mom will survive. If she needs some therapy or some extra care, she could always stay with me for a while."

The doctor nodded then walked away.

Aunt Debbie patted Jamie's arm. "I'll help as much as I can."

Hank glanced between Jon and Jamie. "You know I'll make sure your mother has whatever she needs."

"Thank you. We appreciate it." Jon ran his hands through his hair and tugged on the ends. "This is just—I don't know what to do. I wish I could split myself in two. Kato landed in Ottawa, and he's on his way to the FBI sub-office. He plans to dig into records and gather info for when I get there. But Mom needs me."

"The doctor just said Mom will survive. The rest of us can take care of her." Jamie rested a hand on his shoulder. "David is sick. You need to go to Ottawa. Mom would want you to catch him."

Jessica remained silent and allowed Jon to process. She agreed with Jamie, but she didn't want to push Jon in a direction he would come to regret. He needed to draw his own conclusions since he would have to live with the consequences of his decision.

Jon met Jessica's gaze. "Jamie is right. I hate to leave you all behind with Mom in the hospital but the situation with David—his real name is Bradley Kingston by the way—can't wait."

Jessica nodded. "I think you're doing the right thing. We'll manage fine without you."

Aunt Debbie said, "That's his real name? Are you sure?"

Jessica explained how they'd tracked down Bradley's identity with his DNA sample.

Aunt Debbie smiled. "That's wonderful. You're on the right track. I can feel it. Go find him, Jon. Make him pay."

Despite her misgivings about Jon leaving again, Jessica agreed. Something about their investigation felt different. She sensed a breakthrough was near. Hopefully, it happened before Bradley came for them, but somehow, he always seemed to be a step ahead of them no matter what they did.

Chapter Twenty

With candles and roses in hand from the florist, Nathan strode the few blocks back to Main Street where Amy waited for him inside his truck. As pretentious as it was, he always went the extra mile to ensure he maintained the image of a loving and kind husband.

The first person the police looked to while determining if a death was an accident or a suspicious death, was the spouse. Keeping himself above suspicion enabled him to get away with murder and collect insurance money time and time again. And he only needed to make it through this one last sham marriage.

She smiled with rosy-red cheeks as he climbed into the driver's seat. "You're so sweet. I'm so lucky to have you. I picked up coffees and sandwich wraps from that quaint little café. I found a few books there too."

"I don't think we'll be doing much reading tonight."

She chuckled. "No, I suppose not."

He'd convinced her to stay in and order takeout. Although he had a new face, he still didn't want to parade himself around in public and land himself on camera footage. For an early dinner, they ordered steak entrees, dessert, and a bottle of champagne for later.

Silence spread between them as they ate. Unsurprisingly, Amy was quiet, more like the insecure, bashful girl from early on in their relationship. The typical virgin except she was in her late twenties instead of her teens. Her bashfulness was the one annoying thing about her.

He resisted the urge to roll his eyes. Once he popped her cherry, she'd get past it. If she didn't it would be a long month or so to get through. He'd already applied for the life insurance policy in her name on the day of the wedding. Brazen, but as long as the policy paid out, he didn't care if the authorities sniffed around because he'd be long gone with Bryce.

She pushed her half-eaten food away. "Do you mind if I take a quick bath and freshen up?"

"Of course not. Go ahead. I'll set up while you're in there."

Amy glanced over her shoulder, met his gaze, and smiled before closing the bathroom door behind her. She'd given him an ideal window for subterfuge.

Perfect.

He used the cheap corkscrew provided by the hotel, twisted it into the muselet and tugged. A pop filled the air as it dislodged, and a trickle of champagne spilled out of the bottle. He filled two glasses close to the top, pulled a small Ziploc bag out of his pocket, and dumped a fine powder of crushed sleeping pills into one of the glasses. The champagne inside the glass fizzed, and he stirred the amber liquid to dissolve the powder.

The bathroom door opened. "I forgot my toothbrush in my bag."

He clutched the empty bag and jammed it inside his pocket. "Okay." He winked. "But stay in there this time. I want to surprise you."

"I will. Let me know when you're ready for me to come out."

He blew out a breath as the bathroom door shut

behind her. If she'd come out a minute sooner, she would've ruined everything. It's hard to explain away dumping powder in a glass of champagne.

At least the rest of his preparations were less nefarious. His agitated energy slipped away as he settled into his usual wedding night routine. He plucked fragrant red rose petals from their blossoms and created a trail from the bathroom door to the bed.

The sweet scent of the flowers permeated the air as he lit candles and placed them around the room. He flicked the light switch and the candle flames danced in the darkness.

"Amy, you can come out now, darling."

She opened the door then stood inside the doorway in a black silk negligee and a matching robe. She glanced around the room. "This is so sweet. I'll always remember this night."

He handed her the champagne, then held up his glass. "A toast. May we have a long and happy marriage."

She clinked glasses with him and took a sip.

Nathan took the glass from her hand and placed both of their glasses on a table. One sip wouldn't make her drowsy, but he couldn't allow her to have more until later. His goal was to get her to drink the rest after they slept together, then he'd be free to prowl the night with her unaware of his absence.

Sally's accidental gas leak hadn't made news. He didn't yet know whether she'd perished or not and that irked him. No matter. On the off chance she survived, the family would be traumatized by the 'accident'. He wasn't finished torturing the Kents yet anyhow.

But first, he needed to take care of his new wife. The

minute she'd let him move in, he'd kicked his planning for her into gear. He kissed Amy softly and she yielded to him and deepened the kiss.

She broke their kiss then lifted the hem of his tee and pulled it over his head. "Make love to me, Nathan. I love you."

Spare me the emotional crap. "I love you, too." He grabbed her bottom, lifted her into his arms, and carried her to bed.

After he was finished with her, Amy sat up in bed glowing with a bigger smile than ever on her face. He retrieved their champagne. "Here, darling. Drink up. No sense in this delicious champagne going to waste."

"Thank you." Amy took a sip and made a face.

She wasn't much of a drinker which made it hard to discern if she didn't like the champagne itself or whether the pills had made it bitter. She drank just over half of her champagne. "I'm tired. I think I'll go to sleep now."

He kissed her then lay down in bed next to her the same way he had the night he murdered Emily. "Goodnight, darling." With her small size, and no tolerance to sleep medication, half of what he'd given her should put her into a deep sleep.

He curled up beside her and put his arm around her.

Within half an hour, her breathing slowed.

He waited a while longer then slipped out of bed.

She didn't stir.

His clothes were scattered around the bed. Eager to be on his way, he collected them and dressed quickly. With his cap pulled low on his head, he slipped out of the room.

Chapter Twenty-One

Jon caught a late flight out of Great Falls and landed in Ottawa the next afternoon. During his layover, he checked in with Jamie. Their mother still hadn't woken from her coma. As he turned the airplane mode off on his phone, he prayed for better news. The longer it took her to wake, the worse he feared her prognosis would be. It would be difficult, but he needed to compartmentalize and attempt to forget about his mother laying in the hospital bed.

He hadn't checked any luggage, so at least he didn't have to follow the crowd to the baggage carousel. Instead, he slipped out the nearest exit to where a line of taxi cabs waited for fares. The lingering sulfuric smell of exhaust fumes confirmed he found himself in a city once again. One of the last places he wanted to be. He'd take horse and cow manure over the scent of garbage and pollution in the city any day of the week.

Jon opened the door of the nearest cab and slipped into the back seat. "Good afternoon, sir." He gave the driver the address of the FBI sub-office.

His phone connected to a wireless network and no news greeted him. His mother must still be in the coma. He texted Kato and set up a meeting point outside the building. As a retired agent, it would be easier if Kato vouched for him on the way in.

As they neared the downtown core, Ottawa gave off

the air of a nation's capital with the stunning neo-gothic elements of the historic Parliament Buildings anchored by the Peace Tower. He took a deep breath and spared a minute to appreciate the beauty of the city. Minutes of quiet would be few and far between until they captured Bradley.

Near the address Kato had sent him, Jon spotted Kato standing on the curb. "Could you let me off here, please?" He hadn't bothered to get Canadian currency, so he handed the driver two American twenty-dollar bills for his thirty-five-dollar fare. "Is this okay? No change needed."

The driver smiled. "Yes, sir. Have a great day."

Jon climbed out and joined Kato on the curb. "How's it going with the investigation so far?"

Kato led the way inside the building. "The authorities here have been helpful. Bradley Kingston held a driver's license in his own name. The photo quality on the license isn't fantastic, but they're running it through facial recognition."

"That's great. If the photo isn't too poor, and he followed the same pattern back then, multiple licenses should surface with the same face on them. I've often wondered if he travels locations in a discernible pattern. We might be able to guess at where he could be."

Kato held up his visitor's badge at the reception desk. "My friend needs one of these." He turned to Jon. "We should also have Bradley Kingston's foster records by the end of the day. We served our warrant to the Ministry of Social Services this morning. Jessica guessed right about him landing in care. With no father in the picture, there was no one to take him in."

The receptionist said, "Can I see some

identification, please?"

Jon handed his driver's license to the officer manning the reception desk and signed the visitor's log. "We'll get to know him better if we dig into his past and conduct a few interviews, but our main concern is finding him. I don't think it's safe to stay here for any length of time. In two days, tops, I need to head back. We've been careful, but I can't help but wonder if Bradley is monitoring our movements."

"If necessary, I can stay behind and keep digging. Or I can follow the evidence to wherever it may lead." Kato's phone pinged. "I've got a picture of Bradley as a teen from his high school year book. I'll forward you the image."

Jon's phone pinged and he opened the file. "That initial FBI sketch of Bradley after the apartment building fire was close, but there are some differences. As strange as it is he looks familiar. I'm sure it'll come to me."

Kato led the way past the reception desk and through a sea of cubicles to a small desk and two chairs tucked in a corner. "They assigned me this as a temporary office. At least I can connect to their WIFI."

Jon set his bag on the floor and dug out his laptop. "Can I have the password?"

"Sure. I'll send you what I've found so far. We know Bradley attended school from elementary through high school in Vankleek Hill. I'll send you his records. The most notable entries are from public school."

An email from Kato appeared in his inbox. He opened the attachment and started reading. Although he hated Bradley for all the deaths and trauma he was responsible for, he couldn't help but be disturbed.

Page after page from various teachers listed

concerns and reports were made to child social services. They described Bradley as overly skinny, and they suspected malnourished. His teachers brought an extra lunch to school for him because he so rarely ever had food of his own.

Worse, Bradley came to school running high fevers, sick with stomach bugs, and with various injuries like bruises, cuts, a broken arm, and cigarette burns.

Socially, they described him as withdrawn. When questioned about his injuries, he looked away and wouldn't answer. Besides being a loner, no other behavioral issues were listed in the records.

Jon closed the attachment and met Kato's gaze across the desk. "What did you make of this? Clearly, he was abused, and I don't understand why with the reports filed he wasn't removed from the home. I expected to find more incidents in his school records. The bathroom trash being lit on fire or fights—just something."

"I agree. But it makes me wonder if he took so much abuse until one day he cracked and set his house on fire, killing his mother. At age twelve, as an adolescent with hormones raging, I could see that as a critical age for him to boil over."

"That makes a lot of sense. Maybe once he got a taste for fire, murder, and ultimately power, he enjoyed it and kept going."

Kato's computer pinged. "We have his foster care records. He was placed with the Levesque family in Vankleek Hill within walking distance of the high school. He stayed there for six years until he aged out of the system."

"That could be a gold mine. We need to pay them a visit."

Kato typed away on his keyboard. "They're still at the same address."

Jon stuck his computer in his bag. "Let's go. Maybe by the time we get back, they'll have an update on facial recognition."

With no idea where Bradley was, they couldn't possibly be close to him physically, yet somehow Jon was overcome with a sense of hope that they were getting closer to him than they'd ever been before.

Chapter Twenty-Two

With Kato next to him in the passenger seat, Jon drove to the address listed as the Levesque home and parked on the street. The two-story home stood on a big lot. A few acres separated them from their neighbors on either side. Around the corner of the house, two children bounced on a trampoline.

Their laughter carried to Jon as he stepped outside the black sedan borrowed from the FBI sub-office. Not all foster homes were happy ones, but this one gave off a cheerful air with the potted mums on the front porch and the fairy statues in the garden boxes placed between bushes.

Kato smiled. "They seem like good people. Bradley must have been ruined by the abuse he suffered by the time he got here."

Jon climbed the porch stairs to the front door and rang the doorbell. "Or his mental wiring was off from the beginning. I don't think we'll ever know."

A short man with salt and pepper hair opened the door. He wore a 'kiss the cook' apron over his golf shirt and jeans.

Kato held up his badge. "Alain Levesque?"

The man nodded. "Can I help you, gentlemen?"

"I'm Agent Kato Chen and this is Retired Agent Jon Kent. We're with the FBI. We'd like to ask you questions about a child you fostered almost twenty years ago.

Bradley Kingston."

Alain frowned. "If you're this far north talking to me, this must be serious." Hurt clouded his gaze. "I'd like to say I'm surprised, but I'm not. Come in. My wife is out back with the kids. We were about to grill our dinner."

Jon said, "Would you like us to come back later?"

Alain shrugged. "Up to you. I don't mind throwing a few extra burgers on the barbecue."

Jon wanted to stay, and he got the sense from Alain's reaction they would be engaging in a long conversation. He glanced at Kato.

Kato nodded.

Jon stepped inside. "That's very kind of you. Thank you."

Alain led them along a hallway past a dining room with a long table, a living room with toys scattered around the area rug in front of the television, then out the back door into a large backyard.

A woman with short, light brown hair stood by the grill.

Alain walked up to her. "We have guests, Lorraine. FBI Agents. They need to talk to us about Bradley."

She spun and smiled. Smile lines crinkled around her kind brown eyes. "Oh, hello. Nice to meet you. Have a seat."

Jon settled into one of six lawn chairs surrounding the patio table beside the grill. "Thank you, Mrs. Levesque."

Alain said, "Can you watch the grill for a minute longer? I'll be right back. I'm grabbing another few burgers. I think this will be a long talk."

She pursed her lips. "Likely will be." She glanced

up at the two girls who'd stopped bouncing and now sat on the trampoline. Keeping her voice low, she said, "We did everything we could for that boy. But his mother put him through hell, and no matter how many times he visited the psychiatrist, he would never talk about it. He bottled it up inside. You should see the scars on his back. It looked like someone put out cigarettes on his skin. And not one or two, more like twenty. They told us there was evidence of broken bones and they suspected other abuse from what his teachers reported."

Jon cringed even though he'd read the information in Bradley's foster records on the way to Hawkesbury. He couldn't help but think of Bryce and how young and innocent he was when Jessica first fled to Lewistown before Bradley kidnapped him and stripped him of his innocence.

How sick would Bradley have to be to kidnap Bryce and traumatize him that way after what Bradley himself had been through as a child?

Alain returned with the burgers, and they sizzled as he dropped them on the grill. "Did I miss anything?"

"I was just telling them about Bradley's injuries. Oh, and he was starving. The poor boy. We could count his ribs. His clothes were barely holding together at the seams," Lorraine asked, "So, what happened to him?"

Jon sighed. There would be no point sugar coating the answer. "He's a wanted serial killer. We're digging into his past to try and figure out where he might be."

Lorraine sat hard in the chair across from Jon. "We knew he was troubled, but I never imagined he'd kill people. The last time we heard from him, or his foster sister Simone, was before they moved away. It hurt, but I always imagined they'd settled down in Saskatchewan somewhere and wanted to forget their painful pasts."

Kato asked, "What was Simone's last name? Given what we know about Bradley, we need to track her down to see if she's still alive."

"Girard." Alain flipped a burger and opened a bag of buns. "Why wouldn't she be alive? I can see him killing others, but he'd never hurt her."

Jon's thoughts travelled along the same path as Kato's. "Bradley has murdered his wives on numerous occasions. We're still combing records and searching for his victims. He's been changing identities and moving around Canada and the United States marrying women, taking life insurance policies out on them, then staging accidents and cashing in."

Lorraine's eyes filled with tears, and she turned her head away from the little girls on the trampoline. "That's just horrible. I wish we had done more. Tried different therapists."

Alain placed a hand on her shoulder. "How do you think I feel? Where do you think he got the knowledge of insurance from?" He glanced between Jon and Kato. "I'm an insurance broker. I have my own firm in town."

Jon said, "You two aren't to blame. You took him in, and I'm sure you gave him a loving home. I hate to say it, but some people are just born this way, and some end up this way after serious abuse. If anyone's at fault, it's the social workers who left him in the care of his mother after the school made numerous reports to them from kindergarten on."

Kato nodded with a solemn expression on his face. "From his records, that failure to act led to eight more years of abuse."

Alain shifted the cooked burgers onto a platter.

"Girls, dinner is ready. Time to come inside and set the table for dinner."

Lorraine wiped her eyes. "We'll have to continue this discussion after we eat."

The two girls climbed off the trampoline, then held hands, giggling, as they ran inside ahead of the adults.

Jon longed for home as he watched the girls pull placemats out of drawers ahead of sitting down for a family dinner the Levesque family had so kindly invited them to join. Once the girls set cutlery and plates out for everyone, Lorraine and Alain carried the platter of burgers and two bowls of salad to the table.

As they ate, the girls who were both in the third grade, filled the silence telling stories about their school and friends. Eventually, they managed to eat most of their burgers which had to be cold with how long it took them to eat between tales.

Lorraine stacked their plates. "Bath time, girls. Head upstairs. I'll be there in a minute." She patted Alain's shoulder in passing. "I'll take care of them while you continue answering questions."

"Sure, Lorraine." Alain stood. "I'll make coffee."

Jon shifted his gaze to Kato who sat beside him. "I sense he has something to tell us."

"I think so, too." Kato sighed. "I texted our host at the field office and asked them to locate Simone Girard. I don't think they're going to find her."

"Me neither. He had the tenacity to learn about Alain's business and then use it for his own gains. I doubt he felt any closer to his foster sister with how nice Lorraine and Alain are."

Despite already knowing how sick and disturbed Bradley was, the hairs on Jon's arms stood on end at the thought of him living with his foster sister for years and then killing her. That meant that even as a twelve-year-old child, all Bradley could think about was his next mark. Given Bradley was now thirty-eight, that meant the man had been planning and executing murder for twenty-six years.

The comforting smoky aroma of coffee wafted into the room as Alain carried in a tray with mugs, sugar, cream, and spoons. He set it in the middle of the table and then sat across from Jon and Kato with the same somber expression he'd worn before dinner. "Okay, let's talk."

Jon asked, "During the years Bradley lived with you, were there any incidents or behavioral issues? Fires? Suspicious deaths?"

Alain stirred cream in his mug. "I think it's best to start at the beginning. I'm assuming you know how his mother died."

Kato said, "Yes. And we think there's a good chance he's responsible."

Alain nodded. "After the fire, he came straight to us. I can understand him having mixed feelings about losing his mother with the abuse, but he never grieved. He didn't shed a single tear, and he never asked to visit her grave. That's when we knew something was wrong with him."

Kato sipped his coffee. "Were there any other signs? Was he quick to anger? Did he act out?"

"Not that we saw, and that's what made it difficult. He went to school and did chores without giving us trouble. His teachers never complained about his behavior, but they were concerned about his social skills.

"Besides Simone, he didn't make friends. He

interacted fine with adults, but never other kids his age. Bullying could explain some of it. From what we understand, the other kids were horrible to him over the years because of the way he was neglected. Dirty hair and clothes. It's terribly sad."

"It is. I have children, and I can't understand how any parent could be so neglectful." Jon understood Alain's sadness for Bradley's suffering. How could anyone not pity a child who endured that kind of abuse?

"We tried getting him to talk. When he didn't, eventually, we let it go. He seemed to be fine. He got good enough grades, and he showed an interest in my business." Alain drank from his mug. "But now that you're here asking about fires, I can't help but wonder."

Sensing Alain was about to answer his original question, Jon placed his elbows on the table and leaned forward. "What is it you suspect he did?"

Alain looked him in the eyes. "Over the years, five of his classmates and their families died in house fires. Only one was ruled an arson, the first one that killed Francis Castonguay, his two younger siblings, and their parents. We thought he was in bed sleeping that night, but he could've snuck out. At the time, after how his mother died, I remember wondering if he could be responsible. He wasn't acting out, so I dismissed it. But now…I can't help but feel the weight of those deaths on my hands."

Sweet Jesus. Just when I think he can't get any sicker. "No, sir," Jon spoke with conviction. "You are *not* responsible. He's too smart for his own good. He fools everyone around him, including countless women who have married him not realizing they were signing their own death warrants. You couldn't have known."

Chapter Twenty-Three

Debbie sat in a chair next to Sally's hospital bed and held her best friend's hand. The permanent antiseptic odor and the constant beeping reminded Debbie of her time in the hospital after recovering from being shot in the basement of the so-called safe house in Hawaii. There she'd hunkered down with Jon, Jessica, Bryce, Cynthia, Trent, and Thomas while the FBI assessed the risk to their lives after Hugh Jones' death.

Little did they know that before Hugh Jones had died, he'd discovered their flight plan to Hawaii and had sent a group of criminals after them. Hugh's men had attempted to surprise them in the middle of the night, planning to murder them in their beds. In the end, the thugs had all ended up dead instead, but so did their dear friend Thomas. Debbie had managed to cheat death but had spent a long time in the hospital regenerating her damaged liver after emergency surgery.

An unwelcome memory.

She prayed Sally would wake soon without any lasting cognitive impairments. Then they'd be able to get her home and avoid the hospital for a long time. She also prayed Jon and Kato would find something that led them to that horrid David—no, she needed to stop calling him that—his name was Bradley Kingston. They needed to catch him before he came after them again.

"Sally, please wake up. I need you. And your kids

and grandbabies need you, too. Hank took charge, and he's taking care of that stupid hot water tank. All you have to do is wake up."

Sally's hand moved in her grip.

"That's it, Sally. Come back to me, you hear?"

Sally's eyelids fluttered a few times, then she held her eyes open.

"Sally?"

Sally blinked and her gaze shifted sideways to Debbie. She croaked, "Debbie? What's going on?"

"You're in the hospital. You had an accident. Carbon monoxide poisoning from a gas leak. I better go get your doctor."

Sally's pupils dilated and she squeezed Debbie's hand with a surprising amount of strength for a sick woman. "No! Call Hank then Jon."

Debbie took her phone out of her pocket. "Why?"

"It wasn't an accident. I heard someone leaving my house. By the time I got out of bed, they were gone, and I thought I imagined it. But someone must have poisoned me."

"I'll get Hank over here. But you'll have to wait to see Jon. He's in Ottawa following a lead on— Bradley Kingston."

Hell in a handbasket!

Debbie's hands vibrated as she searched her contacts for Hank's name. The only person that Debbie could imagine messing with Sally's hot water tank was Bradley Kingston. After what he pulled lighting Debbie's barn on fire—it had to be him. None of them were safe.

****

Jessica shut the cover of Bryce's graphic novel and

133

kissed his forehead. "Goodnight, buddy. See you in the morning."

"Mom?"

"Yes, buddy?"

"I think I saw my dad on the first day of school. He looked just like he does in his picture and none of my friends saw him."

Her breath caught, and the room tilted. It must have been Adam trying to reach her in the cornfield and on the baby monitor. "Why are you only telling me this now?"

"I didn't want to make you sad, and I didn't think you'd believe me."

"Oh, Bryce. You can tell me anything, and I'll always believe you. Your father watches over us all the time. I've seen him before, too."

"You have?"

"Yes. I swear."

Bryce smiled then rolled over and faced the wall. "Goodnight, Mom."

She tugged his blanket up to his chin, then triple-checked the lock on his window. With Jon and Kato out of town, an air of foreboding and tension hung in the air. Trent and Cynthia would be arriving soon to stay the night in the guest room.

Their presence comforted in one sense, but in another, having people in the house set her on edge. Especially since they didn't have faith in her and chalked up her strange experiences to mental stress even after everything they'd been through together.

Jessica yawned as she tiptoed past the nursery on her way to the kitchen to make her bedtime cup of tea. She set the kettle to boil and then stuck a chamomile tea bag in a mug. The kitchen door opened behind her, and

Cynthia and Trent came in.

Cynthia shut the door gently. "Hi, how are the kids?"

"Asleep. Do you guys want tea?"

Cynthia came to lean on the counter beside her. "Yes, please."

"I'd like some too, please." Trent set a thick envelope on the kitchen table. "I found this stuck in the gate when I did my rounds."

"Oh, yeah. A delivery guy buzzed earlier and I told the driver to leave it there. I completely forgot about it." Jessica grabbed two more mugs from the cupboard. "Just in case I'm at the hospital, could you guys keep a look out for a bigger delivery? My mom and my sister shipped me some boxes of stuff from my house in Cochrane earlier today. Hopefully, with the housing market up, a buyer will look over the house's past."

Cynthia grimaced. "Sorry about the two men I killed in there. That couldn't have been good for property value."

The kettle whistled. Jessica turned off the burner and poured water into the mugs. "You had no choice but to shoot them, and that's old news now. The area is growing like crazy with people moving in from out of town and there isn't much on the market. The realtor told my sister the property value shouldn't be affected."

Cynthia carried two of the mugs to the table. "Good. I feel better about it then."

Trent asked, "Any updates on Sally?"

"No, she hasn't woken yet. I was thinking of taking the kids to see her for a few minutes tomorrow. If she can hear us, I'm sure she'd appreciate knowing we're there for her." Jessica sighed. "Bryce told me something interesting at bedtime. He thinks he saw Adam in the schoolyard on the first day of school."

Cynthia's brows furrowed. "How sure are you he saw Adam?"

Jessica said, "I've had photos of Adam all over the house his whole life. He'd know his own father, and he says no one else saw him. But just in case, can you keep a closer eye on the recess yard?"

Cynthia said, "Of course. Wait, that's around the same time you thought you saw him in the field and the baby monitor happened, right?"

"Yes. And with Bradley on the loose, it makes sense Adam would be worried and watching us."

Trent pursed his lips. "I'm still having trouble coming to terms with the ghost thing, but that warning in Hawaii when the thugs were coming for us was accurate and I can't explain that. But for argument's sake, why wouldn't he communicate with you?"

"Every time he tried to tell me something before, he'd disappear when he said too much. I'm guessing he's trying to work up the energy to share something huge and specific that he's not allowed to say. With the holes in our knowledge, like where Bradley is right this minute, that makes sense to me." Jessica turned to face Cynthia. "I think that makes a lot more sense than waking dreams since nothing has happened since."

"I agree. As crazy as it might sound, after everything that's happened, it's the most likely scenario." Cynthia fiddled with the string of her teabag. "I will keep Bryce close though, just in case."

Jessica yawned. "Thank you. Do you need anything else before I turn in? That midnight feeding will come soon enough."

Trent carried his mug to the sink. "No. We're fine."

Jessica's phone buzzed on the counter and Debbie's name showed on a text message notification. She picked up her phone, facial recognition accepted her identity, then the message showed on her screen.

—*Good news. Sally is awake and the doctor's assessing her now. She's talking and she seems lucid. The bad news is she thinks someone was in her house messing with her hot water tank that night. She didn't see this person, but we both know who would do something like that.*—

"Oh no." Jessica turned to face Cynthia and Trent.

Cynthia asked, "What's wrong?"

"I got a text from my aunt. Sally is awake and talking."

Trent said, "Well, that's good news, right?"

Jessica wrestled away the urge to panic. "Yes, but it wasn't an accident. Sally heard someone in her house that night."

Cynthia sat up straighter in her chair. "She might have been disoriented from the carbon monoxide. Do you know if she saw this person?"

Jessica clenched her phone in her hand. Why were these two always so quick to doubt everything? Even after what seemed like the breakthrough, they'd just had a few minutes earlier. If she didn't have the kids' safety to worry about, she'd kick them out of her house and off her property. "No. But don't you guys see what's happening here? Bradley Kingston has a history of making deaths look like an accident. He has to be behind this. He likes to circle and taunt. Look what he did to Debbie. I don't care what you two want to believe as long as you're prepared and vigilant. Because this is him. I know Jon will agree with me."

Chapter Twenty-Four

The next morning, Jessica sat at the kitchen table with the unopened envelope and the one cup of coffee she allowed herself every few days. Cassie had already fed and went back to sleep, and Trent was out helping the ranch hands. Cynthia was still asleep, likely worn out from the school week and their slightly heated exchange the night before.

Since it was Saturday, she didn't have to worry about waking Bryce and going through the school routine. She had a moment to herself for a change. Later, they'd go visit Sally. Thank heavens the early assessments showed no lasting cognitive impairments. Hank had taken the possible threat seriously and posted a guard outside Sally's room.

Jessica sipped her coffee, savoring the flavor and warmth that traveled all the way to her toes. She returned her attention to the thick envelope in front of her. Likely, it contained paperwork from her desk in Cochrane, and had come through customs ahead of the rest of her boxes.

She stuck her finger under the edge of the envelope and tore it open. Inside, she found a thick stack of papers and flipped through them. They didn't belong to her. They were internal documents from the FBI, and Jon's name was all over them.

Jessica broke out in a cold sweat and shivered.

In search of a return address, she picked up the

envelope and flipped it over. No return sender. She never pressed Jon for information about his time at the FBI because he hated talking about it, and what little he'd told her was horrible. While undercover collecting evidence, he'd been forced to stand by while people who owed debts were tortured and killed by Hugh Jones. He'd retired because he couldn't handle that dark lifestyle anymore.

Whoever had sent the files intended to hurt her and Jon both. Reading those pages would only give the sender what they wanted. It would be easy to throw the stack of paper in the fireplace and erase it from existence. If she didn't read the files, then she would always wonder what Jon ran away from and what dark secrets he kept locked away.

He had a nasty habit of trying to shield her from the truth and lying by omission.

She suspected this was the only chance she'd ever get to learn the truth about that phase of his life, and what had morphed him from the young man she grew up with to the haunted man he'd become. The answers wouldn't be pretty, but she needed to know.

Jessica inhaled a deep breath through her nose then exhaled through her mouth, steeling herself for dark truths. She started with the first page on the top of the stack.

****

Fourteen years earlier (March 4, 2010)

In the middle of the night, Jon, deep undercover and going by the name of Knox, held onto the Jesus handle as he rode shotgun in the passenger seat of a cube van next to Stevie. The man drove like a crazed maniac, but Jon didn't dare say anything to him about his crappy driving skills. Stevie had a screw loose and was the one in charge of the operation tonight.

After three months of assimilating himself into the trafficking operation, the big boss, Carlo Lombardi, still didn't trust Jon enough to let him in on inside information. He needed more evidence and information on the network beyond Carlo's operation. Then his bosses at the FBI would have enough to move in and lay enough charges to break up the whole ring on the US side of the border. Efforts were always made to coordinate with the Federales in Mexico.

The plan was to collect a shipment from a container at the dock in San Diego and drive it to the warehouse downtown. Jon assumed it would be another load of drugs or weapons of some kind—a poisonous load, contributing to addiction, violence, and death.

The tape on his chest holding his wire in place made his skin itch, especially in the heat of Southern California, but he didn't dare scratch it and draw attention to himself. That itch acted as a constant reminder of the danger he placed himself in each day.

Stevie parked beside a container. "All right. Let's get this over with. This load might be a pain in the ass."

"Why?"

"You'll see."

Jon opened the door of the van and shuddered as muffled screams and bangs emanated from the shipping container. A large padlock shook as someone pounded on the door from inside.

Human trafficking was the lowest of the low and the one crime Jon absolutely despised being complicit in. If an opportunity arose, he'd inform his handler. It would be taking a huge risk, but maybe Agent Reynolds could get local law enforcement to pull them over on a traffic stop on the way to the warehouse.

Stevie flipped through a key ring, then shoved a key in the lock. "Whatever you do, don't let them bite you. These girls aren't the cleanest if you know what I mean."

"That's just gross, Stevie."

Stevie opened the door, and the stench of urine and body odor combined with cheap perfume escaped from within.

Jon forced himself to look inside at the faces of about twenty Latina women chained to the walls, likely brought up through Mexico from further south. The women recoiled from them and plastered themselves against the wall, crying and shivering. The one closest to them on the right had soulful, terrified brown eyes in the face of a teenager.

That face would haunt Jon forever. He had to save her and the others.

Stevie grinned crookedly. "I know how you are with wanting your girls wholesome and all. I'm not as picky. Maybe I'll have a go with one before we unchain them and load them up."

Sweet Jesus, forgive me. "I'm not one for watching. I'll wait out here." Although he couldn't save Stevie's chosen victim from rape, he could sound the alarm to rescue them all.

Stevie shrugged, "Your loss," then stepped inside. The screams inside the container intensified as he pulled the door closed.

Jon resisted the urge to padlock Stevie inside. At times like these, he struggled to hang onto the bigger picture and how many lives would be saved when the operation crumbled. Of course, another criminal enterprise would step in and take their place, but it slowed the flow in the area temporarily while the authorities worked to take down the next big fish in the ocean of crime plaguing the United States.

Overall, a depressing state of affairs, but every life saved counted for something.

Jon hurried inside the cube van and dug the burner phone out of his pocket. He dialed Agent Reynolds, grateful when he answered.

"It's Jon. The shipment tonight is a load of young Latina women. Stevie is having his way with one of them now. You have to inform the local police to make a traffic stop. I'll give you the plate."

Agent Reynolds sighed, "If I do that, the whole operation will be compromised. You know this."

"No. Stevie won't talk. He's too afraid of Carlo. Arrange things so that it looks like I got out on bail, and I'll still be undercover."

"You know I can't. Getting the whole organization comes first."

"Have I ever been wrong about something like this working? Why won't you just trust me? It's only one load. We've been letting every other shipment get through. They won't suspect anything."

"No. I'm sorry, Jon. Goodbye."

The line went dead.

Jon erased the call from the burner phone. Without the support of the FBI, he couldn't risk calling the local police. Agent Reynolds would know what he'd done. He'd face suspension and no law enforcement agency would ever hire him. He had no choice but to help move the women as gently as possible and carry on with the investigation. In the end, Carlos and Stevie would answer for their crimes.

****

Present Day

Jessica's coffee churned in her stomach. She flipped the report upside down, but she couldn't erase the words from her mind. How could Jon have let Stevie rape that woman and help transport them into the hands of more criminals where they'd be violated over and over again?

Soft steps approached from nearby.

Jessica lifted her head as Cynthia walked into the kitchen.

Cynthia frowned. "What's wrong, Jess? Is it Sally?"

"No nothing like that. She's doing well." Jessica shoved the stack of paper aside. "That envelope Trent brought in last night was filled with copies of internal FBI documents. I only read the first report, and it's the most awful thing I've ever read. I can't stomach reading anymore. What Jon did undercover is just despicable."

"Can I see that report?"

Considering Cynthia had been married to Jon during this incident, it only seemed right to share it with her even though Jessica still wasn't over their exchange last night.

Jessica handed the report to Cynthia. "Don't tell anyone else what's in there. I'm not one for secrets, but the kids can never know this about their father."

"I promise I won't tell anyone."

Cynthia's forehead creased as she read through the pages and paled near the end. "This is really bad. I can understand why you're upset. Jon always refused to talk about his work. I knew it was bad, and he did try to intervene. But this…"

"I know. I don't know how to reconcile this with the

man I know. It's no wonder he snapped and walked away from the FBI. We need to burn this whole stack of paper right now."

Cynthia carried the stack over to the wood burning fireplace in the living room. "Are you sure?"

Jessica reached for the box of matches tucked behind a family photo on the mantle. "Yes." She lit the match then ran it along the edges of the paper, making sure it all burned, then topped it with kindling. An unsettling thought crossed her mind—the sender. "There was no return address on the envelope."

Cynthia kneeled beside her next to the fireplace. "Right. And whoever sent you these obviously has copies. This is one of those times where Trent's badge will come in handy." Cynthia pulled out her phone. "I'll let him know what was in the envelope."

"Do you have to? He might be able to access the files, but I'd rather he didn't know."

"I won't give him details. Telling him you received internal documents meant to hurt Jon is enough." Cynthia's fingers flew across her phone screen. "The local office of the delivery company is more likely to give him information than they are us. If nothing else, they can tell him where the package was sent from."

"The sender obviously isn't a friend. I hope it wasn't sent from anywhere near us." Jessica grabbed Cynthia's arm. "Oh my God."

"What?"

"The timing. Do you think whoever did this knew Jon was out of town with Kato? Bradley Kingston couldn't be behind this, could he? I can't picture him having an FBI contact."

"Shit. The timing is suspect, isn't it? These

documents wouldn't be easy to get, but we know dirty agents exist. The thought of someone helping Bradley from the inside is just sickening though. It has to be a messed-up coincidence."

"Are you up for some exercise? I'd like to go over everything you've taught me again."

Cynthia wrapped an arm around Jessica's shoulders. "I'd love to. I'm so proud of how far you've come in the month and a half since we started getting you into shape. The baby weight is pretty much gone, and you're a fighting machine now."

"Thanks to you. I feel so much better about my ability to protect the kids." The urge to punch the filling out of the punching bag warred with the instinct to wallow in fear. Jessica refused to let fear take over. She shut her eyes and pictured how good it would feel to pummel Bradley's face with the old boxing gloves on.

Jon's face flashed through her mind as well. What he'd been complacent in during his undercover work sickened her, but he had tried to help those women. The criminals in that organization, including Stevie, were hopefully rotting in jail for a really long time. Someday soon, Bradley would be joining them.

With the enemy circling, she couldn't afford the distraction of dwelling on Jon's past. After things settled, somehow, she'd work through what she read in that awful report.

Chapter Twenty-Five

Jon only managed a few hours of sleep and would have to rely on adrenaline and coffee to get through the day. They'd gotten back to their hotel in the city late after their interview with Alain and Lorraine, then he'd received the welcome news from Jessica that his mother had awoken along with the disturbing message that someone might've tampered with the furnace.

Jessica wasn't wrong to fear that Bradley Kingston could be the one behind it. That sort of torment with choosing an unguarded target fit with his modus operandi. Jon also didn't doubt his mother's hearing, and neither did Hank. His mother should be safe at the hospital with it being a public place and her room guarded. Hank promised to spend as much time with her as he could manage.

What churned Jon's stomach was the distance between him and his wife and children. They had a sophisticated security system and two capable protectors guarding them, but Bradley possessed such intelligence and diabolical tendencies. He might only be one man, but he had killed so many.

He sat in a chair next to Kato at the small desk in the corner of the FBI sub-office in Ottawa. The skunky odor of burned coffee permeated the whole floor, but they didn't have a choice but to put up with it. They needed to access the FBI's internal system to locate Simone

Girard.

Kato had found her birth certificate and social insurance number which they hoped would lead to a driver's license, employment records, tax information, or a death certificate that could yield an address. But so far, Kato had found nothing, as if she'd disappeared off the face of the earth.

Jon opened a browser window. He typed 'Simone Kingston' into the search bar and results came up. He scrolled through the social media listings that popped up at the top of his search, comparing them to the photo they'd gotten from Alain. Age could change a face, but none of the women bore a close resemblance to their Simone.

He scrolled further down the page and touched a link to an obituary in a local paper. "I think I found her. She's dead. Search for Simone Kingston in Prince Albert, Saskatchewan, and I bet you'll find official records to confirm. He married her using his real name and she died in a house fire."

"Yes. I found the death certificate and the dates and place of birth line up. How could a young man like Bradley Kingston, manage to get away with arson so many times? It's baffling, Jon."

"I know. I can't get the image of my ranch burning out of my mind. It's a wonder I'm not having nightmares." His phone vibrated and a number with an area code from Georgia flashed across his screen. "Hello, Jon Kent here."

"Jon, it's Matthew Evans. We've been through Emily's things a bunch of times. But Heather wouldn't give up. She found a folded scrap of paper inside a small zipper pocket in one of those tiny purses women carry to fancy events. It has a username and a password on it."

"That's great, Mr. Evans. Thank you." Jon grabbed a sheet of paper and a pen from the desk. "Can you spell them out for me?"

"Yes."

Jon wrote the information down, thanked him again, then ended the call.

Kato glanced at the paper. "That might finally give us an active lead. Are there any more avenues of investigation you'd like to pursue here?"

"Not that I can think of, but I don't know if my head is in the game. The ranch has a ton of security, but I'm on edge after discovering all these arsons."

"I don't think there's anything else to be learned in the Ottawa area. If we were to keep pursuing each individual case and following his trail, I think we'd be wasting precious time. After he's captured, the authorities here can sort out his crimes and extradite him after he faces charges in the US."

"I agree. I want to go home. We can look into this username and password from anywhere. If he's using one dating site with one alias, we might be able to figure out where he is now and save the next wife from being murdered. I'm forwarding the information to Beachgirl71. If she's willing to help, she'll get results faster than the FBI without the red tape of legalities."

Jon and Kato's phones pinged at the same time with a group text from Trent.

—We received an envelope yesterday addressed to Jessica. It was filled with internal FBI documents about you. The women burned them before I saw them, but the gist is they were meant to make you look bad.—

Jon's heart raced as his fingers flew across the

screen.

—Tell me she's okay.—

Bubbles appeared on the screen, then Trent's response.

—Yes. She's fine. Someone from the field office in Great Falls is coming to collect the envelope for DNA testing. I contacted the delivery company and they're tracing the origins of the envelope. Maybe we'll get a lead on the sender that way if we can get camera footage.—

Kato's brows furrowed. "We need to get to the airport right away."

Jon stood, grateful they'd taken their luggage with them and checked out in case they decided to follow a lead on Simone. "What was I thinking leaving Jess and the kids? That sick bastard might've been in Lewistown, trying to kill my mother, and who knows what else this whole time and now this envelope."

"You don't believe Bradley Kingston is behind that envelope, do you?"

"He could've gotten those documents from Hugh Jones. Or there could be someone else connected to the FBI that has it out for me. Neither is a great thought."

On the way to the airport, while Kato searched for flights, Jon took out his phone to text Jessica. After getting past the initial shock, the idea that the documents were meant to make him look bad sunk in. He'd made a point of hiding that part of his past from her. A lot of what he'd had to do undercover filled him with enough shame to bury him under an avalanche of snow so deep it would kill him.

What did the love of his life think of him now? Trent had been the one to tell him about the envelope and the footage, not her. Was she avoiding him?

Only one way to know. He typed a message and pressed send.

—*I'm on my way, sweetheart. I'm not leaving town again until he's dead or captured. Preferably dead. I'm so sorry I left you and the kids.*—

She responded. —*We're fine. I refuse to panic. I'm not the meek woman you married anymore. Sheriff Hank is checking the few local hotels to see if he can find Bradley. Trent and Cynthia are both here and we have the weapons ready and loaded.*—

—*You've come a long way and I'm so proud of you, Jess. I know you can handle yourself. Take care of everyone until I get home. I love you.*—

My God, did he love her, and he prayed that whatever she'd read hadn't changed how she felt about him. When this nightmare ended, he vowed to spend the rest of his life showing her who he really was inside. The man she loved.

With Kato's efficient searching skills, they managed to board their first flight to Chicago within an hour of arriving at the airport. There was nothing like an FBI badge to speed up the process of customs and security.

The plane picked up speed beneath them. A sensation that normally made Jon uncomfortable, but today the idea of rushing home overrode that anxiety. Although he'd never admit it, he hated take offs and landings. His and Kato's phones pinged in unison with an incoming email. The sketch had finally arrived.

Jon touched the attachment and the image loaded on his screen. The face looked so familiar. Where had he seen it before? The photo of Jessica's first husband hanging in his hallway. He broke out in a cold sweat and shivered. "This can't be accurate."

"Why not?" Kato narrowed his eyes at the image. "Where have I seen this guy before?"

"You saw a man that looks like this in a photo hanging on my wall. He's almost a doppelganger to Jessica's dead first husband, Adam. This could be a culmination of too many witnesses, but I don't think so."

Kato finished his unspoken thought. "You think Bradley had his surgeon rearrange his face this way on purpose to mess with Jessica's head."

"Exactly what I was thinking. What better way to disturb Jessica's psyche and inflict pain."

Jon scrambled to send a text message to Jessica. She needed to see this sketch and wrap her head around it. It would be harder on her than it was on him, but it needed to happen, the sooner the better.

—Make Trent show you the sketch. I think Bradley went to great lengths to upset you with his new face. I love you. I'm flying home now.—

Chapter Twenty-Six

Tension hung heavy in the room as Jessica sat at the kitchen table with Trent and Cynthia. The idea that Bradley might've been in town and tried to murder Sally wasn't a pleasant thing to wrap her head around, combined with the tension between her and Trent.

With Sheriff Hank's connection to Sally, they couldn't step on his toes. They were stuck waiting for him to check the hotels and businesses on Main Street for any signs that Bradley might've stayed in the area.

If only Jon and Kato weren't away, then they could've investigated instead of stretching the resources of the small local police force. Their chances of capturing Bradley, if he really did turn out to be in town, would've been a lot better. Although Hank had stepped up in the past when she'd needed him.

If only Bradley hadn't survived falling off the cliff the first time he'd come after her a year and a half earlier. The man wasn't a superhero or a cat, yet he seemed to have nine lives. No mere mortal survived that type of fall. And as irrational as it was, she couldn't help but think the man was invincible.

Jessica's phone pinged. "I got a text from Jon. The sketch is done, and Bradley made his new face disturbing somehow. At least Jon and Kato are on a plane now."

Trent picked up his phone. "Yes, I have the sketch here."

Cynthia frowned. "Why weren't you paying closer attention to your emails?" Her voice raised. "This guy is gunning for Jess."

"You're one to talk." Trent turned his laptop to face them, then brought up the image. "Why did you two burn evidence? What the hell were you thinking? There might have been DNA on those pages and then we would know for sure who was behind this delivery."

Cynthia clenched her coffee mug. "Jessica had the right to burn those pages. Besides, DNA is usually found on the envelope. Get over it already."

"Keep it down. The kids are sleeping. Besides, we're on the same team here." Jessica focused on the image, and blinked, unable to believe her eyes. She clenched her fists, resisting the urge to scream. Nothing this man did should surprise her, but this…"If he really does look like this now, he's sicker than I ever gave him credit for."

"Why?" Cynthia leaned closer to her and stared at the screen. "And why does he look familiar?"

Jessica struggled to keep her voice down. "Because he looks like Adam."

Trent shifted the computer away from them. "It's a sketch based on imperfect memories from people who hadn't seen him in months. It's probably just a coincidence. I think you and Jon are reaching."

Oh, God, no! Jessica gasped and grabbed onto the edge of the table. "What if…"

Cynthia rested a hand on her arm. "What's wrong?"

Jessica forced her erratic breathing to slow. "What if Bryce saw *him* in the schoolyard and not Adam's ghost? What if *he's* the one I saw in the hayfield? That would mean he's managed to figure out a way past the security system and can avoid the cameras."

Trent said, "I believe Bryce could have seen him near the school, but to get past security here? I don't know. It would take a highly skilled hacker to get into the security system without setting it off."

Jessica gritted her teeth and resisted the urge to scream. "Is it that much easier to believe I'm crazy? Really? After how smart he's proven himself to be, you still think I'm nuts."

"You're right. I'm sorry. I should have more faith in you," Trent said. "I'll contact the office in Great Falls again and get them to send the security expert to examine the system and look for breaches."

Cassie's low cries came through the baby monitor sitting on the table.

If Jessica hurried, they wouldn't escalate into a full-blown wail. "Thank you. Can you send the sketch to the printer in Jon's office? We need to show it to Bryce when he wakes. I don't think we can keep him in the dark anymore."

Lightheaded, Jessica hurried along the hallway into the nursery. She couldn't wait for Bryce to wake any longer. She'd have to make breakfast after feeding Cassie and keep his plate warm. "Hi, baby. Mommy's here."

Cassie quieted and turned her sweet little face towards her mother.

Jessica held her close as she carried her to the changing table. She didn't regret having Cassie for a minute, but if only she'd known the danger that would enter life during her pregnancy and up until this point. She'd never taken risks or thrown caution to the wind, yet her children weren't safe. One of the sickest men in the world circled them.

After nursing, Jessica set Cassie in her crib. Before she made it out of the nursery, the security system buzzed, and Cassie's eyes popped open.

She sighed. *Great timing.* Breakfast would have to wait.

Jessica grabbed the baby sling from the hook on the back of the door, draped it over her head, and settled Cassie inside of it. She'd lost weight since the last time she used the sling a few weeks ago, and the sling wasn't as snug as she'd like it to be. She held Cassie's head to keep her stable as she walked to the kitchen.

"It's Sheriff Hank. Trent's waiting for him at the front door." Cynthia stood. "Your sling is loose. You've lost weight. Hang onto her, and I'll re-tie the knot between your shoulders."

"That would be great. Thanks." Jessica turned her back towards Cynthia.

"Sorry Trent bit your head off earlier over the burnt pages. I think he's wound up because Bradley might be nearby, and Jon isn't." Cynthia tied the fabric tighter, and Cassie sat where she should, nestled against Jessica's chest. "Is that better?"

"Much. Thanks." Jessica sat at the table to wait for news and gently swayed side to side. Lately, it seemed all she could do was wait and pray. Cassie's eyes fluttered. She'd be asleep again in no time with Jessica's body heat warming her. "We burned evidence and that might get Trent in trouble. It didn't occur to me he'd be sending it back to the FBI. I panicked. I didn't want those papers in my house."

"In the moment, I didn't think it through either. What we read was so disturbing."

Sheriff Hank came into the kitchen with a tray of coffees in one hand, and the delicious scent of cinnamon wafted out of the box he carried in the other. "Thought you guys might need a boost, so I stopped at The Rising Trout."

Jessica smiled. "Thank you, Sheriff. I'm starving." She bit into a still warm cinnamon roll and the spice and sugar flooded her senses.

"I want to reassure you again that Sally is under guard. I have a man there and an FBI agent showed earlier, so she has two watchers now." Sheriff Hank stayed standing as he sipped from his cup. "I took an old image of Bradley Kingston from his David era around town. One of the staff at the hotel claims a man bearing a resemblance stayed there with his wife, but he checked out yesterday. The credit card used to book the room was under the name Ben Green, but he paid cash. He drove an older dark blue Dodge Ram."

Trent turned his computer to face Sheriff Hank. "We have a brand-new sketch for you now. This just came through from the field office in Georgia."

Sheriff Hank said, "Yes, I know. Jon sent it to me, too."

Jessica pondered Sheriff Hank's words. *His wife.* Why would Bradley bring his new wife to town and risk being identified or captured? The FBI had kept their investigation low key. Maybe Bradley believed his ploy had worked and everyone still thought him dead.

"Sounds like we missed him." Trent frowned. "I doubt that name will get us anywhere, but it's worth looking into. If we could get the license plate, then that might lead us to him. But if I were him, returning to the scene of his crimes, I'd use a stolen or fake plate. The wife makes no sense at all."

"Who knows? But it's worth looking into him even if he isn't Bradley Kingston. We'll know one way or the other." Sheriff Hank reached into his pocket, pulled out a USB drive, and put it on the table in front of Trent. "This is a copy of the video footage from the lobby and the parking lot. I haven't watched it yet. I'd like to keep canvassing the area around Main Street to see if I can find more sightings or video with the new sketch."

Jessica swallowed the last bite of her roll. "We appreciate it."

"I'm headed out," Sheriff Hank said. "If you find anything on the footage let me know.

Trent clutched the USB drive. "We will. Thank you."

The sheriff tipped his hat. "I appreciate being involved this time instead of finding out after the fact."

Bryce came into the kitchen. "Yum. I smell cinnamon rolls."

How much did Bryce hear? Either way, he didn't know the name Bradley Kingston. He only knew him as David Hayes. Jessica pulled out the chair next to her. "Sit. I'll get you a glass of milk. It isn't the healthiest breakfast, but it's fun to have a treat."

Cassie stayed asleep as Jessica stood, got a glass from the cupboard, and poured milk. With her thoughts swirling, she almost overfilled the glass as she debated whether to tell Bryce about him. If Bradley had been in town, it almost sounded as if he'd left. She didn't want to dredge up memories of Bryce's kidnapping unless she had no other choice.

The same question remained. Why would Bradley risk bringing his new wife to Lewistown? The fact that

Trent had also questioned the presence of a wife made her wonder. If Bradley didn't know they were onto him, it would make perfect sense. He would need to keep up his pretense as a normal husband and couples took trips.

But if he timed his trip for when Jon was out of town, that would mean he'd monitored them somehow. How could he possibly have done that without noticing Trent and Cynthia nearby, plus the extra security? Especially if he'd stood in their hay field.

Unless he thought they'd updated security because of Hugh Jones. And perhaps the timing was coincidental, and he didn't know Jon wouldn't be around. Or this man might not be Bradley at all. If it was Bradley, Jessica prayed they'd catch him before the poor woman he married ended up dead.

Chapter Twenty-Seven

Jon took his phone off airplane mode the minute the plane touched down in Montana just after ten o'clock at night. A text popped up on his screen from his brother Jamie. He'd left the hospital an hour earlier. Two guards watched over their mother, and her condition had improved.

Her legs shook as she walked, but she could walk, which meant no motor impairments. She needed to regain her strength, and then she would be released and sent home. Only days had passed since the accident, but the longer she took to wake, the scarier the situation had become. Thankfully, she'd survived.

Kato stowed the paperback he'd read during the flight inside his jacket pocket. "Any news?"

"My mother is recovering well. Nothing from Jessica or Trent. Things at the ranch must be quiet. I was hoping Trent or Hank would've found something on that video footage by now."

"After a good night's sleep, we'll watch it ourselves."

"Sounds like a plan. I'm hoping Beachgirl71 gets back to me by then. She hacked into the clinic within a day the last time, but with only a username and no website to link it to, it might take a whole lot longer."

"Speed is important." Kato had taken the aisle seat, so he stood and collected the carry-on suitcases from the

160

overhead bin. "After what we've learned, it's more important than ever to capture him quickly, especially if he has a new wife."

"I wish they'd hurry up and let us deplane. The idea of him possibly being close by with us not there is giving me horrible indigestion. With what we know, and after seeing that sketch, I don't believe Jess saw Adam's ghost in the field that night. It was Bradley Kingston. He would also be the type to mess with the baby monitor to scare her."

"This could all be a crazy coincidence. It's possible both Bradley and Adam's ghost are afoot."

"Maybe. But this situation reeks of Bradley," Jon said. "He's pulled psychological stunts on Jess in the past, and he'd scout out the ranch before making a move. As far as he knows, we upped security because of Hugh Jones. Not because we know he's alive. That would make him brazen enough to attempt getting onto the property to screw with her head."

"I hope you're wrong. If he got past security while you weren't there, I don't think he'd spy. I think he'd go in for the kill."

"He likes to circle his prey, and he wants me too. Not just her. Besides, why has he continued with the murders and the insurance scams? Maybe he needs money to accomplish whatever it is he has in store for us."

The flight attendants opened the doors and Jon followed Kato and the flow of people off the plane. Without traffic in the way, Jon put the gas pedal of his trusty Ram to the floor, and they came upon the high fence enclosing the ranch in an hour and a half.

He pressed his thumb to the sensor and the metal

gate swung open to admit them. They'd relied on the security system and the high fencing so far, but what if it wasn't enough?

A strong wind fanned the last crop of hay for the year, bending the stalks sideways. Rather than leave it grow for a few more weeks, he'd have Chip bring in the harvest tomorrow. The land surrounding the main house and the guest house where the cows didn't graze also needed to be mowed.

The sightlines needed to be clear.

Padlocking the barn would be annoying for Chip and the ranch hands going in and out throughout the day, but it had to be done. If there was a weakness anywhere, it was the forest behind the guest house past his property line. The owners of the neighboring ranch had agreed to motion sensors and cameras, but they wouldn't let him cut the forest down.

Who could blame them? People lived in rural Montana to enjoy nature, not destroy it.

Jon parked around the side of the house, and they entered through the back door into the kitchen.

Trent sat at the kitchen table alone with bags under his eyes. "How was your trip?"

Jon took the chair next to him. "We learned a lot about Bradley Kingston's younger years and pinpointed when his insurance scams began. The most promising lead is a username and password the Evans's found in Emily's purse in Georgia. Did you find anything on the video footage Hank dropped off?"

"This guy kept his head tilted away from all the cameras in a way that had to be deliberate." Trent rubbed his eyes. "I might have something though, but it isn't concrete. The man at the hotel drove an older dark blue truck. The license plate was mudded over, but you can see what looks to be the start of the letter 's' in cursive writing. To me, it looks like the right location to be the word 'Scenic' on the license plates for the state of Idaho."

"So, he could be living one state away from us, allowing him to come and go and scout us out," Jon said. "That's good detective work. We may as well sleep and pick this back up in the morning."

Kato asked, "Should someone stay awake to keep watch?"

Trent shut his computer. "Since this man checked out thirty-six hours ago, I would guess he's back in Idaho. Unless he's sightseeing in another town nearby."

Jon paced the kitchen as he cycled through ideas. "Okay. So, we have a lead on what state he could be in. That's good. Tomorrow morning, if you two don't mind taking care of things here, I'll go into town and talk to people. They know me, so I might get more from them. One small detail could narrow things down."

Trent nodded. "Of course. With it being Sunday, Cynthia will be around to help Jessica too."

Jon walked Kato and Trent to the door. "Thank you both so much for everything. Having your help is a game changer."

After locking up behind them, Jon tiptoed along the hall with his suitcase in hand. The door to the nursery was open enough for him to stick his head inside. The sight of his precious daughter, fast asleep, warmed his heart, chasing away the darkness clinging to him after diving into Bradley's past.

He opened Bryce's door. The hinges squeaked in protest, but it would take a lot more than that to wake his stepson who slept like the dead. Tufts of Bryce's hair stuck out from beneath his comforter as he lay facing the wall.

With no other children to check on, he couldn't put off entering his own room. The door stood partway ajar. He paused in the hallway, facing it with trepidation. While preoccupied with worries for Jessica and their children's safety, he hadn't had time to reflect on one of his biggest fears being realized. He'd never wanted his wife to know the details from his dark times undercover and the man he used to be.

Would Jessica hate him after what she'd read about his past?

Slowly, he opened the door and slipped inside. Jessica slept in a fetal position, facing the baby monitor on the edge of the nightstand beside her. He left the door cracked open the way she always left it to be attuned to any foreign sounds in the night.

Would there ever come a time when they could enjoy the solitude of the ranch without maintaining a constant watch for danger?

He climbed into his side of the bed, taking care not to jostle his wife. Her quiet breaths weren't enough to lull him to sleep with his troubled thoughts and danger nearby. But at least at home, in his own bed, he could watch her sleep and keep her safe.

Chapter Twenty-Eight

Cassie's whimpers carried through the crack in the door. Jessica opened her eyes, squinted at the alarm clock, then scrambled out of bed to the nursery. Cassie had slept six hours since her last feeding around eleven the night before, a record for her. She had to be hungry and wet.

"Hey, sweetie." She picked Cassie up and carried her to the changing table, taking care to avoid the damp spots of her sleeper around the edges of her diaper. "Thanks for letting me sleep. Let's get you a clean diaper and dry clothes."

After her feeding, Cassie stared into Jessica's eyes, wide awake and smiled for the first time.

Heat spread through Jessica's chest, warming her from the inside out. "Aren't you the sweetest little girl in the whole world? I bet Daddy would love to see that smile."

"I heard my name." Jon stuck his head inside the nursery and the corner of his mouth raised into his signature lopsided grin.

Mixed emotions—happiness, grief, love, and anger—ran through Jessica's mind at the sight of her husband. The most dominant one was love. "She's smiling for the first time."

Jon came to stand beside the rocking chair. "Ahh. Look at that smile. Hey, pretty girl. I missed you and

Mommy. You're wide awake this morning."

"Probably because she almost slept through the night."

"I barely slept more than a few hours. Mostly, I watched you sleep. The idea of Bradley Kingston being nearby has me on edge." Jon glanced at his feet and sighed. "Do you want to talk about what you read in that file?"

Did she? "I don't know. I think I need time to come to terms with it."

"Which case was it?"

She sighed, wanting to ask a question but afraid of the answer. "Carlo Lombardi. Please tell me Stevie is rotting in jail."

"That was one of my worst cases. Stevie, the other men in the inner circle, and the big boss Carlo are all serving consecutive life sentences. I hit paydirt about a month after that incident with the women, and although those women went through hell, we were able to rescue them and send them back to their families in South America."

Jessica inhaled a deep cleansing breath. "Oh, thank God."

"Do you think less of me knowing what I let Stevie do?"

"The truth?"

Cassie stayed quiet as she watched them talk, almost as if she sensed the importance of her parents' conversation.

He nodded with that troubled expression that surfaced whenever they talked about his time with the FBI.

"When I look at you, I feel love. I knew you did

undercover work, and that some of it was awful, but that was hard to read. It bothers me that you didn't intervene, but you were only following orders that kept you alive and let you get the job done. I'll get past it with time."

"I love you, Jess. I'm not that man anymore, and I never will be again. I'm a rancher for life, a husband, and a father to our amazing children."

"I know. I love you, too. I want this whole thing to be over, so we can live like a normal happy family again. I hope you have a plan. Trent's lead is promising with the license plate."

"I'm planning to talk to the folks around Main Street today. Since they know me, they'll be more willing to talk to me than they would Trent or Kato."

Jessica bit her lip. "There's something else I haven't told you yet. The night the package arrived; Bryce told me he thought he saw Adam on the first day of school in the forest behind the recess yard."

"Dammit! Bradley was near Bryce at school, too?"

"Yes, but behind a fence outside the property away from the yard and the school building. I must have seen *him* in the hay field that night, and I bet he messed with the baby monitor. The security hasn't stopped him. He's been toying with us for months. Why? Why not try to kill us and put an end to it?"

"He burned down Debbie's barn to torture you. He likes sick games. Maybe he wants to cash in on another insurance scam first. That would explain the new wife which was the one thing that threw Hank and Trent off about the hotel sighting."

"What do we do?"

"I contacted Special Agent Pruitt and asked her to send a specialist out to look at the system and analyze for hacks. If they detect any breeches, she said they'd hire a private security company to man the entry gate. I texted Chip late last night and asked him to cut down the hay today to clear our sightlines of the property."

"I've been wrestling with whether to tell Bryce about Bradley all weekend." Her breath hitched. A memory flooded her of the night she had watched Bradley running away from the ranch with Bryce thrown over his shoulder. Bryce had pounded on his back while screaming for her as she ran after them. "Knowing what was happening didn't stop Bradley from kidnapping Bryce the first time he came after us, but it can't hurt for him to be extra vigilant. He's a year and a half older, and he's had way too much experience with bad guys for a nine-year-old."

"We've saved him from the truth for as long as we can. I think we need to tell him. After breakfast, we'll sit him down together."

She swallowed, trying to moisten her dry throat. "Okay."

An unusual silence hovered over the breakfast table as Jessica forced herself to eat. With the calories she burned nursing and working out, she needed the nutrition to keep up her strength. After Bryce finished his last bite of toast, she set her fork aside and met Jon's gaze.

Jon cleared his throat. "Bryce, son. We need to talk."

Bryce glanced between her and Jon. "Are you finally going to tell me what's going on around here? The big gates, Cynthia, and Trent, why I can't take the bus. I know something is wrong. Who's after us this time?"

Jessica's eyes prickled and she fought the urge to cry. She needed to put on a brave front for her son. "Bryce, we thought David was dead when he fell off the side of a mountain at Judith Peak. But he's alive. He's the one who told Hugh Jones where to find us. We found out the day your sister was born. The FBI sent Trent to tell us. That's why he and Cynthia are here until David is captured."

Bryce frowned and his skin paled. "Maybe that's why Dad reached out to me."

Jon asked, "What do you mean, son? How did I reach out to you."

"Not you. My real father. Adam."

Jessica gasped. "Buddy, he's dead."

Bryce shook his head. "No, he stood on the other side of the fence at school and left a note in my locker. He said he's in witness protection and he's coming to visit me soon."

A tear escaped and trickled out of the corner of Jessica's eye. "I saw his body, Bryce. We had an open casket at his wake."

"I'm going to show you a sketch." Jon grabbed his laptop from the kitchen counter and set it on the table in front of Bryce. "Is this the man you saw?"

Bryce studied the screen. "Yes, that looks like him. Who is he?"

Jessica held Bryce's hand. "That's what David looks like now. He had plastic surgery. His real name is Bradley Kingston."

"I have to show you something. I'll be right back." Bryce tugged his hand away, ran down the hallway to his room, then returned with a creased and folded sheet of paper. He handed it to Jon. "This is the note."

"Thanks for showing me this. This might lead us to him," Jon said. "Why didn't you tell us about this sooner?"

"He said not to. That Mom would look for him, and she'd end up getting hurt."

After all the revelations of the past twenty-four hours, this one hit Jessica the hardest. That monster had been inside the same building as her son, and she hadn't been there to protect him. That sick bastard was toying with them, and they were no safer behind the tall metal fencing. "You know what this means, Jon. Bradley got inside the building. It seems no one saw him, including Cynthia. Bryce isn't safe at school."

Bryce groaned. "Mom, I don't want to home school again. I want to see my friends."

Jon rested a hand on Bryce's shoulder. "I know, and I'm sorry. But Mom is right. You need to be home until he's captured. But you know what?"

"What?" Bryce said.

"This sheet of paper is an access point to him. I can try to lure him out of hiding. With this, and the Idaho symbol on the license plate of the truck we think he's been driving, I'm going to find him soon."

"Do you promise, Dad?"

Jon nodded. "Yes, son. This will all be over soon."

"Please get him, Dad." Bryce lifted hands from the tabletop, leaving behind a sheen of sweat from his nervous palms.

A fierce and fiery burst of rage flooded Jessica with warmth, and she clenched her fists, resisting the urge to scream. She hated the fear in her son's eyes. She visualized what it would be like to obliterate David's head with a shotgun slug, slice his throat open, or bury a knife in his vile, blackened heart. Whether or not those thoughts made her a bad person, she didn't care.

Forget rotting in jail, Bradley needed to die.

Chapter Twenty-Nine

Pent up energy, and a rage Jessica had only experienced a few times in her life, set her on edge as she scrubbed the counters and cupboards in the kitchen with more force than necessary. She couldn't sit still. Jon had headed into town to try and find another lead while Trent and Kato kept an eye on the grounds and Chip managed the hay.

Bryce sat in the living room racing carts around the track on his gaming console. She sensed her boy needed the extra screen time to manage the horrible news they'd dropped on him that morning.

Cynthia came into the kitchen in her workout gear. "Do you want to hit the punching bag with me? Maybe spar? We could bring the baby monitor."

"I know we'd only be going to the basement, but I don't want to leave Bryce alone even though he barely knows I'm here now anyway."

"You need to take care of yourself, too. And right now, you need to get that energy out. I'll text Trent to come inside for an hour and keep Bryce company."

Jessica nodded. "Thank you." She understood why Jon had fallen in love with Cynthia. Despite their connection of having married the same man, which would be stressful for any women in their position, Cynthia was such a considerate and caring friend.

Cynthia's presence had made Jessica's insecurities

come to the surface after Cassie was born. Although Jessica had never said anything to Cynthia, it was almost as if the other woman had sensed her inner struggle and endeavored to help her. And while Hugh Jones was on his rampage, Cynthia had watched over her and Bryce from a distance and had only made herself known to save Jessica's life.

How many people would behave so selflessly and risk their lives that way? Not many.

Jessica had more confidence in her appearance and in her ability to protect her family than she'd ever had before but doubts still wormed their way through her consciousness.

If it wasn't for the kids, would Jon have stayed with her? Or would he have gone back to Cynthia?

The back door opened, ending the unproductive train of Jessica's thoughts.

Trent kicked his boots off by the back door and took off his hat. "You ladies blow off some steam. I'll be here."

"Thanks." Cynthia kissed his cheek. "Come on, Jess."

Jessica followed Cynthia past the guest room and down the basement stairs to the punching bag.

"You go first." Cynthia pulled boxing gloves onto Jessica's hands. "Remember, use your core strength to fuel your strikes. Elbows and knees whenever you can so you don't break your hands. Move fast, and always hit your target. We're both average-sized women and we need to use any advantage we can get. Against a big man like Bradley, your speed and agility are everything. You need to move faster than him to keep him from gaining control of the situation."

Standing at the ready with the gloves on took the edge off some of Jessica's excess energy. "Like you did in the bathroom with that thug at the Edmonton airport?"

"Yes, I chopped him in the carotid artery which cut off the blood supply to his brain. But it was easy because he didn't see me coming. In a pinch, you can jam a pencil or a pen into that artery and it's fatal."

"Right. I don't imagine I'll get a chance to sneak up on Bradley like that, but I'll keep that trick in mind." Jessica hit the bag with a series of strikes, visualizing nailing Bradley in the temple, the throat, the gut, and the groin. "Apparently, during his fall off the cliff he broke his leg badly enough to need surgery. That might be a weakness we could exploit."

What was harder to visualize was his reaction. How would he move? He wouldn't stand still and let her wail away on him, but if she got an opening, at least she could hit him in the right places. With each strike, her head cleared, and she regained control of her thoughts and her body.

She wouldn't be clueless and timid the way she had been the first time he threatened her in the grocery store. She'd never forget the scent of his musky aftershave worming its way up her nostrils, nor the weight of his massive form pinning her in place against the metal shelf on the cracker aisle.

Never again would she let anyone make her feel too weak to defend herself or her children.

She pulled the sweaty gloves off and handed them to Cynthia. "I really needed that."

"We should practice some basic stuff again. Do you remember how to break out of the choke hold?"

"I think so. Let's try it."

"Remember, never waste time pulling on the hands trapping you. You have six seconds to break out of that hold before you're unconscious." Cynthia stepped behind her out of sight. "Get ready. I'm going to put you in a rear sleeper hold."

An arm wrapped around Jessica's neck, along with the familiar floral scent of Cynthia's body wash or deodorant. Even with that recognition, Jessica's adrenaline kicked in and her heart raced.

Don't panic. Think.

She turned her head to the right, grabbed Cynthia's bicep, and tucked her chin into her neck while raising her shoulders at the same time. It gave her room to breathe. She bent her knees while keeping her weight forward then stepped to Cynthia's right, the same side Cynthia was choking her on, and locked her foot behind Cynthia's. "Then, I'd take your leg out and throw you down."

Cynthia let go of Jessica and clapped. "That's perfect! I'm so proud of you. Only a month and a half of training and you've come so far already."

"Thanks to you. I couldn't ask for a better friend."

****

Jon drove along Main Street, trying, but failing, to push the fear in Bryce's gaze out of his mind, along with the rage in Jessica's eyes. No matter how things shook out in the end, two of the people he loved most in this world would be forever tainted by the touch of pure evil. All because Bradley Kingston happened to move in next door to Jessica.

How could fate be so damn cruel?

He parked in front of the Rising Trout Cafe, a favorite destination for locals. Through the window, he recognized Lydia behind the counter. If Bradley and his wife had been in town, chances were high they'd frequented this coffee shop. But timing could be everything. If they'd passed through during the morning or lunch rush, Lydia might not have caught any useful tidbits of information.

As Jon climbed out of his truck, he inhaled a deep breath of clean mountain air. Shoving emotion aside, he focused on the case. They had the partial print, the state from the license plate, Emily's login information, and the chat room from the sheet of paper left in Bryce's locker.

Kato had agreed to come up with a plan for the chat room. Knowing who was behind the conversation, Jon didn't trust himself not to type the wrong message and tip Bradley off. It would be a delicate operation since Bryce, thankfully, had never responded to any of the messages left for him. Jon had also sent the chatroom link to Beachgirl71 to see if she could somehow find an IP and narrow down the location of origin.

All they'd gotten so far was a trail of breadcrumbs. With each morsel, they inched closer to finding that monster. And sometimes the tiniest morsel, in connection with another small detail, could blow a case wide open.

A chilly wind gusted, carrying dried leaves on the breeze, and rustling a string of orange pumpkin lights hanging on the awning of a shop. Halloween would be upon them in a few weeks, a holiday he normally enjoyed. His heart wouldn't be in it this year unless they caught Bradley.

Jon stepped inside the welcome warmth of the busy café, caught Lydia's eye, and tipped his hat. He sat on a stool and waited until the line of customers in front of the counter had their orders to approach. "Hey, Lydia. How are you today?"

"I'm good. You?"

"I'm worried. A wanted serial killer may have been through town in the past few days with his wife." Jon took the sketch of Bradley out of his pocket, unfolded it, then handed it to Lydia. "Did he come in here over the past few days?"

"I don't think he came inside, but I saw someone that looked like him standing on the sidewalk by a dark blue truck. His wife did come inside. She had thick glasses and commented on the book display. Her name is Amy, and she works as a librarian in Idaho. She was here on her honeymoon."

Jon's heart raced with adrenaline. This could be a coincidence. A man resembling Bradley could have honeymooned in Lewistown. But what were the odds? Bradley had a knack for slipping away and evading capture, but this was the best lead they'd gotten. "Did she happen to mention a last name or her husband's name? Possibly where in Idaho she lives?"

"No. It was busy, so I ended the conversation. Sorry." Lydia studied the sketch. "Are you sure he's a killer? The wife seemed so nice. I can't picture her having anything to do with murder."

"If he is who we think he is, then the poor woman doesn't know he's a murderer. Please, if you see either one of them again, call Sheriff Hank and then call me."

"I will. Can I get you anything?"

Jon tucked the sketch in his pocket. "You know me. I can't leave without a box of cinnamon rolls and large black coffee."

She smiled. "Coming right up."

While Lydia poured his coffee, Jon yanked his phone out of his pocket and sent a group text to Kato, Trent, Cynthia, and Jessica.

—Bradley might be married to a librarian named Amy in Idaho. Let's get the ball rolling and find out how many Amys are librarians in Idaho.—

Bubbles appeared on his screen, then a message popped up from Trent.

—On it. I knew that was an Idaho plate.—

With just under two million people in Idaho, finding a librarian named Amy shouldn't take too long. By the end of the day, they'd have found her or would be close to finding her. He could keep questioning shopkeepers, but his gut told him this was the best lead he'd find.

Jon's desire to hunt when they did find Amy, warred with the instinct to guard his family, but his family won out. As much as it killed him to trust other FBI agents to investigate their new lead, Jessica and the kids needed him close. He wouldn't leave them exposed again. Especially not after the possibility that their state-of-the-art security system had been breached.

Jon thanked Lydia for his coffee and cinnamon rolls, then climbed in his truck and floored the accelerator to the ranch. He pressed his thumb to the sensor and drove up the winding gravel road to the house.

Chip had made good progress with the hay already. If the ranch hands kept up their pace, the hay stalks would all be cut down by that evening, opening up their sightlines all the way to the forested area on the property line behind the rental house.

Jon parked in front of the house, then stepped inside the kitchen door. Trent and Kato were sitting at the kitchen table. "Any word on when the security expert is coming?"

Trent glanced up from his screen. "Not until tomorrow. The best tech, Shandru Anand, is at his daughter's wedding. I figured that since our possible suspect just skipped town it was worth waiting the extra day for him."

Jon set the cinnamon rolls in the center of the table. "I agree. We need the best available person. Lydia identified Bradley from the sketch just like Bryce and the hotel staff did. It's seeming more and more likely Bradley was here."

Trent said, "There are 137 public libraries in Idaho. I should have a warrant by the end of the day for their employment records. When the offices open tomorrow morning, we shouldn't hit any hurdles getting the information we need. There can't be many librarians named Amy."

Jon sipped his coffee. "Kato, how's it going with the chatroom?"

Kato said, "In the last part of the message to Bryce, Bradley said he'd be coming to visit him when he could. So, I thought about it from a child's perspective and looked up common spelling errors for a child Bryce's age. Then I sent a message asking Bradley when he's coming to visit. It's the simplest way to hopefully lure him out. Since he kidnapped Bryce once, I'm guessing that was his goal. To use Bryce as leverage to get to you and Jessica."

Despite the warmth of his kitchen and the coffee, Jon shivered. He'd already drawn the same conclusion. But having someone say it out loud brought back the horrific few hours he'd endured after Bradley kidnapped Bryce. He'd never forget Bryce's screams as Jon had pursued Bradley through the woods, desperate to catch up to him, and the sense of utter devastation when Bradley made it to his vehicle and got away with Bryce.

Chapter Thirty

Amy brewed coffee while Nathan showered. For the first time in days, her thoughts were clear without fuzz around the edges. Ever since they'd married, she'd slept a lot, and during the day murky fog swirled around her brain, scrambling her thoughts. At first, she assumed it was all the marital fun and losing her virginity, but maybe she'd picked up a virus of some kind.

She poured coffee into a travel mug for Nathan and set it on the table. He'd taken a job moving a load of pumpkins to Northern California and planned to be home by tomorrow night. As much as she loved having her new husband around, she looked forward to having the apartment to herself.

Since Nathan had moved into her apartment, he'd unwittingly cramped her lifestyle. But she'd adjusted in exchange for the satisfying feeling of loving and being loved by someone. She enjoyed the companionship and the end to her constant, lonely solitude. But her brain needed exercise.

She loved books, and working as a librarian meant she could be surrounded by comforting shelves that didn't judge her the way people did. But her same, everyday, monotonous routine at the library didn't satisfy her need to overcome intellectual challenges. With Nathan gone, she'd be free to assume her alternate online persona for a while. She kept that part of her life a secret as some of the things she did weren't exactly on the up and ups.

He whistled as he came into the kitchen and leaned on the counter beside her. "It's nice waking up next to you every morning, darling."

Parker stopped eating his food, glared at Nathan, growled, then ran into the living room and curled up underneath an end table.

"I thought he'd get used to you by now. It's so weird."

He shrugged. "Give him time. Maybe a man abused him and now he's afraid of all men."

"Maybe." The scent of his Old Spice aftershave reminded her of the sensation of his stubble brushing her skin as he trailed kisses along her collarbone. Why this attractive man had asked her out, and then married her, she'd never understand when he could have any woman he wanted. Her cheeks warmed. "I'll miss you tonight."

"I'll be back before you know it. The sooner I leave, the faster I'll be home." He picked up his mug and quickly brushed his lips against hers.

Too fast a kiss for her liking. "Bye."

The door shut behind him and she sighed with a mixture of relief, longing, and excitement. After eating a big bowl of her favorite apple cinnamon oatmeal, she refilled her coffee mug, then took it to their second bedroom that she used as her office. Their bags from their trip to Lewistown glared at her from where they sat in the middle of the carpet in the way of pulling out her computer chair.

Amy set her coffee on the desk, then picked up the bags and carried them to the bedroom. She dumped her dirty clothes out of the main pocket into the laundry hamper, set the paperback she was reading on the table next to her side of the bed, placed her toiletries in the bathroom, then tucked her empty duffle in behind the clothes hanging on her side of the closet to get it out of the way.

Should she unpack Nathan's bag? Early on in their relationship, she didn't want to set the precedent of cleaning up after him. Although, he did wash his own dishes and use the laundry hamper. She shrugged. What could it hurt to unpack one bag?

She opened the main pocket of his bag and dumped his dirty clothes in the hamper. As a pair of his jeans landed on the top of the pile, something rattled in one of the pockets. She reached inside the front pocket of Nathan's jeans and pulled out an unlabeled pill bottle.

During their short relationship, she'd never seen him taking these pills or handling this bottle. Maybe he had a health condition of some kind he hadn't mentioned? Her mind forced her to consider another more likely option given the missing label—drug addiction. But wouldn't she have noticed if he was getting high around her?

Speculating would accomplish nothing. She set the pill bottle on the table next to his side of the bed, and planned to ask him about the pills when he came home. She stowed his empty bag in the closet.

With the unpacking done, she could focus on her hacking without that task hanging over her head. She sank into her chair and booted her computer. The screen came to life, and she entered her password. Over a week had passed since she'd last checked her email, but since she reserved this one for limited communication with a few online friends, she only had a page of emails to contend with.

An email from Thomas' friend Jon Kent caught her eye. Thomas had been a great guy and she still missed him. They were both introverts, but they'd connected, and their chats had been stimulating, and on occasion a bit racy.

She clicked on the email.

Hello Beachgirl71,

Thanks again for helping us get into the records from Belleza del Sol. With your help, we were able to track Chris White to a victim named Emily. He drugged her and made it look like an accidental overdose. He managed to foil the authorities and cashed in Emily's life insurance before skipping town.

We have reason to believe he has a new wife. A librarian named Amy from Idaho. We fear for her safety, as well as our own since he may have been spotted in my hometown of Lewistown while on his honeymoon.

Emily's parents found a username (Emslookingforluv) and password (Parker45). We don't know what website it's for, but we're hoping it's for a dating site since she met Chris White online.

This could be a shot in the dark as well as labor intensive. But if you're willing to dig into this, we'd really appreciate it as it could lead us to the new wife in time to capture him before he harms her or us.

Thank you,

Jon

"No! It can't be!" Amy trembled and her breakfast churned in her stomach. *And he drugged her...those pills. Ohmigod! Did he drug me too?*

Nathan couldn't be the sick, twisted killer tormenting Jon and his family. This whole thing had to be a crazy coincidence, like Emily using the name

'Parker' as her password. She opened a new browser window and brought up the dating site where she'd met Nathan, then entered Emily's username and password.

Emily's profile loaded.

Okay. She used the same website. So, what?

Thousands if not hundreds of thousands of other people used this particular dating site touted to have a high success rate at matching people. She scrolled through Emily's many chats It seemed she'd engaged in conversation with over forty men, yet somehow, she'd managed to pick a serial killer.

Amy's breath hitched as she scrolled down the screen and spotted a familiar profile picture beside the name Chris W.

Oh my God!

She jumped out of her chair, ran to the bathroom, and kneeled in front of the toilet. Her stomach heaved and heaved as her breakfast made a comeback. The whole time one thought rolled through her mind on repeat.

I married a serial killer.

Parker nudged her hand with his cold nose and whined.

After the heaving stopped, she rinsed her mouth out with cold water. "I'm okay, baby. Now, I know why you don't like him." Her voice hitched. "He killed your mommy." She picked up Parker and returned to the spare bedroom. She collapsed into her chair with Parker in her lap. Not able to stand the sight of her husband's picture, she closed the browser window.

How could she have been so stupid and pathetic? She'd had the power at her fingertips to dig into Nathan Kirk, and she hadn't done it. An attractive man paid her the least bit of attention, and she threw caution to the wind, including not digging into his identity online even though she was an expert hacker.

She covered Parker's ears then screamed as loud as she could, letting out the anguish of her broken heart and the rage building inside of her that this charming killer had made it through her defenses. Once the beating of her heart and her anger subsided, she picked up her phone.

Jon had included his phone number in the first email he'd sent her, and it would be a lot easier to speak to him than it would to try to string together words with how fast her thoughts and emotions raced inside of her.

Chapter Thirty-One

Jon sat on the couch in front of a roaring fire with Jessica tucked into his side. His eyes needed a break from scrolling, and the crackling of the wood burning had a way of steadying him. While they waited for the warrant to be served the next morning for the library staff records in Idaho, they'd started searching individual libraries' websites for staff listings. Some of them listed staff and others didn't, and so far, they hadn't found Amy.

His phone vibrated in his pocket. "I don't recognize the number, but I think it's an Idaho area code." He accepted the call. "Hello?"

A woman's voice with a hysterical edge to it asked, "Are you Jon Kent?"

"Yes."

"This is Amy, the librarian from Idaho. You know me better as *Beachgirl 71*."

Holy cow! What are the odds? "So, you're the new wife."

"Unfortunately."

Jessica clutched his arm and mouthed, "What?"

Jon nodded and mouthed, "We found him." He asked Amy, "Where's Bradley now? Are you safe?"

Jessica leaned her ear towards the phone and Jon angled it so she could hear the conversation.

Amy said, "Bradley? I know him as Nathan Kirk.

But he was Emily's husband Chris White. She met him on the same dating website I did."

Jon vibrated and resisted the urge to stand and pace. "But again, are you safe? Do you know where he is?"

"He left about half an hour ago. He said he was taking a load of pumpkins to Northern California, and he'd be back in a few days, but who knows? He doesn't own a smartphone, so I can't track him. He might've headed back your way. I live in Ketchum, Idaho. I'll text you the address. I'm guessing the FBI will want to stake our apartment out and wait for him to come home."

Damn. It was too much to hope he was in the area. "He always evades capture. We'll come up with a solid plan to catch him. You'll be kept in the loop. Does he have any idea you're onto him?"

"No, I only figured it out when I read your email just now. What do I do now? I don't want to stay here and wait for him, but I also want to make sure you get him."

Jon asked, "Does he have a life insurance policy out on you?"

"I haven't taken out a policy or signed any paperwork, but who knows? He could've bought the policy and forged my signature. He took his laptop with him, and I've never snooped. I'm a total idiot. I fell hard and married him without hacking him first."

"You aren't the first to fall for him, but hopefully you'll be the last." Jon clasped Jessica's hand and kissed her palm. "Do you have anywhere you can go for now where he wouldn't know to look for you while we get things in motion?"

"He knows where my parents live, and I don't have friends. He never comes home before he says he's going to. I should be fine here at least until tomorrow. I'll hack into some servers to see if a policy exists in my name. Does he use the same insurance companies, or does he move around?"

"He switches from one company to the next, but he usually chooses big companies. Send us anything you find. But be careful."

"I have a fuzzy profile picture of him from the dating site," Amy answered. "It could be enhanced. I'll email it to you. Also, before you ask, the license plate on his blue Dodge Ram is 1AGH785."

Jon grabbed a pen and wrote the plate number in the margins of his notes. "That's perfect. Thank you. Send us anything you find. But be careful."

"I will. Keep your eyes open on your end for him. Stay safe."

"We will. And we'll talk soon." Jon ended the call. "Did you hear all that, Jess?"

"I did. Bradley's not a step ahead of us anymore. We've finally caught up to him. He hasn't killed her, so he'll return to that apartment."

"He will. But who is he planning to kill first? Us or Amy?" He stood and crossed the room to the kitchen. "Kato, Trent, stop looking for Amy."

Trent turned to face him. "Why?"

Jon said, "Because Amy found us. She's Beachgirl. And she's emailing us a profile photo he used on a dating website. She says it needs enhancing. I'm sure we can get that fast-tracked. She also gave me his license plate number."

Trent's eyes widened. "Wow, talk about a crazy coincidence. Send me the info. I'll send an urgent request in to clean up that photo and update the BOLO."

Jon said, "I'm not sure if we want that information

getting to the Idaho police force until our team is in place. If they up their presence around Amy's apartment building, they might spook him. Then he'll be in the wind again."

Trent leaned back in his chair and pursed his lips. "You have a valid point there."

"I agree with Jon, but this is a fantastic break. Now we don't have to wait another nine or ten hours for that information." Kato asked, "Where's our guy? He hasn't responded to the message I sent him in the chatroom he set up for Bryce."

Jon ran his hand through his hair. "He could be on his way here. He left Ketchum, Idaho less than an hour ago. He told Amy he was taking a load of pumpkins to Northern California. For all we know, he could be subsidizing his insurance income by trucking, but chances are he lied to her."

Trent glanced between them. "Since Assistant Director Pruitt's taken charge of the case, we'll have to inform her of what's happening."

Jon said, "I'd like to be the one to make that call. I'm hoping she'll agree to delay notifying law enforcement and keep this away from the press. If they start plastering Bradley's face in the media, we'll never catch him."

Jessica clasped Jon's hand with more strength in her grip than she had before. Worry lines creased her forehead. "This can't continue with him in the wind and waiting for him to come after us. It's sheer hell."

"I know, sweetheart."

Cassie's whimpers emitted from the baby monitor speaker.

Jessica raced out of the room and along the hallway,

then stepped into the nursery, disappearing from view.

Jon didn't know how to feel about her new lean, sculpted muscles. He admired her determination and the quiet confidence she exuded, but he hated that her experiences and fear had driven her to this point.

While she took care of Cassie, Jon collected the cordless phone from the charging port and headed to his office in the basement where there would be no distractions. This conversation could be the most important one he'd ever have.

Energy thrummed through his fingertips as he dialed Pruitt's direct line. He tapped his foot on the floor to let loose some of the excess energy.

"Assistant Director Pruitt."

"It's Jon Kent with an update. Can you talk?"

"Hold on." Her voice was muffled in the background, then a door shut. "I don't have much time before my next meeting. I instructed my secretary to postpone if necessary. What's happening?"

"We have a break in the case. Bradley Kingston is currently going by the alias of Nathan Kirk. He's married to a librarian named Amy and living with her in an apartment in Ketchum, Idaho. He just honeymooned with her here in Lewistown, right under our noses."

"That's great news! This wife is still alive, and I'd like to keep her that way. We'll send in a team to pick him up right away."

"You can't. She says he left this morning, claiming to be moving a load of pumpkins to Northern California. He said he'd be home tomorrow sometime. The thing is…well, I don't know if I trust your team to do the job. Sam brought in who he thought were the best people and they made critical mistakes."

"With an exact location, rather than a huge swatch of forested land, it shouldn't be an issue."

"Please tell me you won't involve local law enforcement or the media."

"I won't involve the media unless he slips away, and we have no leads at all, then I wouldn't have a choice since he's a danger to the public. His sketch was already sent to local law enforcement across the country. It'll have to be reissued with his current alias. I'll make a point of instructing the police in Ketchum, Idaho to stay away from the area surrounding his residence while our people are on the ground."

"I understand. But could you wait to recirculate the sketch until you send your team in?"

She sighed. "As you well know, that goes against protocol. Are you in communication with the wife?"

"Yes, I am. She's on our side, and I've urged her to be cautious. I have her phone number and I promised to keep her informed of our plans."

"Can we trust her not to blow the whistle and warn him we're coming?"

"Yes. She was a trusted friend of Thomas Gaines'. I've already involved her in the investigation as she's an experienced hacker. She put us on the trail of Chris White, and she contacted me when she realized we were looking for a librarian named Amy living in Idaho. If she wanted to help Bradley Kingston, she wouldn't have called me."

"All right. I'm trusting your judgment. I'll hold off on reissuing the sketch for thirty-six hours. Since we have a day to get into place, I'll hand pick the best agents. Trent Cooper and Kato Chen would be good choices, but I don't want to leave you unguarded."

"How about we send Kato to Idaho and leave Trent here? I'd feel better knowing Kato was running things on the ground. I trust him."

"Done. I'll nudge that security expert to get out to your ranch asap."

Chapter Thirty-Two

Nathan sat in the back corner of an older, camera-free coffee shop not far from his apartment building with his cap pulled low and his laptop computer open. Using his foot, he nudged the empty chair across from him into a better position, then stretched out his surgically repaired right leg. The worn chair wobbled, and he grimaced as a bolt of pain travelled along a nerve. All the driving from Lewistown to Idaho had caught up with him and the area around the metal rod in his leg throbbed.

Staying at home with his leg up would've been the best thing to do for this discomfort, but he needed some space from Amy to plan in peace. She hadn't changed the way he'd expected she would since their wedding night, and he didn't know what to make of it. Every other woman he'd married had used their wiles to try to manipulate him.

His first wife and former foster sister, Simone had taught him a painful yet valuable lesson—all women possessed an evil disposition. They'd spent their teen years together in the same house, and Simone had understood him in the way few others could.

She'd starved and experienced neglect at the hands of a drug-addicted single mother like he had. A scar in the shape of a slightly curved line travelled from under her armpit to her waist where she'd impaled herself with the edge of a metal shelf, trying to reach a box of cookies.

He'd fallen in love with her. He'd trusted her in a way he hadn't allowed himself to trust anyone besides Mr. and Mrs. DeGuire, the elderly couple next door. They took care of him when his mother went on benders and disappeared for weeks at a time.

After high school, he'd wanted nothing more than to run away and start a new life with Simone. He'd mistakenly believed the slate could be wiped clean, and that all the bloodshed and deaths in his past could be left behind.

At first, things went well for them. Simone got a job waitressing, and he'd become a licensed insurance salesman. They'd rented a tiny, old house with persistent drafts in the winter, and that baked them in the summer, but they made the most of their life together.

Before they'd saved enough money for a down payment on a house of their own, their life together shattered into a million pieces. He'd remember the fateful day their relationship ended forever.

****

Twenty years earlier

On a cold winter day, heavy snow tumbled from the sky, and the wind gusted hard across the flat, unforgiving prairies. A sheet of pure white blanketed the world outside the windows of Bradley Kingston's old Honda Civic, cloaking the world beyond the hood of his car.

With the weather conditions forecasted to get worse as the snow accumulated, Bradley's boss, the manager of their small, local insurance branch had made the decision to close at lunchtime and had sent everyone home early.

Bradley had stopped by the diner expecting to see Simone, but she wasn't there. According to the manager, she wasn't on the schedule for that day, yet he'd swear she'd told him she would be at work. With the storm raging, she was safer at home anyhow.

He clenched the steering wheel, struggling to stay on his side of the one-lane highway. Lights in the shape of a big truck shone through the blizzard in the middle of both lanes, coming straight for him. Surely, the driver would see him and move into his own lane.

Sweat coated Bradley's palms, making it harder for him to maintain his grip on the cracked leather.

The truck came closer and closer, and still the driver wasn't moving over.

Christ! This idiot is going to kill me!

Bradley pounded on his horn three times as he swerved right to the edge of the road, perilously close to the ditch. If the truck didn't move, he wouldn't have a choice but to steer into the ditch.

The truck jerked to the left at the last possible moment, tires spinning and skidding, scrambling for purchase.

Bradley gritted his teeth and braced for impact as the truck moved past him, an inch from the driver's side mirror. He took a deep breath and steered into the middle of his lane again. Hopefully, he wouldn't encounter any more idiots on the way home.

The wipers battled to keep the windshield clear against the snow blanketing the surface. He cranked the defroster to speed the melting of the snow, bolstering the wipers' efforts. He turned onto the unplowed side street that led to their house, taking care not to drive too slowly. The last thing he needed was to get stuck in the middle of the road.

Finally, he made it to their small house. But he couldn't pull into the driveway because there was an old, red Ford truck parked next to Simone's Mazda station wagon. He parked along the curb in front of the neighbor's house instead, then rolled his eyes and groaned.

After dealing with people at work, the last thing he wanted to do was entertain. It made sense that Simone would have company over during the day while he worked. She understood his introverted personality and his need to shut people out.

The front door of his house opened, and a man he'd never seen before stepped outside onto the porch.

Why is there a strange man in my house in the middle of the day while I'm supposed to be at work?

The dark recesses of his mind screamed she was two-timing him, but Bradley shook off the devil sitting on his shoulder. It could be a repairman sent by the landlord. They lived in an old house and things broke all the time. The faucets dripped, and the wiring was old. A few months ago, the oven had broken down.

Simone appeared in the entryway smiling at the stranger with a seductive gaze, twirling a long strand of her red hair. She waved to the stranger, then blew him a kiss. The man smiled then waved. He jumped into the old, red Ford and drove off.

With her focus so intent on the stranger, Simone didn't even look in Bradley's direction before she turned and shut the front door—twisting a knife in his heart.

A strangled cry escaped his lips, and he pounded on the steering wheel with his fists.

Bitch! How could she betray me like this?

After years of living together in the same foster home, they'd become lovers and best friends—dependent on each other for happiness. They'd even moved two provinces west to escape the past and start over. At their townhall wedding she'd promised to be faithful and pledged herself to him forever, til death do them part.

Death.

The life insurance policy in her name sitting in his desk at work could make him a rich man. Their crappy house in need of constant repairs could have a believable flaw that caused it to burn to the ground with her in it. When presented with a logical, non-nefarious answer, the authorities were quick to accept it and move on without digging any deeper and making their jobs harder.

He'd tried so hard to be a good man for Simone. What a wasted effort. He should've known better. Women were poison, without exception. No matter what he did, violent thoughts and darkness followed him everywhere he went.

****

Nathan crumpled his empty coffee cup with more force than necessary, trying to crush Bradley's old memories out of his consciousness. The one memory that wouldn't leave him, no matter how hard he tried, was the sight of their crappy rental house enveloped with flames while Simone had lain in bed unconscious. The acrid scent of plastic siding melting still lingered in his mind like muscle memory, and every time he lit a house on fire that same smell brought back that painful memory like a dagger to the heart.

A notification popped up on his computer. He'd gotten a response in the chatroom he'd set up for Bryce.

—When are you coming to visist me?—

Given it had been almost two months since he'd left the note in Bryce's locker, he was skeptical the message was from the boy. Would a child that smart make that spelling error on a simple word like 'visit'? And why would he have waited so long to send a message?

On the chance the message had come from Bryce, he responded.

—Soon. As soon as I can. —

With his head tilted to the floor, Bradley tucked his computer under his arm and wove his way through the small tables in the shop. He deposited what was left of his cup in the garbage on his way outside. He stepped onto the sidewalk and inhaled a deep breath of mountain air to cleanse away the memory of plastic burning.

Of all the places he'd lived during his travels, he liked the mountain climates best. That's why he'd decided to make Bolivia his next home after the Kents' were dead. He'd settle near the Andes with Bryce where he'd teach him the realities of the world and mentor him. Even if Bryce figured out his deceit about his claim to be Adam, Bryce would eventually come around when he learned the truth anyhow. Especially with his mother dead and no other alternatives.

Chapter Thirty-Three

In the middle of the afternoon, Jessica stood next to Jon by the window in the entryway waiting for the security expert. He'd texted Jon a few minutes ago letting him know he would arrive soon.

They'd stood in the same spot that morning as Kato had driven his rental car up the winding gravel road and out of sight. Sending him to Ketchum to lead the FBI team planning Bradley's capture made sense, yet she couldn't shake the sense that it was the wrong decision.

She chalked it up to fear and anxiety. "I felt better having Kato here."

Jon wrapped an arm around her shoulder and kissed the side of her head. "I get it. I don't like the idea of him leaving either, but I trust him to organize the team in Idaho. He has good instincts, and he doesn't make mistakes."

The security system buzzed. The display panel mounted on the wall next to Jessica turned on, showing a delivery truck at the gate. She turned her head to face Jon. "Do we let him in? I'm expecting a load of stuff from my house in Cochrane."

"Let's take a closer look at the driver." Jon zoomed in on the camera feed. His apple-shaped face and ample cheeks didn't come close to resembling Bradley. "It should be safe." He touched the microphone icon. "Please, leave the boxes on the front porch, sir. Thank you." He hit the button to open the gate.

Having those boxes and getting her house on the market should be a relief, but letting go of the house she bought with Adam threatened to bring tears to her eyes. That part of her life had ended the day she'd fled that house with Bryce, and she needed to move on.

Jon asked, "What's wrong? You look like you're going to cry."

"Those boxes are the end of an era for me and Bryce. We'll never step foot in our old home again. I wasn't expecting it to be this hard after all this time."

"I know exactly how you feel. I never did sell my old house in D.C. because I didn't want to let it go. Seeing how brave you're being with moving on, I decided to do the same. When this is over, it's going on the market, and I'm giving Cynthia half the proceeds. Yes, it's not easy letting go, but we have an amazing future to look forward to."

"After Bradley is in the ground, we're definitely looking ahead and letting go of the past. The kids need that. They need normal. School, preschool, playdates, family outings, and family trips."

Jon gazed into her eyes. "I promise you we'll have all that and more. And I'll be ripping all that horrible black metal out of the ground."

"That's a relief. This is a ranch. Not a prison."

On the security feed, the delivery driver placed the last box on the porch, then climbed in his truck and drove away from their house.

"I better get those boxes inside." Jon stepped outside.

A shiver travelled up her spine. "I'll watch your back."

Jon made quick work of stacking the eight boxes inside the entrance.

Bryce approached from the direction of the living room where he'd spent the morning gaming. "What's in the boxes?"

Jessica resisted the urge to flatten a section of his hair that was standing on end. Under stress, Bryce hated to be coddled. "It's boxes from our old house in Cochrane. One of them has your name on it."

"Can I take it to my room?"

Jon handed it to him. "Of course. Here you go."

"Thanks." Bryce turned and headed for his room.

Hopefully, a box of old treasures would be a good distraction for him. Jessica eyed the other seven boxes, debating which one to open first. The top one was labelled paperwork, not the most exciting. She set it aside for later.

The two boxes beneath that one contained her books. She ripped the tape off the one stacked on top and opened the flaps. Like an old friend, her romantic suspense books greeted her and offered comfort. She carried the box over to the bookshelves in the living room. It would be a tight fit, but she'd make room somehow.

The panel by the front door buzzed again.

Jessica called to Jon from the living room. "Is it the security guy?"

"Yes. It's Shandru. I recognize him from the photo they sent me."

"Good." The expert would either validate her sighting of the man in the hayfield and confirm that Bradley Kingston had found a way around their security, or he might also question her sanity. Neither would be a welcome conclusion, but they needed to know.

"I'm stepping out to chat with him and answer his questions if that's okay. I'll get him to come inside to give us both his conclusions after he does his thing."

"Sounds like a plan."

While she waited for Jon and Shandru, she turned the books on the shelves to stack them vertically to make room. It took some trial and error, but once she double layered the mass market paperbacks, all the books fit on the shelves.

Jessica stood back to examine her work. Although it was only books, and possessions were just things, in a sense, she'd merged her old life with her new one. And it didn't bring on the wave of sadness she'd expected.

She broke down the empty boxes and carried them to the backdoor in the kitchen to go out for recycling later. The screen of Jon's laptop came to life on the kitchen table with a notification. She didn't have his fingerprint to activate the screen, but the notification banner showed a preview of a text message from Kato.

—*Bradley responded with soon, very soon.*—

Jessica cursed under her breath at the menacing yet frustratingly vague message. She'd expected nothing concrete. Bradley wouldn't give away his location that easily. All she could hope for was that Kato might be able to get the FBI techs to get a location from where the message was sent.

If Bradley was on the move, that information might not help them find him. Thankfully, they knew where he lived. She lowered her head and folded her hands, then prayed he'd return home before coming after them. She also prayed the FBI wouldn't bungle his capture again.

Wanting to break out of that train of thought if only

for a while, she put the kettle on to boil, then she stood by the sink in front of the kitchen window. With the hay cut, she could see beyond that field to the others where the cows grazed. Hopefully, they'd get their fill of grass. The weather app forecasted a shift in the jetstream, bringing them colder temperatures slightly below freezing with the possibility of flurries overnight.

Barring a deep freeze, the pumpkins on the porch should be fine outside. She'd gotten burnt a few years ago in Cochrane after leaving the pumpkins outside during frigid weather and they'd turned to mush inside. Bryce hadn't been impressed and they'd rushed to the store, managing to get the last straggling pumpkin with a bizarre shape and broken stem that no one had wanted.

They'd need to carve the pumpkins ahead of Halloween in the coming days. Although, it wouldn't be a festive holiday this year, and kids wouldn't be coming to their door. Trick or treating took place in town rather than on the more remote properties. The past two years they'd taken Bryce to Main Street to the local businesses and the neighborhood houses in that area.

Unless Bradley's capture happened fast in the next week, trick or treating this year would be taking a risk. But at the same time, if they stuck to the businesses in the public areas of town, they should be safe. They'd have to assess and make a decision closer to the day. After making the decision to keep Bryce home from school, the notion of taking something else away from him made her want to cry.

Jon and Shandru came around the back corner of the house from the direction of the rental and through the kitchen door. Shandru stood half a head taller than Jon, but had a slimmer, wiry frame.

Jon said, "Jess, meet Shandru. Shandru this is my wife, Jessica."

The corners of Shandru's mouth lifted in a half-smile. Almost as if it was forced. "It's a pleasure, Jessica."

"It's nice to meet you, Shandru." She didn't like the troubled expression on Jon's face either. "Would you like tea? I just put the kettle on to boil."

Shandru shook his head. "No, thank you."

Jon gestured to the kitchen table. "Have a seat. I'll get your tea, Jess. Shandru can explain to you what he just told me."

Jessica sat in her usual chair and stared at Shandru, willing him to talk and give her the answers she needed.

"I logged into your wireless system and ran some analytics. Now, the thing with wireless systems is that they all have one weakness. Scramblers. Simple devices that scramble your signal and can interrupt your feed." Shandru cleared his throat. "With a system as sophisticated as this one, it should not be an issue. There are safeguards built in to prevent it, and they have always worked in the past."

"Worked in the past?" Jessica asked, "Are you saying our system failed?"

"Yes. My theory is the person behind the breech must possess a state-of-the-art model scrambler, likely purchased on the dark web. I found two instances of brief disruptions around ten minutes long both times. The system should have alerted you to an interruption in the signal, but it did not. I recalibrated the software to make sure it alerts you to any disruptions on every panel in the house and device logged onto the network."

Jon set a steaming mug in front of Jessica. "Will the

system recognize the disruption as it happens or only after the scrambler is turned off?"

"It should pick up on it immediately as it happens. As a backup, we can install a second older system that is hardwired around both houses with a loud alarm that will also alert emergency services, similar to the systems they use at jewelry stores and banks. They are not as sophisticated, but they don't have that vulnerability. Yes, the wires could be cut, but our suspect will not be expecting something like that. He will likely assume all the sensors are connected to the same system."

Jessica's palms moistened. "By the time that alarm goes off, he'll already be close to breaking in. I thought the whole point was to keep him from getting past those huge metal fences. How is he getting in? Is he scrambling the keypad at the entrance and driving in?"

"No. There would still be camera footage of him approaching that gate on more than one camera," Shandru said. "I think he is coming through the side where the forest is by the small house, using the trees for cover and possibly using them as leverage with rope to get over the fence. Cutting down the trees near the gate is not an option?"

Jon drummed his fingers on the table. "We can only take them down on our side. The neighbor complained about the few trees we trimmed on his side to make way for the fence. He'll never agree to take them down which means he can still use those to gain access anyway."

Shandru said, "What if you cut the neighbor's trees down anyway? What is the worst that could happen? A lawsuit? You replace the trees?"

Jon sighed. "This isn't the city. When someone trespasses, you protect your property first before you call the Sheriff's office. My neighbor is the type of surly bastard who would shoot the person who tries and ask questions later."

"Well, that isn't an option." Shandru said, "What I propose then is we add onto the metal structure of the gate back there to make the fence taller, and we install the extra separate security system. Also, we will ask the FBI to hire a private security company as the system failed."

Jessica forced a sip of tea down her thick throat. "That's it? That's all we can do. You can't change the software or do more to stop him from hacking it?"

"I am sorry, but that is all I can do."

Jon took her hand. "It's not perfect, but it improves on what we have. The idea with having the second system is a really good one. Until Bradley tries to break into the house, he won't know about it. Also, private security companies work for celebrities. They're the experts on keeping people safe. It'll make it a lot harder for him to get onto the property again. The only other option is we go into hiding again until the FBI catches him. We're getting really close. The decision is yours."

Jessica took a minute to consider their options. "Running didn't work the last time, and now we have a two-month-old. With us, Cynthia and Trent, a security company, and all these alarms, we have a good chance of defending ourselves here. Besides, like you said, we're close to catching him."

Chapter Thirty-Four

Amy's head throbbed after not sleeping or eating much since discovering she'd married a serial killer. At least Nathan had stayed away as he'd promised, giving her time to hack servers in her search to find an insurance policy in her name. Thankfully, she hadn't found one yet, but that didn't mean a policy didn't exist. Her naivety didn't extend far enough for her to believe herself immune from her husband's diabolical ways.

Knock! Knock!

She stood on stiff and slightly numb legs, from sitting in her computer chair for hours on end, and hurried to the door, then put her eye to the peephole. A man she didn't recognize stood waiting with a compact build and black hair peppered with a few strands of gray running through it.

She cracked open the door. "Hello. Can I see some identification?"

He held up his FBI badge. "I'm Agent Kato Chen. Jon Kent told you to expect me."

"Right. He did." She opened the door the rest of the way. "Come in. Can I get you anything to drink? Coffee?"

He stepped inside. "No, thank you. I won't be staying. I came to reassure you that I have a team of plain clothes agents watching the streets, snipers on the roof, and another team of agents stationed around the parameter of your neighborhood." He handed her a business card. "Put this number in your phone. If Bradley Kingston slips by us somehow, send me a text message, then find an innocent excuse to step out of the apartment and run to the parking lot. Say you're doing laundry or taking garbage out. Something simple he won't question. We don't want you harmed in the crossfire."

Goose pimples rose on her skin, and she rubbed her arms to warm up. "It sounds like you have everything under control, but I'll be ready for him in case something goes wrong."

"Have you found anything? Jon mentioned you planned to keep digging."

"I've been up all night searching and nothing yet, but I plan to keep at it. I'll text you if I find anything."

Kato bowed his head, opened the door, and stepped into the hallway. "Thank you. Take care."

"I will." She shut the door behind him and turned the deadbolt, nauseated by the fact that Nathan had the key.

Having an empty stomach would only make her feel worse, so she popped bread in the toaster and made a fresh cup of coffee. She took her snack back to her desk and continued searching for a backdoor into the server of one of the biggest insurance companies around she had yet to breach.

Finding a backdoor required experience and finesse, digging through individual files of code to find them. Not all websites had them, but most did. If a site didn't have one, she'd insert one of her own. After scrolling for another ten minutes, she spotted a familiar line of code, granting her access to the company's client files.

She typed her name into the server and this time it

didn't give her an error message. A policy in her name and at her address existed for one and a half million dollars and Nathan was the beneficiary.

That slimy, manipulative asshole!

She gritted her teeth and resisted the urge to scream only because she didn't want the neighbors calling the police or banging on her door.

Chapter Thirty-Five

Nathan awoke rejuvenated to the light shining through the thin curtains of the motel room he'd rented the night before. After all the uncomfortable places he'd rested his head over the years, including vehicles, the ground, and a cavern, crappy motel beds weren't an issue. All he needed was to be alone and undisturbed by a wife. Last night he'd slept like the dead after his busy nights in Lewistown on top of the sixteen hours of driving in both directions.

His thoughts flowed with a clarity, allowing him to decide on when to time his next move and how to go about it. With the warm, not quite hot water of the small shower trickling on his head, he pondered his current options. Killing someone while making their death appear accidental was difficult in apartment buildings.

Too many possible witnesses, and unlike Emily, Amy didn't take any prescription medications he could manipulate. It might be easier to take Amy somewhere else to do the deed—an accidental drowning, a tumble off an embankment or a cliff, or a drunken stumble into traffic.

If he waited long enough, she'd show her true self or betray him in some way and earn her death. Time should be on his side. After faking his own death then altering his face, no one should be looking for him. He'd even taken the extra precaution of changing names after collecting the policy on Emily, yet an unexplained sense of urgency spurred him to get on with it.

Maybe it stemmed from the desire to settle and take a break somewhere after years of pulling scams and moving from one wife to another. For once he didn't have to bother with dating websites and lining up his next victims.

Before the water turned any colder, he stepped out of the shower and dried off with a ratty, rough towel. He pulled on the dark hoody and jeans he'd packed, then dropped his key at the deserted reception desk. The diner a few blocks away called his name where they served a mean steak and eggs.

Rested with a stomach full of protein, he climbed into his truck. He could stall for longer and find another coffee shop, or he could go home to his wife. He needed to keep up the pretense of the loving husband long enough to convince her to go on a drunken cold picnic somewhere along the Sawtooth Mountain Range this weekend.

He took the less direct route back to the apartment building using side streets as he always did when Amy wasn't in the truck with him. It probably wasn't necessary, but he'd evaded capture with his good habit over the years of never letting his guard down.

Even though his was the only vehicle at the intersection, Nathan signaled a right turn as he approached a four-way stop that would bring him to his building. He stopped and scouted the street. Four black SUVs sat along the curbs on either side of the road. With limited spaces in the apartment building lot, street parking was at a premium, and the same vehicles usually occupied those spots.

None of them were black SUVs—often the vehicle of choice for the FBI in mountainous terrain.

Instead of turning, he drove straight through the intersection and wove his way through residential side streets, navigating further into the neighborhood. He parked close to a walking path, leading back to his apartment building. He needed to double back and take a closer look at the situation before deciding how to proceed. The FBI could be there on an unrelated matter unless they'd somehow figured out he was alive and behind Emily's death, then trailed him here.

That seemed unlikely unless one of Hugh Jones' former crew got in trouble and then sold him out. Always a risk when involving others in your crimes, but he'd needed Hugh Jones to get him out of Lewistown to the plastic surgery resort in Columbia.

The brisk fall wind carried fallen leaves in the air, leaving the trees along the streets bare. With the chill in the air, he could disguise himself without standing out. He tugged the hood of his sweater over his lowered ballcap, zipped his black puffer jacket up to his chin, and walked with his shoulders hunched and his head lowered.

His furtive glance travelled the streets as he walked, ensuring he didn't come close to anyone else on the streets. There could be plainclothes agents in the area, although most of them would stick to busier areas and closer to the building. For a group of experts with behavioral specialists among them, they dropped the ball with their own predictable behavior patterns.

A group of four older teen boys clustered at the end of a driveway, laughing at something. They could be useful.

He approached them casually with his hands tucked in his pockets. "Hey, guys. Want to make a quick hundred?"

The biggest one, gauging by his letter jacket, a linebacker on his football team, scrutinized him through his sunglasses. "We aren't going to blow you if that's what you're thinking."

Jesus! What's wrong with kids these days? "That's just disgusting. No. I'm dodging one of those annoying people who thinks they're your friend when they're not. You know the type."

Another kid with surfer dude blond hair down to his shoulders nodded. "Yeah, man. There's this one kid at school who follows us around like a lost dog. Total loser."

Nathan bet that kid was smarter than this goofball. "Anyways, this guy is standing outside my apartment building just up that path, and I can't handle his shit today. All I want is for you four to walk inside the building with me. He's not brave enough to approach with other people around. I'll even give you the money upfront. What do you say?"

The big guy shrugged. "One hundred split four ways doesn't buy us all a decent *V-Buck* pack. Double or nothing."

Nathan resisted the urge to roll his eyes. "Okay fine." He pulled out his wallet. "Here's the cash. Let me walk in the middle."

With his head down amongst this group of kids, he blended in. Hoodies and jeans were universal and wouldn't give away his age. As they made their way along the path, he didn't participate in the pointless conversation about girls and video games sure to repel most adults. Guaranteed the surfer dude was lying about rounding second base with the head cheerleader. His friends snickered as he told his tall tale, but no one called him on it.

Nathan's heart rate ticked up a notch as they approached the entrance to the building, but no one stopped them as he pulled out his key and let them inside. "Thanks, guys. If you walk through the lobby, it'll take you out the back entrance."

"Yeah, whatever." The big guy led the way holding his stomach and laughing. "Can you believe that old geezer just paid us all that cash not to look like a loser walking alone?"

Nathan ignored the barb and pressed the button for the elevator. The jock didn't have the brain cells to imagine that he'd helped a serial killer move around undetected. Nathan stepped into the elevator and rode it to the second floor. The hallway leading to his apartment stood empty and some of the pent-up tension left his shoulders.

Maybe his paranoid, overly cautious mind had blown the situation out of proportion. He unlocked the apartment door and stepped inside. "Darling, I'm home."

Amy came around the corner with flushed cheeks and the laundry basket tucked under her arm. "I'm so happy you're home. How was your trip?"

"Great," He lied. "Traffic was light, and I got those pumpkins delivered fast."

"Okay, I'll be right back. I'm throwing in a load of laundry before I have to go back to work tomorrow. I grabbed your stuff, too. Could you put the kettle on?"

"Sure."

"Thanks." She stepped into the hallway and shut the

door behind her.

Was it his imagination, or had her hand tremored slightly on the doorknob? His presence still flustered her from time to time. That had to be the reason. He filled the kettle with water and flicked the button on to boil the water. The sink was filled with mugs as if she'd been drinking coffee or tea for hours on end. Maybe that was the source of her jitters.

Nathan went into their bedroom to change into jogging pants. He paused at the sight of the pill bottle he'd stashed Emily's medication in sitting on his night table. Then cursed himself for not moving the pills into the backpack he took with him on his shorter trips.

Amy had unpacked his bag, something she'd never done before. He'd have to be more cautious in the future. If she asked about the pills, he would claim they were his. What else could he do? The best lies were the simplest ones.

Multiple sets of heavy, fast footsteps thundering along the hallway reached his ears through the thin walls.

Oh, no!

They couldn't be racing down the hall for anyone else.

Nathan pulled on the second set of running shoes he kept in the bedroom closet, grabbed the revolver hidden beneath a stack of sweaters on the top shelf, and tucked it in the back of his jeans. He opened the sliding glass doors to the balcony off their bedroom, then stepped outside. He had to be about twenty feet above the ground.

His options included dropping to the ground in a roll and praying his surgically repaired leg held up, or he could jump onto one of the balconies on either side of him. If the neighbors were home, how would he explain himself?

"FBI! Bradley Kingston, come out with your hands up!"

Fuck! Worst case scenario!

They had called him by his name at birth which meant they knew he'd survived that fall off the cliff. If they caught him, he'd be going down for so many crimes, he'd never see the outside of a jail cell again. Something from one of his worst nightmares. Amy turned out to be a bitch after all. She must have helped the FBI and told them he was in the apartment. He'd get revenge someday, but first, he needed to escape this mess.

Nathan climbed over the side of his balcony, using his upper body strength to hold onto the concrete edge. His legs dangled precariously. He could either scream for help and rot in prison, although some of the states he'd committed murders in had the death penalty, or he could risk a tactical drop onto the thick dead grass below. His upper body could only hold his weight for so long.

Miraculously, no one stood below staring up at him in anticipation of a daring escape bordering on stupidity. After ridding humanity of so many awful women, he prayed that if a higher entity existed, he'd protect him and aid his escape once again.

Nathan let go of the balcony and tumbled through the air. He tucked his chin into his body and turned to land on his left side. Steadying his breathing to keep blood flowing to his muscles and prevent them from tensing, he braced for impact.

His body slammed into the dead grass with a thud, and his left shoulder and hip screamed as he rolled away. The grass might've cushioned his fall somewhat, but most importantly it muffled the sound of his landing.

Either way, he needed to move fast.

He shifted his weight onto his right leg as he stood and ran around the side of the building. His left leg held him, and he could withstand the pain in his hip which suggested painful bruising that would heal without medical intervention. However, his left shoulder hadn't faired so well.

Each time he pumped his left arm, sharp pains radiated from the edge of his shoulder to his neck. But he had to keep running until he made it to his truck. Hiding and waiting for the FBI to gather more reinforcements and bring in the dogs would be sheer stupidity. Too many idiots were captured that way.

The truck wasn't registered to the state of Idaho, and he used fake plates that he swapped out on a regular basis. They wouldn't be able to track him if he could make it out of the area.

Only one man walked along the path between his building and the residential neighborhood where Nathan had parked his truck. The man reached inside his coat pocket.

Nathan slowed to a jog and placed his hand on the revolver tucked into his waistband. Firing a bullet would draw the attention of everyone around, but if that man pulled a gun out of his pocket, Nathan wouldn't have a choice.

In slow motion, the man pulled his hand out of his pocket.

A phone. Only a phone.

Nathan ran past him. By some measure of insane luck, the FBI must not have figured out he'd dropped from the balcony. They must have assumed he'd fled inside the building before they got to his door.

He emerged from the path into the world of American suburbia once again. Single homes lined both sides of the street. A street not unlike many of the ones he'd lived on in the past. His truck sat within view a few yards away.

Despite the odds stacked against him, he'd made it. He stopped in front of the driver's door, fumbled in his left coat pocket for his keys, then pressed the key fob to unlock the doors.

"Freeze! Hands on the hood where I can see them!"

Nathan lifted his head in the direction of the voice. A lone man, one of Jon's buddies, Kato Chen stood in front of the truck with a handgun aimed at him. The only way to gain control of the situation would be to act compliant. If Chen planned to cuff him, he'd have to holster that gun. And he stood a whole head shorter than Nathan.

Nathan placed his hands on the truck. "I'll cooperate. Don't shoot."

Kato kept the gun trained on him as he moved behind Nathan's back. "I have the suspect by his vehicle. Requesting backup."

The wind had died since Nathan first arrived home, and the street was quiet besides a bird chirping in a nearby tree and cars in the distance. Kato's footsteps betrayed his location. When Kato stopped walking, Nathan glanced over his shoulder.

Kato crooked his arm and lowered his head.

I can't miss.

Nathan threw his right elbow backwards and connected with Kato's neck. The momentum knocked Kato backwards onto the blacktop and his gun skittered away.

The pain in Nathan's left shoulder intensified and black spots danced in his vision. Despite his height and size advantage, with his injury, he might not win the fight. Instead of attacking, he yanked the keys hanging from the lock in the driver's door and climbed into the truck. He locked the doors, then started the engine.

In his side mirror, he could see Kato picking up his gun near the back of the truck.

Oh, no you don't!

Nathan shifted into reverse, slammed his foot on the gas pedal, and aimed his truck for Kato.

Kato dove away from the truck.

Nathan adjusted his steering to compensate.

Thud!

His truck lifted on the driver's side as his back tire drove over Kato Chen. For good measure, he kept his foot on the gas pedal and ran him over with the front tire. He stayed in reverse until Kato Chen emerged on the road in front of him, not moving with a leg twisted in a direction it shouldn't be. To make sure Kato wouldn't cause him any more problems, he ran him over again.

Sirens wailed in the distance. Nathan needed to get out of there and get ahead of his pursuers. Thankfully, he'd prepared in case he needed to make a quick getaway. He wove his way through residential streets to the back of an old strip mall and parked next to a mid-sized sedan he'd left there with a full gas tank.

Ignoring the worsening pain in his shoulder, he shoved his backpack and his guns into the trunk of the car next to the camping stuff and tech equipment he'd stored there. He grabbed the magnetic key box from underneath the back bumper, climbed behind the wheel, and drove away.

Chapter Thirty-Six

With the FBI searching for Bradley Kingston in Idaho, Jon's nervous energy made it difficult for him to focus. He couldn't shake the feeling something horrible would happen and Bradley would escape once again. To center himself, he went into the barn.

The comforting scents of hay, manure, and leather welcomed him along with his favorite horse, Daisy. He plucked her brush off the hook by the door. "Hey, girl. Want an extra brushing?"

Daisy swung her tail as he approached.

He offered her an apple and she took it from him gently and munched. Trying to keep Jessica and Bryce's spirits up under the circumstances was near impossible, but at least he could keep Daisy happy.

Jon trailed the brush along her back and a small measure of peace settled over him until his phone rang, breaking the spell of calm and solitude he'd woven for himself in the barn.

"What now, Daisy?"

He pulled his phone out of his pocket. Assistant Director Pruitt's number flashed on his screen. "Darn, I have to get this girl. I'll come visit you again later." He swiped to answer, then headed inside the house to find Jessica. "Hello."

"Jon, I have an update for you, and it isn't good news. Bradley Kingston went home to his apartment in

Ketchum, Idaho, but our team wasn't able to capture him. He got away. We can't figure out what tipped him off, but something or someone did.

"We didn't find any surveillance equipment in his apartment, yet he knew to use a group of teenage boys to slip past our team and into the building. To escape after our team entered his apartment, he jumped off a second story balcony conveniently located away from both entrances. The agent placed on that side of the building trailed him and radioed his location to the team, but they weren't fast enough to stop him."

He found Jessica in the kitchen, took her hand, and led her to their bedroom. "Is Amy okay?"

Jessica shut the bedroom door and sat on their bed as he paced the room.

"She's shaken, but unharmed. We have her in protective custody. She discovered a one and a half million-dollar policy in her name shortly before Bradley Kingston came home. She alerted Kato Chen and left the apartment."

"I had hoped with Kato Chen in charge this wouldn't happen."

Pruitt sighed. "While the team stormed the building, Agent Chen was stationed by the older blue truck from the surveillance video in Lewistown. He waited for the suspect there as a backup plan in case he made it that far.

"A witness from a home across the street saw Kato attempt an arrest. Kingston appeared to be compliant and then he landed an elbow to Agent Chen's neck knocking him to the pavement and dislodging his service weapon. While Agent Chen attempted to retrieve his gun, the suspect climbed into his truck and backed over him. He ran him over twice then fled the scene ten seconds before our team arrived at the location."

Jon's stomach clenched. "Did Kato survive?"

Jessica paled and covered her mouth with her hand.

"Agent Chen is in critical condition. He's in surgery now to repair internal bleeding, and one of his legs is shattered in multiple places. They aren't sure if the limb can be saved, and they won't attempt to fix it until he's stable."

Sweet Jesus, no! Not another one of my friends dead because of me. "Thank you for letting us know."

"I'm sorry, Jon. I wish I had better news. We sent out the updated sketch and an all points bulletin. Our team and local law enforcement will be searching hard knowing he harmed one of their own. We know what vehicle he's driving and the fake plate number he's using. I can't see him getting far."

He resisted the urge to give into his despair and weep like a baby. This situation was about the worst possible outcome. "Lewistown is only eight hours away from Ketchum, Idaho. And he switches vehicles when the heat is on him, so unless you find him in the next hour you can't rely on that information. This is a huge mistake on your part."

"Again, I apologize. I received the recommendations from Shandru Anand and I'm approving all of them. I'll have a private security team out there by the end of the day. Let me know if there's anything else you need."

"Could Bryce be given a security detail so he can continue to attend school? Staying home has a negative impact on him."

"Yes, of course."

"Thank you." Jon hung up and sat beside Jessica and

took her hand.

Jessica said, "Oh my God, Kato. I knew I had a bad feeling about letting him go to Idaho. I could hear bits and pieces. Internal bleeding?"

"Yes, and a badly shattered leg that might not be salvageable."

"This all comes back to me. If I had ignored the noise Bradley made when he moved Sarah's body in the middle of the night, instead of looking outside and calling the cops, none of this would be happening."

He gazed into her eyes. "He's the murderer, *not* you. We've had this discussion."

"Here I am criticizing you for your past, and I'm just as bad. I killed a man to protect you, and you've killed multiple people over the years. We might not be cold-blooded murderers, but we're killers, Jon. To believe otherwise is naïve. I can't help but wonder if this is karma coming back to get us."

"We're decent human beings who killed for the right reasons. That isn't the same, and I don't believe we deserve to be punished for it, do you?"

"I guess not." She lowered her head and stared at the carpet as she deflated in front of his eyes. This situation had a brutal hold over their family. Jessica most of all.

He lifted her chin. "You're an amazing mother and wife. Don't let that scumbag make you doubt who you are. I love you." He brushed a gentle kiss against her lips.

She fisted his shirt and fell backwards onto the bed, pulling him on top of her with her newfound strength. "Kiss me the way you used to. Like you actually want me."

Is that how I've made her feel? Like I don't want her? "Are you kidding me? You're the sexiest woman in the world. I've only been holding back because I didn't want to push after you had Cassie. You have to know I always want you."

He lowered his mouth to hers and this time he didn't hold back. All the tension between them erupted in fast and passionate flames as they let their love burn strong. His heart and soul reconnected with hers and they became one again.

Chapter Thirty-Seven

Jessica rested her head on Jon's chest and inhaled his musky scent mixed with sweat. The smattering of hair tickled her cheek. They needed to get out of bed, but neither one of them moved. This moment of peace wouldn't last, so she clung to him, taking in as much comfort as she could after this latest blow.

Cassie would wake soon, looking for an afternoon feeding, and Jessica wanted to tidy and clean the kitchen before dinner. "Aunt Debbie called just before Pruitt did. Your mom is being released from the hospital this afternoon, and she wants to celebrate her freedom by having a family dinner of pizza with us here at the ranch."

"Well, at least something good is happening today. I bet Mom would love it if we invited Jamie and the boys over. I think Pat is working, so it'll save Jamie some cooking."

"Pat is on shift. Noah and Oliver would be an excellent and much needed distraction for Bryce. They might not be cousins by blood, but they act like it. Your family has been so welcoming."

"I'll text Jamie and let you know."

"Sounds good. Hank is on duty, so Aunt Debbie is driving Sally and the pizzas over to the ranch later." She lifted her head and batted her eyelashes. "I wasn't exactly in the mood to entertain earlier, but I am now.

You took the edge off the depression. Poor Kato."

Cassie's cries came through the baby monitor on the night stand.

Jessica climbed out of bed. "That's my cue."

"We can't get a moment to ourselves, can we?"

"Lately, no. After this nightmare ends, we might need a vacation."

Jon tugged his boxers and jeans on. "I'm holding you to that. We'll let Bryce choose the destination."

"It might be a long time before that happens. Whenever Bradley escapes capture, he disappears and regroups. You said yourself that if they didn't find him fast, they wouldn't find him at all. What if he has surgery again? What if he waits years to come back? The FBI isn't going to cover the cost of private security long term."

"We'll get through this. He didn't disappear for that long after his tumble off the cliff."

"Just over a year. That's long enough." A pang of guilt clawed at her stomach as she made her way to the nursery. They'd talked about vacations and planning a family dinner while Kato fought for his life in the hospital. But if they gave in to the depression and the darkness pressing in on them, then they wouldn't have the strength to fight back.

After getting to know him over the past month, she firmly believed Kato wouldn't want them to do that.

****

Jessica hit the button on the control panel to let Aunt Debbie and Sally onto the property. In the sling around Jessica's front, Cassie's eyes were wide open. Her brother-in-law Jamie and his sons Noah and Oliver had arrived half an hour earlier. Rather than play videogames, Bryce and his cousins had spent their time together working on a 'Welcome Home, Grandma' banner that Jon had hung for them over the dining room table.

She and Jon made the decision not to tell Bryce about Kato's injuries and Bradley's escape. He didn't need that dark cloud hanging over his head while he had his grandma, uncle, and cousins around to cheer him up. They also hadn't mentioned the security company and the possibility of him returning to school.

She hadn't yet determined if they should send him back to school or not. She wanted Bryce to have as normal a life as possible, and Jon assured her that royals and celebrity children attended school with a security detail safely all the time. They couldn't keep him home indefinitely. He'd tolerated homeschooling during their time at the safehouse in Utah, but he'd missed being around children.

If only the phone would ring with news of Bradley Kingston's capture, then she wouldn't be forced to make such a difficult decision. Thankfully, Jon's phone had rung with other good news earlier. Kato had survived his initial surgery, and the doctors believed he'd live. Whether or not he'd lose his leg remained to be seen.

The kitchen door opened, snapping Jessica out of her own head and back into the present.

Sally held on to Jon's arm as she stepped inside. Her face lacked her usual color, but her smile warmed the room.

Jessica said, "It's wonderful seeing you up and about again."

"Hello, Jess. I'm happy to be here." Sally touched Cassie's cheek. "You, my sweet granddaughter saved my life." She shifted her attention back to Jessica. "If Debbie and I hadn't made plans to go shopping for baby clothes, then I wouldn't be here. She's such a blessing."

Jessica gazed into Cassie's blue eyes and smiled. "Yes, she is."

Aunt Debbie stepped inside the house with a stack of pizza boxes, and the delicious scent of baked cheese, meat, and veggies permeated the air. "Pizza's here, folks."

"Thank you, Debbie." Jon took the boxes from her and set them on the dining room table. "Come sit down, Mom. The boys worked hard on this banner."

"That's so sweet. Thank you, grandsons." Sally kissed the tops of Noah, Oliver, and Bryce's heads as they laughed and tried to squirm away.

Jessica sat while Cassie was content and preoccupied by all the faces and voices at the table. Bryce wore a massive, carefree smile, sitting between Noah and Oliver. A feeling of comfort and camaraderie settled over her. The special type of feeling that came from being surrounded by family or friends in a relaxed space, sharing a meal.

The kind of love and happiness worth fighting for.

Chapter Thirty-Eight

On a Saturday, two weeks before Christmas, Jon lowered the tailgate of his truck and unloaded one of the two blue spruce trees he'd picked up in town. One for the ranch house and one for Cynthia and Trent to decorate at the rental. He'd already hung lights on the exterior of the house and added a wreath to the front door. Maybe with luck they'd get snow in time for the big day to blanket the brown landscape.

He couldn't believe Cassie's first Christmas was almost upon them. Although she'd have no memory of it, he wanted it to be special.

Jessica also needed a mood booster. After Bradley's escape, she'd managed well after they'd returned to making love regularly, retaining the closeness they shared as a couple. All the workouts and Cynthia's companionship also helped. But for the past week, she seemed off, distracted and bothered. With Bradley on the loose, he couldn't blame her.

He'd struggled with depressed thoughts from time to time. But with the holiday season upon them, he refused to let the dark shadow cast by Bradley Kingston suck the life out of their happy home.

A month and a half had passed since the FBI had botched taking Bradley Kingston in. Even though the media had plastered his face everywhere, the FBI had no leads on his whereabouts. At first, tips had poured in from all over the place, but none of them had panned out. Gradually, fewer people reported sightings as Bradley became old news.

After Kato's extensive leg surgery, he'd returned home to rehab his leg and regain his strength. He'd insisted on staying involved in the investigation, interviewing witnesses remotely, and following up on leads from home. He apologized once a week for not apprehending Bradley and blamed himself even though other agents on the scene had failed to track him moving in and out of the apartment building.

Trent wandered over from the barn. "Need a hand getting those trees inside?"

"Sure. This one is for my living room and the other is for yours. I was about to leave this one here and drive the other to your place."

"You didn't have to go to the trouble of getting us a tree."

"I wanted to. I know you're assigned here and getting paid and all, but I've kept you away from home for months now."

Trent grinned. "I've had worse assignments. Cynthia signed a contract until June, so she'd be staying in town no matter what."

"Jess likes having Cynthia around. It's remarkable how close they've become given the circumstances."

"Shared trauma creates a bond. They went through a lot during Hugh Jones' rampage between the shootout in the parking garage and at that house in Hawaii. It's only fitting we're all together again to put an end to Bradley Kingston."

Jon hefted the tree by the trunk. "If there is an end to Bradley Kingston. Slimy, slippery eel. He's as hard to catch as Pablo Escobar, and he doesn't have an organization to help him."

Trent picked up the other end of the tree. "He'll surface. He has to eventually."

"If he set up a hideout somewhere remote or a doomsday bunker, then maybe not. I'm starting to think that's the only possible explanation. I think the surgeries were more to allow him to be out in public and continue the insurance scams for income." Jon opened the kitchen door and called out. "Tree's here."

Bryce emerged from the hallway. "Mom's in the nursery with Cassie. Want me to hold the tree stand for you, Dad?"

"That would be a big help. Thanks."

Jon and Trent maneuvered the tree into the stand while Bryce held it in place.

"That's a big tree." Jessica came into the room, patting Cassie's back.

Jon kissed the side of Cassie's head. "It's a seven-footer. I thought this little girl would like a big tree to look at for her first Christmas."

Bryce crawled out from beneath the tree. "Can we decorate it today?"

Jon said, "Yes, I'll dig out the lights and the decorations from the basement after we bring Trent's tree over to his house."

Despite, or more like to spite Bradley Kingston, they'd have a great Christmas. Their Christmas Eve wedding last year would be hard to top, but Jon vowed to try his hardest.

Chapter Thirty-Nine

In a cabin hidden in the Montana wilderness, Bradley had prepared to end Jon and Jessica Kent once and for all. The couple who'd built the cabin were government hating, reclusive survivalists who lived off the land. No one would be looking for them and if they did, they wouldn't find much left of them after the wildlife feasted on their dead bodies. Humanity was better off without them anyhow.

Bradley had a warm place to live and supplies, and some of the weapons the survivalists had gathered were useful in a warped way. But in essence, he was living in forced seclusion with his face plastered all over the media. He needed to finish the job, grab Bryce, and flee to the remote area of Bolivia he wanted to make his new home.

Throughout the six weeks his fractured collarbone had taken to heal, he'd accomplished quite a lot. Online shopping had revolutionized the world in so many ways. All anyone needed was a post office box or an address. He'd acquired two sets of colored contact lenses, two wigs, and a professional prosthetic kit and makeup to alter his face.

After hours upon hours of practice, he'd mastered blending a prosthetic nose onto his face with makeup. With the prosthetic in place, he'd taken photos and obtained high-quality fake passports. When they used the new passports would depend on Bryce.

If Bryce bought the lie that he was Adam and came willingly, then he might be able to head to Bolivia right away. More than likely with his intelligence, Bryce knew better. He'd probably already asked his parents about Adam and showed them the link to the chat room.

Bradley would have to spend time with him at the cabin, bonding, and teaching him the ways of the world until he could trust the boy enough to bring him out in public. Only then could they begin their new life together.

The big pile of chopped wood, along with all the food and winter gear he'd amassed, would allow him to keep Bryce at the cabin for six months if needed. Some time away from all the modern-day crap like the internet and gaming would also allow him to get the boy used to what life would be like in the immediate future. He couldn't be allowed any way to reach people from his past life until he'd forgotten about them.

To get to that point, his parents would have to die.

That meant Bradley needed to bypass the guard from the new security company, and he'd have to get over the metal fencing. His state-of-the-art jammer would take care of the security system. One guard on a sleepy assignment in the middle of nowhere in the winter wouldn't be too much of a hindrance either.

The biggest obstacle would be the fence since they'd raised the height of it above the tree line in the forested area between Kent's property and the neighbors. In the past, he'd scaled a tree and rappelled over the fence. That wouldn't work anymore, but he'd found a way around the problem.

Close to midnight, Bradley crept around the motel,

picked the lock to room four, and let himself in. He turned the deadbolt, flipped the light off, then stood beside the door in the dark with a syringe full of pentothal.

Soon, Rennie Vega, a security guard from the company guarding the Kent ranch would be coming through the door. His shift ended at midnight, and with any luck, he would be good and tired after a boring day on the ranch. He wouldn't be expecting an assailant waiting inside his room.

All humans fall victim to complacency given enough time, no matter how big the threat.

Time passed, and Bradley slapped his cheeks and shifted around to keep himself from settling into a complacent state. Rennie must have made a stop on the way to the motel which made sense. The only food he'd find on site came from vending machines. But he'd surface eventually.

Headlights shone through the window, sweeping across the room. An engine clicked off. A car door banged shut. Then a key slipped in the lock and turned. The doorknob twisted, the door opened, and Rennie Vega stepped in the room wearing a leather cap with furry earflaps.

In one swift movement with a steady arm, Bradley plunged the needle into Rennie Vega's neck, then depressed the plunger.

Rennie spun to face him. "What the hell?" His eyes grew wide, and he reached for a gun from the holster belt around his waist. "It's you." He staggered with the gun in his hand and lifted his arm.

Bradley dove over the bed, crouched on the other side, and peered over the edge of the mattress, praying for the sedative to take effect before Rennie squeezed the trigger. If Rennie fired a bullet, the noise would draw the attention of anyone who was staying in the motel, then the police would respond, realize who the guard was, then his plans for the entire night would be foiled.

Rennie staggered around the bed, then his eyes rolled, and he fell forwards, face planting on the worn, green carpet.

To buy himself more time, Bradley injected him with another dose, then zip tied Rennie's wrists behind his back and his ankles. He rifled through Rennie's pockets until he found his car keys, then stole the ugly hat off his hat. He put the hat on and pulled the earflaps down, then he cracked the motel door open and peered outside.

No one.

Bradley climbed in Rennie's compact sedan, turned it around, then backed into the parking spot and popped the trunk. He scanned the parking lot again and the windows of all the rooms nearby. The last time he'd moved a body into a vehicle was the time that nosey bitch, Jessica, saw him loading Sarah's body into his truck bed.

Again, no one.

The stakes were higher this time. He could not afford to have any witnesses interfering on this of all days.

Bradley sprinted inside the room and dragged Rennie by his bound ankles to the car. So far, his tender shoulder hadn't complained. Luckily, the small car sat low to the ground. He dropped Rennie's feet inside the trunk, then bent and tucked his arms under Rennie's back. Using his legs and his back muscles, he hoisted

Rennie inside. He bent Rennie's legs at the knee and folded them inside the cavity, then shut the trunk. A tight squeeze. Thankfully, Rennie was under six feet and slim or he wouldn't have fit.

He drove Rennie's car around to the back of the building and parked next to the old truck he'd borrowed from the survivalist cabin owners. He grabbed his gear from the back seat of the truck and moved it into the backseat of Rennie's car and sped off into the night.

Phase one of his plan was complete. Now it was time for phase two to begin. Driving Rennie's car while wearing Rennie's hat on his head should fool the other guard, Matt, into buzzing him onto the property. If all else failed, he had a drugged-up Rennie in the trunk with a thumb that would open the gate.

Few cars passed him on the roads at this late hour, and none of the drivers paid him any mind. Most probably had designs on getting home to bed. Ranchers that woke with the crack of dawn tended to long be in bed at this time. With a baby in the house, he expected the Kents to be asleep unless the baby woke for a midnight feeding.

The Kent property had a peaceful air about it as he approached the black metal gate. If they thought hiding behind a barricade like a king in a medieval castle would keep him away, they had another thing coming.

He stopped in front of the gate with his head facing the road to avoid making eye contact with Matt sitting in the booth. Time to find out how well this guard did his job. The sensor on the panel beside the thumb pad turned green and the fence swung open.

Child's play.

Bradley chuckled, switched on the jammer in his

pocket, and drove through the gate. He parked beside the other sedan next to the booth. Having gained entrance to the Kent property, he didn't need to keep Rennie alive anymore, and Matt also needed to be dealt with.

Bradley popped the trunk, then climbed out of the car, whistling a tune to appear nonchalant. The dormant, brown ground crunched beneath his boots as he walked to the back of the car. He left the trunk only partially ajar to conceal his load and contain the mess he was about to make. He pulled the 9mm Glock from the holster on his belt, fitted with a silencer, and fired a single round through Rennie's temple.

He shut the trunk then strolled towards the booth with his hand behind his back to conceal the gun.

Matt glanced at him sideways while keeping his gaze fixed on the monitor in front of him, alternating between the cameras on the property. "Did you forget something, Rennie?"

Bradley put the gun to Matt's head and squeezed the trigger, splattering the guard's brain matter on the glass wall of the booth. "No, you moron. I didn't forget anything."

Chapter Forty

Jon's eyes flew open. Something had woken him, but he didn't know what. The blackness of the night outside the windows, combined with the fuzziness in his head, meant it had to be the middle of the night. He searched the shadows in the corner of the room and tuned his ears to his surroundings.

His phone vibrated in the pocket of his pajama pants, and a vague recollection of his leg vibrating returned to him. He retrieved his phone and discovered an empty banner notification from the wireless security system. Neither alarm system had gone off, nor any of the motion sensors.

Jon reached over Jessica, catching a whiff of her strawberry shampoo, and picked up her phone from her nightstand. Her phone had gotten the same blank notification, so it wasn't his phone malfunctioning. Apps had bugs. Normally, he would dismiss something like this, but since learning a signal jammer could manipulate the wireless system, he needed to investigate.

He sent a group message to Matt working the gate, Trent, and George, the owner of the security company.

—We received an empty alert from the wireless security system. Matt, is the property secure?—

He shoved the phone in his pocket and climbed out of bed.

Jessica's blonde eyelashes fluttered, and she

moaned but didn't move. Should he wake her? At one in the morning, maybe he should check the camera feeds before depriving her of sleep.

Jon crossed the room to the window and peered outside. The full moon cast light upon the empty fields, giving off an air that all was well. But his family's property covered over twenty acres, and the hair prickled on the back of his neck in warning.

The hell with it. Better to be safe.

He shook Jessica's shoulder.

She rolled over and opened her eyes. "What?"

"The wireless system sent an empty alert to both of our phones. I don't know what to make of it, but after Shandru's warning about the scramblers, we should take it as a threat."

Jessica sat up in bed. "What do we do?"

He touched Trent's icon to dial his number. "I'm calling Trent. I already texted him, the security guard on duty, and his supervisor. We also need to check the camera feeds. I don't want to go outside and get a nasty surprise."

She scrambled out of bed, shed her nightshirt, and pulled on athletic wear.

Trent's phone rang four times and then prompted Jon to leave a voicemail. He hung up and tried again, getting the same result. "He's not picking up."

"Right. Well, he could just be in a deep sleep. Has the guard responded?"

"No. His supervisor sent a second text to the group, prompting Matt to respond and nothing." Matt or Trent alone not responding, maybe nothing. Both being incommunicado could mean something horrible had happened to them.

Adrenaline flooded his system, making him jittery.

Jessica tucked her phone into the side pocket of her pants, then pulled open the drawer of her night table and grabbed her revolver. "I'm checking on the kids. Then I'll message Cynthia while I bring up the vests and the guns from your cabinet in the basement. You call Sheriff Hank and check the cameras."

Jon grabbed an assault rifle from the top shelf of their closet. "Right. Double check the locks on the kids' windows, too. Then meet me at the kitchen table."

Chapter Forty-One

Filled with an abundance of fear and energy, Jessica raced to Bryce's room. She placed a hand over her heart at the sight of her precious firstborn asleep facing the wall with his comforter tugged beneath his chin. That monster would never get near *her* boy again.

She'd checked the locks on his windows before bed, but the glass wasn't a big enough obstacle. She pushed a tall, heavy dresser in front of the window, proud she possessed enough strength to move something like that on her own.

Jessica kissed the top of Bryce's head and whispered, "I promise to keep you safe, baby." She didn't voice the rest—*or die trying*.

Carefully, she shut his door and crossed the hall to the nursery. Cassie slept with her mouth in a cute little bow, and her arms over her head. Jessica wanted to kiss her, hold her close, and make her the same promises, but Cassie wasn't as deep a sleeper.

The dresser in her room was too short to block the window, but the changing table flipped on its side was tall enough to do the job. Alone, the table wasn't much of a heavy obstacle, so she leveraged the dresser against the changing table.

Jessica let her eyes linger on Cassie for a moment longer, drinking in the sight of her sweet daughter, then she left the room and shut the door. She sent a quick message to Cynthia.

—*Are you okay? We got a security alert and Trent isn't answering Jon.*—

She hurried to the kitchen. "Anything?"

"Nothing from Matt or Trent." Jon stood at the counter with his laptop open. "Worse, sweetheart, the camera is showing an empty guard booth, and there's gunk on the glass that wasn't there before. Also, the signal was interfered with again, blocking the footage for a chunk of time by the gate, and there's a path of interferences leading to the rental house. That empty notification, and this flagged section of missing footage, was part of the failsafe Shandru installed."

"Cynthia's not returning my text either." She resisted the urge to breakdown and sob at the idea that their friends might be hurt or dead because of them. "He's here, Jon. I can feel it. We need to hurry for those guns and the vests." She sprinted past the dining room and the guest room to the basement stairs.

Jon followed. "Listen, we're going to be okay. Hank is on his way. He dispatched every officer on duty to us, and Pruitt has a team twenty to thirty minutes out."

"We have him outnumbered two to one. We can kill him, Jon. He dies tonight. Because if he gets away, he'll keep coming back." She stopped in front of the weapons cabinet, barely out of breath, like she could run for miles.

Jon unlocked the cabinet and handed her a vest he'd ordered custom for her after Bradley's escape. "I've never understood why he's so determined to kill us. When Todd Collins survived, he never went back for him. Why risk coming here again after his latest identity and face were outed?"

"He hates us more." She tugged on the vest.

Jon studied her face as he strapped on his own vest. "You've been troubled lately. Right now, you need to be focused and alert. If you need to get something off your chest, now is the time. You can tell me anything. I owe you absolution with what you know about me."

She pulled on her weapon belt and stuck her favorite dagger in the leather sheath on her left side and did the thing she hated most—she lied. "There's nothing to tell. It's just the stress of Bradley on the loose."

She'd discovered the ugly reason why Bradley kept returning a few weeks ago, and she'd been carrying the burden of the truth alone. Because despite her belief that honesty was paramount, some truths were too repulsive and damaging to share. Like the details of Jon's undercover work, this secret needed to stay buried ten feet beneath the earth in a padlocked wooden chest.

He mounted a suppressor to an assault rifle, then loaded a cartridge into the chamber. "I love you. And you're right. We can end him ourselves. Let's do this, sweetheart."

"I love you, too. More than anything." She took a deep breath and followed Jon upstairs. Tonight, one way or another, this nightmare would end.

Jon's phone pinged. "It's Hank. The wired alarm system went off at the rental house five minutes ago and the security company alerted the police."

Her stomach knotted with nerves. If she had any doubts about Bradley's presence nearby, they'd evaporated. "No wonder they weren't answering our calls. They had their hands full. This could be good. This could mean they're alive and fighting as we speak, right?"

"It's Cynthia and Trent. They've been in some

scrapes and come out unscathed. We need to have faith that they can handle themselves."

Chapter Forty-Two

Bradley climbed behind the wheel of Rennie's sedan and followed the gravel road. With the vastness of the property, his jammer would only cover so large of an area. He'd been on and off the property three times without pursuit. The alterations they made to the fence along the forest meant they'd discovered the breeches at some point. But not in real time.

If his luck held, they wouldn't see him coming.

At the fork in the road, he steered left and continued to the rental house. He needed to act fast and catch Trent and Cynthia by surprise. He wanted to take them out of the equation in a way that didn't afford them an opportunity to warn Jon and Jessica to expect him.

Bradley didn't like his odds at four against one, even if one of the four was Jessica who wouldn't stand a chance against him. But he did like his odds one on one against Jon. With how easily he'd dispensed of Kato Chen, it didn't appear that the FBI training was beyond Bradley's own skill level.

Soon, Bryce would be with him where he belonged. They'd have a new life together—a new beginning for them both in a new country. Jon and Jessica Kent would turn into a distant and unpleasant memory.

****

Cynthia shifted the pillow under her head and turned onto her side. She couldn't sleep. A sense of restless unease kept her alert. She couldn't shake the feeling, yet Trent snored quietly beside her unperturbed.

What the heck was wrong with her?

Maybe living on constant guard had finally worn her mental defenses down. Having the security detail following her and Bryce to and from work helped, but she couldn't help but look in on Bryce, covertly glancing inside his classroom throughout the day. He understood the danger, but he hated the attention and being singled out.

She couldn't blame him. Navigating the social aspect of school proved to be a difficult enough challenge for children. She'd altered their schedule to arrive at school ahead of all the other children so his friends wouldn't see him being shadowed by the security company. His assigned guard monitored the building from the outside to be as unobtrusive as possible.

Cynthia swallowed saliva, trying to moisten her parched throat. The dry winters in the western states were difficult to adjust to. If she got up for a drink of water, the cool air on her skin would make her even more alert.

Screw it.

She climbed out of bed, pulled on pajama pants, and stuck her feet inside the furry blue slippers she kept beside the bed. She padded along the short hallway to the living room and paused to admire the tree she'd decorated with Trent earlier, inhaling the foresty scent of the spruce. During the years she'd lived alone in Colorado, under an alias to protect her from Hugh Jones, she'd forgone the tradition of a tree.

This year, she planned to enjoy her first Christmas with Trent as a couple. She missed her parents and siblings back in Maryland, and Trent missed his family in Colorado. But they needed to be here. She didn't want to think it, but it crossed her mind that depending on how long this situation dragged out, she may be missing a lot of future holidays with her family over the next year.

Cynthia sighed and padded to the kitchen. She grabbed a mug from the drying rack and turned on the tap. With her thirst quenched, she set her mug in the sink. She turned, ready to return to bed, then paused at an unusual sound so near to their house—an engine.

No one drove around the property at night. The security company stationed a guard at the gate because that was the only way onto the property. Especially since the fence along the forest behind their house had been raised.

The driver could only bring trouble.

"Trent!" She ran to the bedroom and shook his shoulder. "Wake up!"

Trent rolled over to face her and opened his eyes. "What's happening?"

"Listen."

"An engine. That's not Jon's truck either."

"Grab your guns." Cynthia opened the top drawer of her dresser and grabbed her weapon's belt. In case of emergency, she always kept a revolver and a knife in their holstered and ready for use.

Beams of light shone through their bedroom window and drifted across the wall next to their bed.

Trent yanked pants on over his boxer shorts, then grabbed the assault rifle hanging on the bedpost.

Cynthia stood next to the window, staying out of view as she looked outside. "That's Matt's car, and he's almost here. Why would Matt leave his post to drive around the property?"

"Can you see the driver? Is it Matt?"

"I've never seen Bradley Kingston in person, and it's hard to be sure from this distance. But I'm about seventy percent sure it isn't Matt. We should call Jon or Jess."

Trent asked, "You're sure it's Matt's car?"

"Yes, even if it does turn out to be Matt, we should sound the alarm to be safe."

"One of the sensors or cameras might have malfunctioned and Matt could be investigating. I don't want to wake Jon and Jess for nothing. I'm sure the baby is depriving them of enough sleep as it is."

The car drove past the house and out of her view. "The car didn't stop here."

"Tell you what. I'll send Matt a text to ask what's happening." Trent walked around the bed and disconnected his phone from the charger cable. "You're kidding me. My phone is dead. The cable must have stopped working. Of all the times—"

Crack!

Glass shattered, clattering on the floor in another room. Seconds later, the alarm system wailed like a siren.

Cynthia buzzed with a burst of adrenaline. "I don't think Matt was in that car." Bradley had to have broken in. The alarm company would send the police eventually, after they called Jon, but how long would that take?

Jon and Jessica wouldn't hear the alarm going off in the main house. They needed to be warned in case…Cynthia swallowed around a lump in her throat. In case, she and Trent couldn't stop him on their own. But she needed to assess the immediate threat to them first.

Cynthia grabbed her makeup mirror and ran to the bedroom door with Trent on her heels. She angled the mirror, revealing an empty hallway. In the spaces between the alarm beeping, a strange whooshing sound came from somewhere inside the house. It sounded like a pop can fizzing after being opened except louder with more force. Then came a horrible rotten egg odor.

Trent stood behind her with his head perched over her shoulder. "That smell. I think it's gas of some kind, and the masks are under the kitchen sink. I thought Jon was going overboard. I didn't think we'd actually need them."

She resisted the urge to panic. "Should we get them?" Her eyes started to sting and water, and something tickled her throat. "There's definitely something in the air."

"There's no time. The gas is more concentrated out there, and it's highly flammable. One match and this place will go up. We have to climb out the bedroom window."

She shut the door, pulled her shirt over her nose, ran to the window, then yanked it open and pushed out the screen. Her stomach and lungs burned. She stuck her head outside and gulped in the cold air. Still, her eyes wouldn't stop running and her head swam now too. They needed to get out, and the window was small.

She might be able to squeeze through, but Trent would have trouble. He'd have to turn sideways to fit his shoulders through the opening.

Trent coughed, with tears streaming down his face as he yanked the comforter off their bed and stuck it under the door. "Go but be careful. He might be waiting outside to kill you. I'll cover you from inside, then you can cover me while I climb out."

"I'm going." She grabbed her phone off the dresser, then pulled herself through the opening. Her hands slipped on the windowsill, and she fell forward. She tucked her chin to her chest and landed on the hard, frozen ground in a roll.

Cynthia sprung to her feet and yanked her handgun out of her belt. The world tilted beneath her, and she coughed. Using the corner of the house for cover, she glanced around the corner. Matt's car sped away. The driver wore a black hat and bore a large resemblance to the sketch. "It's him. He's headed back towards the ranch house. Trent. Hurry."

"I have to warn them." Cynthia pulled her phone out of her pocket. The screen swam in front of her watery eyes. She typed a quick message to Jessica.

—*911. He's here. He gassed us. Need help.*—

"I just need to catch my breath." Trent released a string of coughs.

She holstered her gun. "Are you coming? Jon and Jess need us."

Silence greeted her in response. She spun to face Trent.

Trent slumped partway out the window with his head facing the ground where his rifle must have dropped.

"Trent!" She ran, staggering towards him and lifted his head.

He'd lost consciousness.

She slapped his cheek. "Trent! Wake up!"

He didn't move.

No! I can't lose you. Don't panic. Think!

With her lightheadedness, and the overwhelming

urge to cough up a lung, thinking wasn't easy. She couldn't administer first aid with him hanging there if he needed it. Weak or not, she'd need to pull him outside.

Trent had wiggled his massive shoulders outside the window before passing out, and the windows were only about five feet off the ground. A fall wouldn't kill him as long as he didn't land on his head or neck.

Cynthia squeezed in between him and the house, wrapped her arms around his back with his head cradled on her breasts, then she yanked him forward.

His body slid out the window, gaining momentum.

She clung to him and used her upper body to slow his trajectory as she flipped him onto his back. "Trent," she coughed. "You have to wake up." She pressed the side of her head to his chest.

His chest rose and fell, and his heart beat thudded beneath her face, but it didn't sound strong. He needed help, but so did Jessica, Jon, and the kids.

What if Bradley Kingston gassed the ranch, too? What if no one was awake?

She shivered. The world spun, and she could barely lift her head off Trent's chest. She couldn't lose consciousness. She had to do something. They didn't have coats and the night was cold enough that their breaths were visible. Going inside the house might kill her. If their body temperature dropped too much before paramedics made it onto the property, with the effects of whatever they'd been poisoned with, they might die anyway.

The car. She had two thick, fleece blankets in the trunk. The cell service was spotty in some areas and in the event of a breakdown or accident, she'd prepared.

Cynthia stood on wobbly legs and collected Trent's

rifle from beneath the window. She stumbled around the house to her car, then slammed the butt of the rifle into the edge of the passenger door window.

The glass cracked but didn't shatter.

She hit the window a second time. The glass shattered inwards. With blurry eyes, she groped for the lock, lifted it, then opened the door and popped the trunk. The thick, fleece blankets sat on top of the emergency kit.

Cynthia tucked the blankets under her arm. Her feet felt like bricks as she half staggered, half jogged back to Trent. Spots danced in front of her eyes, and her strength was waning fast. She wouldn't be any help to Jon and Jessica in this condition, and she couldn't leave Trent alone.

She draped herself over Trent and covered them with both blankets. Between their combined body heat and the layers of fleece, they'd survive until help came. Her eyes wanted to close, but she needed to stay alert in case Bradley tried to come back to finish the job.

Her phone vibrated in her pocket.

She dug it out and swiped her finger across the bottom of the screen.

Chapter Forty-Three

Jon reached the top of the basement staircase with Jessica a step behind him. The floor to ceiling windows in the living room and dining room bothered him. The glass was triple pane, but that didn't mean it wouldn't break.

His phone vibrated in his pocket. He swiped the screen. "Hello?"

"Am I speaking to Jon Kent?"

"Yes."

"The alarm went off in your rental property. I can't reach your tenant, so I dispatched the police."

"Thank you. The police chief has been in touch. We may have a violent, wanted, fugitive on the property."

Jessica stared at her phone, and her face paled. "Jon, get them to send an ambulance. Cynthia messaged me. She says Bradley gassed them, and they need help."

If Bradley gassed their house, Cassie's odds of survival would be low without the infant gas hood the FBI sent them after his mother was poisoned. They all had masks. Why hadn't Cynthia and Trent used theirs?

Jon tamped down the urge to panic. "Send emergency services. We need fire and ambulance. Tell them a toxic gas was released at my rental property."

"Yes, sir. We'll notify them. Stay on the line, and I'll confirm when I've reached them."

"I can't. I have a family to protect." He ended the

call. "Jess, we need the gas masks out of the basement."

"I'll get them. I don't think he'll gas us. Not with Bryce in the house." Jess raced down the stairs, calling over her shoulder, "Can you try to reach Cynthia? I'm worried about them after her message."

Jon dialed Cynthia's number, praying he hadn't gotten her killed, involving her in another one of their messes. Marrying him had proven to be a curse. He thought her dead for years, after she was kidnapped by one of his enemies. The grief and guilt had eaten into his soul. He didn't want to contemplate living with himself if Cynthia and Trent didn't survive.

The phone rang and rang until, finally, she answered. "Hello?" Cynthia dissolved into a coughing fit.

He barely recognized Cynthia's scratchy voice. "Cynthia, are you and Trent okay?"

"I feel awful. Burning lungs and stomach, lightheaded, weak. Trent's unconscious. We're on the ground outside the bedroom window of the house. I covered us with fleece blankets because I don't have the strength to move him. I'm sorry we weren't more help. Keep Jess and the kids safe."

"I will. Ambulance and fire are coming. I'll send them straight there. Hang on, okay?"

Silence.

He checked the screen of his phone. The call was still connected. "Cynthia?"

Silence.

This can't be happening. Cynthia and Trent can't be dead.

Jessica came up the stairs with three masks hanging off her arms, and the special infant hood for Cassie. She asked, "What's going on?"

He held the phone to his ear. "Cynthia." No response. He hung up and stuck his phone in his pocket and shoved back the wave of emotions showering over him. He needed to protect his wife and children. "They're poisoned, laying on the ground outside together. Cynthia said Trent was unconscious, then she stopped responding. I think she passed out, too. They need help."

"Oh my God. How awful." She handed him Bryce's mask and his own, then headed through the kitchen to the hallway. "Is there anything we can do to help them? They're defenseless."

"Not with Bradley on the property. If they're down, he's nearby." He followed her to the space in the hallway between the kids' bedrooms. "I care about them, too. But, sweetheart, ask yourself this. Would they want us to split up with two kids to protect?"

"No." Her voice caught. "They'd die to protect our children. That's why he gassed them. He wanted them out of the equation fast because he's outnumbered." She opened the nursery door and stepped inside.

Jon went into Bryce's room, facing the insurmountable task of waking him up. Bryce was the heaviest sleeper he'd ever come across. He shook Bryce's shoulder and raised his voice in his ear. "This is an emergency, buddy. You have to wake up and put this gas mask on."

Bryce's eyes opened and he rolled towards him. "Dad? Are Mom and Cassie okay?"

"Yes, but Trent and Cynthia's house was gassed. Sit up. I'm putting this on you, and then you need to hide in your closet until we tell you it's safe to come out."

Bryce sat up in bed with wide, doe eyes. "What about Cassie? She's too young to hide. I'll hold her in my closet, so you and Mom can fight *him*. You have to kill him, Dad."

Jon secured Bryce's mask, fighting to contain a swell of emotions—pride, love, fear, and anger. "You're an amazing boy, you know. I love you so much. We'll run it by your mother."

Jessica came in the room donning her mask with Cassie in her arms.

Cassie's mask covered her head and nose, but Jessica had it raised to let her nurse.

Jessica sat next to Bryce on his bed. "I heard my name."

Jon gazed into his wife's eyes, struggling to contain his emotions with danger circling. "Bryce would like to hide in his closet and hold his baby sister."

Tears welled in her eyes. "You sweet, brave, big brother. Of course you can. It's better than leaving her cry in her crib. Make sure she keeps her mask on, okay? Dad and I won't let anything happen to you. We'll keep you safe."

"Don't worry, Mom. I'll take care of her." The gas mask dulled his sweet voice. Bryce ran into his closet, sat on the floor, and held out his arms.

Jon pulled his mask on and positioned his rifle on his shoulder.

Jessica pulled Cassie's hood down and handed her to Bryce. "I love you."

Bryce rocked Cassie gently. "I love you, too."

Cassie's eyes fixed on her brother. She stayed quiet, reached up, and rested her hand on Bryce's mask.

Jessica ran across the hall and returned with her

rifle. Almost unrecognizable in her vest, gas mask, and armed to the teeth. "Now, what?"

"We keep all the lights off. If we're quiet, he might think we're sleeping and clueless. Then we listen." Jon stepped into the hallway and spoke with his voice slightly above a whisper. "Follow me." He leaned forward as he ran behind the kitchen peninsula and kneeled between the peninsula and the bank of cabinets on the wall behind them.

She followed and grabbed his laptop from where he'd left it on the counter.

"Good thinking." He opened it on the floor, and the camera feed around the side of the house displayed fuzz instead of a field. "He's somewhere around that fuzzy area where the basement windows are."

Following his example, she kept her voice low. "Would we hear a window breaking down there?"

"Maybe not, but we can see the panel for the wired system from here, and there are motion sensors on every window connected to wires. Wherever he breeches, the panel will tell us. He can't jam those sensors and he won't be able to cut the wires until he's inside. I wonder if he noticed the new system and if that bought us time."

Jessica asked, "Could he cut the power?"

"When the FBI installed the metal fencing, they also caged the electric meter and the outdoor breakers to prevent it. There's also a backup generator in case of power outages."

"So, we wait for him to break in? Wouldn't it be better to be more proactive?"

"Without an upper floor, it's not like we could watch him from a higher level and shoot him before he comes in." Jon clasped her hand. "We're doing the best we can.

Once he comes in, we circle him from safe vantagepoints and put him down."

Chapter Forty-Four

Jessica's stomach clenched in a tight knot as she knelt with Jon in the kitchen. She didn't want to be afraid. After pounding the punching bag, lifting weights, practicing shooting, sparring, and running miles on the treadmill, she resented her fear. But she loved the hot, rage making the blood race in her veins, filling her with energy and a sense of resilience.

Huddling behind the kitchen peninsula and waiting gave her too much time to ponder their situation. What would Bradley do? How would he attack? Was he rigging the outside of the house to poison them? Or starting a fire?

Not likely if he wanted Bryce.

He didn't seem like the type brave enough for hand-to-hand combat since he resorted to shooting people and using sneaky methods to kill. But who knew? He outmaneuvered Kato and ran him down with his truck.

She scanned her memories for the last time she'd encountered him at Judith Peak, and a detail popped out at her. "He'll be wearing a bulletproof vest under his clothes again. We'll have to aim for his head. Sheriff Hank made that mistake last time."

"Yes, but if he's taking cover and happens to stick out an arm or a leg, aim for the wrist and knees."

The panel on the wall lit up, the alarm system wailed, and the message 'basement window' flashed.

Air burst in and out of her lungs, rattling through her gas mask and fogging up the surface. *This is it.*

Jon lifted her chin to face him, then took exaggerated slow breaths, his breath fogging up the gas mask slightly before it promptly cleared.

She nodded and mimicked his movements, and her breathing came under control.

The panel went dark, and the alarm quieted.

"He cut the wire which means he's in. Come on, Jess," Jon whispered. "Go to the front entrance, and use that wall as cover, then aim your rifle for the basement door."

Jon ran around the other side of the peninsula, and she followed. He stopped at the opening between the living room and the small hallway leading to the basement door, then waved her towards the opposite side.

Although she hated the idea of them separating, she kept going and took up her assigned position. Jon had experience with house clearings and apprehending suspects. She needed to trust in his abilities.

Neither one of them was exposed with where they stood, and they should both be able to get a shot at Bradley when he came through the basement door without risking shooting each other. With the kids tucked away on the opposite side of the house, they should be safe from stray bullets.

Having worked out in that basement more times than she could count, she could attest to how well the soundproofing worked. Without the baby monitor, she couldn't hear Cassie crying in the basement. That meant Bradley couldn't have heard them getting into their positions.

On the flip side, they wouldn't hear Bradley coming until the basement door opened.

Her body vibrated like a frozen pipe ready to burst in anticipation of violence. The last time she'd experienced a danger adrenaline rush was while she hid in the basement of the safe house in Hawaii with Sally and Bryce. The intensity of this rush far surpassed the last one. Because this time she wasn't hiding. This time she would face the beast of all beasts and banish him to Hell.

Jessica peered through the sight, hard to do with a mask on her head, trying to steady her breathing. The door would open in her direction, so she aimed for the space in front of where the door would sit.

Jon had the better vantage point and would take the first critical shot. If he missed, she couldn't.

The basement door flew open.

Two muted shots sounded within seconds of each other. The basement door splintered as a hole appeared. Through the hole, she caught a glimpse of the back of Bradley's head, moving away from her and towards Jon. Bradley wore a dark fitted hat, but no mask.

Bradley continued to underestimate her abilities. He likely didn't expect her to be nearby pointing a gun at him. No, he probably assumed she'd hide in the closet with her children, leaving Jon to face him on his own.

She needed to take advantage. She removed her gas mask and set it silently on the carpet at the entrance.

A few more muted shots fired in the area of the living room, but neither Jon nor Bradley grunted or screamed.

She sped walked on tiptoes to the basement door, then put her eye to the hole.

At the edge of the hallway close to the living room, Bradley stood with his back to the wall, facing the living room—away from her.

Jessica inhaled a deep breath. Once she stepped around that door, she'd lose her cover. She'd need to take one shot, two at most, then sprint for the entrance or the dining area.

Bradley's attention remained on the living room.

She took a few tentative steps around the door, then lifted her rifle, peering through the sight at the middle of the back of Bradley's head. She put her finger on the trigger. Another shot rang out as she squeezed and fired.

A bullet penetrated the wall and flew past Bradley's face. He shuffled backwards, lifting his rifle.

Jessica's bullet missed his head, her intended target, but hit him, nonetheless.

"Ahh!" He dropped his rifle. Blood dripped onto the floor from a bullet hole in his wrist.

He spun to face her and reached into his weapons belt with his left hand. "You bitch!"

Jessica ignored the urge to flee and stood her ground as the monster's eyes oozed malice in her direction. She aimed for the center of his forehead and squeezed the trigger.

Jon came around the corner. "Jess, take cover!"

A wound opened in the center of Bradley's forehead, below the brim of his toque.

"It's over, Jon. I put a bullet in his head." Jessica registered a sharp pain in her left thigh, but she ignored the throbbing sensation. She needed to watch him die. Unlike the first time she'd killed a man in the parking garage to protect Jon, not a shred of guilt or sadness weighed on her. Only a deep sense of relief.

Bradley's surgeon had made his features similar to his half-brother Adam, but his sick eyes and facial expressions bore no resemblance to the man she'd married, or to their son. The malice left Bradley's gaze, replaced with a vacant stare. He slumped to the floor.

"Jessica! Your leg. Don't move and whatever you do, don't remove the knife." Jon ripped his gas mask off and ran towards her.

A handle stuck out of her thigh, and warm blood escaped from around the edges of the blade. Her eyes widened at the large puddle spreading beneath her feet. She felt faint and spots danced in front of her eyes.

He may have killed me, but he didn't get my son. My kids are safe. And no one will ever know the awful truth.

She smiled as the darkness took her.

Chapter Forty-Five

Two weeks earlier

On a quiet afternoon, Jessica faced the remaining two boxes of her stuff from Cochrane sitting in the entrance by the front door. She'd put off unpacking them for months. With the holidays approaching, and their plans to host the whole family for Christmas dinner, the boxes needed to be dealt with.

She clipped the baby monitor to the waistband of her leggings and carried the first box full of random knickknacks to the storage area in the basement. Until Cassie outgrew the curious toddler phase, it made no sense to unpack anything breakable. She placed the box on a shelf with the label facing out.

Taking advantage of any opportunity to get some cardio in, she sprinted up the staircase to finish the job. The only remaining box contained her paperwork, and she wouldn't be able to shove it on a shelf for later. To list her house, she'd need to dig through her files for relevant documents like her property tax assessments.

Jessica carried the box to the dining room table and removed the lid. On top of her files, someone had piled a stack of papers from inside her desk. She flipped through the pages, finding mostly old bills. A piece of lined paper with Adam's handwriting on it drifted from between pages in her hands and landed on the floor beside her foot.

She picked up the paper and scanned the page. He'd written passwords on it for random websites he didn't use often, including the login for his profile on a genealogy site. Ironically, she recognized the name of the website, Family Match. They'd found Bradley's family tree on the same site.

A decade or longer had passed since the last time Adam logged into the website to search for relatives. Maybe someone on his maternal side had uploaded a profile. Over the years, Adam had tried to find his biological mother, but his adoption was closed. His adoptive parents were never given any information about her either.

Jessica carried the paper to the kitchen table and opened Jon's laptop. She logged into the website. A notification icon showed in the corner of the page. She clicked on it and read the message.

—You have one new close family match—possible half-sibling. Bradley Kingston.—

Jessica covered her mouth to stifle a massive scream. Her breathing sped, but she forced her body to take slower, deeper breaths. She couldn't pass out, and she needed a clear head. No wonder Bradley had fixated on Bryce. That explained why he kept coming after them. Bryce was his nephew. Her sweet precious boy was a blood relative of that sick, narcissistic, serial killer and Bradley wanted him.

Bryce can never know!

In her heart, lay an absolute certainty that her son was nothing like his uncle. He wouldn't kill a bug let alone a person. Besides, lots of people had killer relatives and they weren't murderers. Being related to Bradley changed nothing, but that knowledge would only taint

Bryce's image of himself. And what if people treated him differently because of it?

Her thoughts shifted to Jon. If anyone could keep the secret and share this burden of knowledge with her, it was him. He would never see Bryce in a different light. But Jon carried so many dark secrets of his own. Why should he carry the weight of this one?

After preaching honesty and begging Jon to tell her everything for all this time, she finally understood his perspective. He wasn't keeping secrets out of selfishness, but rather he didn't want to place the weight of them on her.

With shaking, clammy hands she went into Adam's profile and deleted his account. She closed the browser window and erased the search history. With all the craziness happening around them, Jon would never dive deeper into his own laptop to recover her trail. She carried the paper with Adam's information on it to the fireplace and threw it in the flames.

Jessica alone would carry this secret to her grave, and she vowed to prevent Bradley from getting anywhere near Bryce. Someday, if Bryce mentioned wanting to use his DNA to find relatives, she'd dissuade him somehow.

Chapter Forty-Six

Jon caught Jessica and lowered her to the floor. Her eyes rolled in the back of her head. She'd lost so much blood. He held the button on the side of his phone to activate voice controls. "Call Sheriff Hank."

Moving faster than he'd ever moved in his life, he dashed into the kitchen to the junk drawer and grabbed a roll of duct tape. He wound tape tightly around Jessica's thigh and the hilt of the dagger sticking out of Jessica's leg.

Hank's voice came through the speaker of his phone. "Jon, what's happening?"

Jon lifted her leg in the air to encourage blood flow to her organs and head. "Hank, we need another ambulance asap. Jessica is the most critical. She has a dagger in the artery of her left thigh."

"I just arrived. We already have two ambulances at the gate."

"Open the gate with your thumbprint." Jon sprinted to the front door. "I unlocked the front door. Let yourselves in."

"Where's Bradley Kingston?"

"Dead." Jon kneeled at Jessica's side and lifted her leg again. "Jess snuck up on him while he was in a standoff with me and shot him twice. Once in the wrist, and then in the forehead. But somehow, he managed to throw a knife at her with his left hand."

Hank bellowed. "All clear. Suspect is deceased in the main house. Ambulance one, take the right fork to the main house."

Jon cut him off. "Hank, I spoke to Cynthia before she lost consciousness. Her and Trent are outside under the bedroom window on the side of the house."

"Ambulance two and fire, left fork to the smaller house. The male and female victims of the gas attack are on the ground by the side of the house. Four black SUVs are coming up the road. Must be the FBI. Too little, too late again."

Jon wrapped his hand around Jessica's wrist. Her pulse beat faintly against his fingers and her skin was cold. He prayed harder than he'd ever prayed in his life that Jessica would survive her mortal wound.

He peered over his shoulder at Bradley Kingston, unequivocally dead this time, leaking blood and brain matter all over the floor. Jon cursed Bradley Kingston, and he cursed himself for not moving faster, in time to stop him from throwing that damn knife at Jessica.

The front door swung open, and two paramedics raced inside. One female and one male. The male said, "We have her, sir."

Jon asked, "Do you have blood on board?"

"No, but we'll get her to the medical center as fast as we can."

The female paramedic wrapped bandages over the duct tape. "You did a decent job taping that wound. You probably bought her time. But her vitals are very weak. Thank goodness we have an emergency department here in Lewistown. We'll floor it."

The male paramedic asked, "What's her blood type? We'll radio to the hospital, so they're prepared to infuse her right away."

Jon swallowed around a lump in his throat. "Type B Positive. I'll help lift her."

The male paramedic nodded. "Ready?"

Jon placed his arms under Jessica's shoulders. "Ready." He lifted her onto the gurney and kissed her forehead. "Fight, sweetheart. Fight. Bryce and Cassie need you." *Oh, my God. The kids.*

The paramedics rushed Jessica out the front door.

Jon followed in search of Sheriff Hank.

Hank stood on the front porch with his arms out keeping the FBI team at bay. "The suspect is dead, but Jon and his kids are still in that house. Give them a minute."

Jon appreciated Sheriff Hank's tenacity. "I need your help."

Sheriff Hank spun to face him. "What can I do, Jon?" He pointed to a young male agent nearby with a mullet, standing in front of a team of agents. "This guy wanted to barge in before the paramedics even had Jessica out the door. Ridiculous. Bradley Kingston is dead. He isn't going anywhere."

Jon wiped his bloody hands on his already blood-soaked jeans. "The kids are in Bryce's closet. I need to get them out of here. Can you have someone cover the body?"

Sheriff Hank placed a hand on his shoulder. "Of course. You must want to get to the hospital. Want me to pack bags for the kids? Sally is staying with Jamie and Pat tonight, and they can take care of Bryce and Cassie."

"Yes, please. There's breast milk in the fridge and frozen in bags in the freezer. Just dump a bunch of sleepers and diapers in the bag hanging on the crib. I'll help Bryce pack."

Sheriff Hank spoke with his usual authority. "All right, you folks can go inside now. You cover up that body until we get the kids out of here."

The male agent scowled but said nothing and continued past them inside with the team on his heels.

Jon squeezed past the FBI team and rushed through the kitchen and along the hallway. He stopped in the powder room and took off his bloody vest and dress shirt and dropped them inside the bathtub. Somehow, his tee beneath his shirt had escaped the bloody mess, and the dark wash of his jeans masked the blood stains.

Not wanting to frighten Bryce, he scrubbed his hands and arms with scalding water and soap. After everything they'd been through in the past few years, Bryce had enough trauma to cope with.

Jon took a deep breath to steady himself, then stepped inside Bryce's room. The absence of Cassie crying brought on unwelcome thoughts of them being unconscious or gone. They hadn't allowed Bradley to get anywhere near the kids.

With his heart jumping into his throat, Jon opened the closet.

Bryce sat on the floor and Cassie slept in his arms.

Jon fought off the urge to breakdown. Both of his children were safe, but they might be motherless if Jess didn't pull through. He couldn't imagine a world without Jessica's smile and laugh. Her warmth and mothering made their family whole.

"You did such an amazing job. I'm so proud of you." Jon kneeled and removed Bryce's gas mask and then Cassie's hood. He took Cassie from Bryce and cradled her in his arms. "Can I have a hug?"

Bryce wrapped his arms around Jon's neck.

Jon held him close. "It's over, Bryce. No more security teams, no more fencing, and no more bad guys."

Bryce stepped back, and his eyes travelled from Jon's head to his toes. "You seem okay. Where's Mom? Is *he* dead?"

"Your mother killed him. He's really dead this time, buddy."

"Where is she?"

Jon inhaled and exhaled a deep breath to hold himself together. "An ambulance is taking her to the hospital. She has a serious knife wound in her leg."

"Just her leg. So, she should be okay, right?"

"She lost a lot of blood, but the hospital is close. Your mother is tough. She'll pull through."

"I want to see her."

"I know, buddy. She'll want to see you too. As soon as she's allowed visitors, I'll get someone to bring you to the hospital. The house is—well it's a real mess. Sheriff Hank is going to take you and Cassie to Uncle Jamie and Aunt Pat's for now. Grandma is staying with them tonight, too. I'll be there for Mom."

Bryce stood and rubbed his eyes. "All right. I'll grab my backpack."

"Good man."

After changing Cassie and making sure Hank had packed everything she'd need, he bundled her into the bucket of her infant car seat. Carrying Cassie, he guided Bryce through the kitchen, making sure his son didn't see the white sheet with blood stains concealing Bradley's body.

After carrying dark memories and taking lives for years, Jon understood better than anyone that the awful events of that night would move to the back of his and Jessica's minds. Occasionally, the memory would haunt them, but they'd move on.

If Jessica survived.

Jon loaded the kids into Jessica's van and handed Hank the key. "Thanks, again. I'll be in touch. Let me know when the kids are settled."

"I will."

With dread knotting his stomach, Jon leaped into the cab of his Dodge Ram and peeled around the FBI vehicles and up the dirt road.

Chapter Forty-Seven

Somewhere in her subconscious, Jessica sensed her body being moved as equipment beeped, then a weightlessness came over her and the beeping ceased.

"Jess, open your eyes. I'm here." Warm hands clasped her own.

Adam?

She opened her eyes and there he stood, smiling. Adam. Tall, dark, and handsome—almost a mirror image of their son, and no longer hazy and cold to the touch. Around them, the fall leaves blazed in all their glory and the sun shone on a crystal-clear lake.

"Where are we? How am I here?" She remembered the knife wound and the life leaving Bradley's eyes. She should be panicked, yet peace enveloped her with warmth. "Am I dead?"

"You flatlined when the ambulance pulled up to the hospital, but the doctors and nurses aren't giving up. A nurse is squeezing a bag of blood into you now."

"I didn't see you in the field by the ranch, did I?"

"No. Ever since I warned you about the gunmen in Hawaii, I haven't been able to reach you until now." He frowned. "Believe me, I tried. I never left your side, and I wanted to warn you Bradley was coming. I prayed you'd never find out he was my brother."

She wrapped her arms around his neck. "You're nothing like him."

"No, I'm not. Neither is Bryce. I'm not making excuses for him, but Bradley had a horrible life. Our mother neglected him and let men abuse him, meanwhile his father, another violent man, was in prison. His soul is tortured, and he isn't moving on."

"You mean he's at the ranch? He's going to haunt Jon and the kids?"

"And you. It isn't your time, Jess. Bryce, Cassie, and Jon need you."

"I need them, too." Something tugged at her body from behind. "What's happening?"

Adam smiled and kissed her forehead. "Your spirit is returning to your body. I don't know if you'll remember this, but if you do, don't worry. I'll be there to keep Bradley in check, and hopefully in time, I can help him find peace and move on. I love you, Jessica."

"I will always love you, Adam. Forever." She shut her eyes and gave into the force tugging her backwards, then darkness surrounded her once again.

****

Jessica roused to familiar voices in the room, and the bitter antiseptic odor that could only be a hospital. She squeezed the hand gripping hers and forced her heavy eyelids open. She blinked at the brightness of the overhead fluorescent lighting as her eyes adjusted.

Jon leaned over her and kissed her forehead. "Hey, Jess. I'm here, and so is Debbie."

Aunt Debbie moved around the bed and took her other hand. "There's my fighting girl. I knew you'd make it. You sure gave us a scare, but good on you for putting a bullet in that creep's brain."

Jessica's throat felt like sandpaper. "Cynthia and Trent. How are they?"

Jon's mouth twisted into his signature lopsided grin which could only mean good news. "They're both on oxygen in another room two doors down from you. Thankfully, they both regained consciousness, and they don't appear to have any lasting neurological issues. They both have lung damage. Trent is a bit worse off than Cynthia, but it shouldn't affect their quality of life too much. They won't be running long distances for a while, but they're going to be okay."

"The kids?"

Aunt Debbie smiled, "They're fine. I just saw them at Jamie's house. Bryce is eager to visit you. He seems happier and more like himself with the stress of Bradley behind us."

"I made sure Bryce didn't see any of the carnage at the ranch." Jon ran his fingers around her palm. "The place is a mess. The FBI finished examining the scene yesterday and took Bradley away. A cleaning crew is supposed to come to the house today, and a local contractor is supposed to repair the damages at both properties."

"Yesterday?"

"You've been out about a day." Jon frowned. "You flatlined yesterday, and your body had to recover from the blood loss. You also had surgery to repair the damage to the artery in your leg. You'll need to take it easy for a while."

Adam's face and the sensation of his warm hands flashed in her mind. "It wasn't a dream, then. I really saw Adam. He told me I'd died, and that it wasn't my time. I'm glad it wasn't. I want to do a lot more living."

With Jon at her side, she wanted to watch the kids grow, graduate, marry, and have kids of their own. There would be more family dinners, holidays, and carefree moments of bliss. They would ride on horseback in the fields and watch the sun setting behind the mountains making them glow golden once again.

****

The next week passed in a blur of happiness and pain as Jessica recovered surrounded by her family. Her parents had arrived an hour after she woke in hospital, and her mother had waited on her ever since. Sally was back to her usual self and cooking up a storm alongside Debbie to keep them, and Trent and Cynthia, fed during their recovery. Although she missed her independence, it was wonderful being surrounded by love.

In the wee hours of Christmas morning, before the sun rose, Jessica stole a moment alone after feeding Cassie and putting her back to sleep. Big snowflakes tumbled lazily outside the floor to ceiling windows. They'd have a white Christmas after all.

She leaned against her crutch as she stood in front of the tree they'd decorated the day Bradley wreaked havoc upon them. Somehow, the tree had escaped damage and welcomed them home the day Jessica was released from the hospital.

Presents filled the area beneath the tree, waiting for the fun to begin. Everyone would be gathering at the ranch later to celebrate—her parents, Aunt Debbie, Cynthia, Trent, Sally, and Jamie and Pat with their kids. The house would fill with love and new happy memories would be born of Cassie's first Christmas, and Jessica needed those memories now more than ever before.

All traces of Bradley were gone, yet whenever she passed the hallway where his body had lain, the image of him standing there lingered in her mind. But it was a single bad memory in a house filled to the brim with good memories—Cassie cooing at the tree, Bryce holding Cassie for the first time, and breakfast with Jon in the kitchen a year ago on the morning of their wedding.

She plucked a Christmas card from the string hanging along the wall, reread it, and shook her head and chuckled. The card addressed to her had arrived while she was at the hospital. It was from an unusual ally, Ed Henson, assassin, and also her and Cynthia's kidnapper who in his own way had saved both women from Hugh Jones.

Inside the card read, *I know you received the documents I sent you. I'm not saying I'm a saint, but I thought you deserved to know the truth about your husband. Do with it what you will.*

Your friend, Ed Henson.

P.S. If ever you want me to kill him, I'll give you a hefty discount.

She didn't appreciate the stress those FBI documents caused, but at least she could move on with her life knowing the truth. She couldn't help but laugh at all the time the FBI spent trying to discover who sent that envelope, only to come up empty. Thankfully, the FBI had never dug deeper into Bradley's family tree. Hopefully, they never would.

She hung the card in its place.

"Ed Henson sure is a character." Jon came into the living room, already dressed in jeans and plaid for chores.

"He is. I'm glad he sent those documents and forced your past out into the open. You don't have to hide who you are from me anymore."

He came up behind her and wrapped his arms around her waist. "Can you really accept that part of me without it changing how you feel?"

Jessica leaned her weight into him, taking some of the pressure off her leg. She wished she could tell him that she now understood the reasoning behind keeping secrets. But if she did, he'd ask why she'd changed her mind. "I love you. In your heart, you're a good man and that's all that's important. We're in this life together. No matter what."

A word about the author…

Michelle Godard-Richer is a multi-award-winning thriller and horror author with an Honours Degree in Criminology from the University of Ottawa. She was named Best Canada Author of the Year by N.N. Light's Book Heaven and earned a Crowned Heart from Ind'Tale Magazine.

Her fascination with crime and human behavior, combined with a lifelong passion for the written word, led her to realize a childhood dream of becoming an author. She enjoys crafting strong protagonists and diabolical villains with realistic and believable characteristics while making their lives as complicated and dangerous as possible.

When she isn't writing, you'll find her in the garden or with her nose in a book. She lives in the foothills of the Rocky Mountains in Alberta with her husband, two children, four dogs, and a cat.

Thank you for purchasing
this publication of The Wild Rose Press, Inc.

For questions or more information
contact us at
info@thewildrosepress.com.

The Wild Rose Press, Inc.
www.thewildrosepress.com